Jack of all Trades

A Novel by

Rich Herschlag

Cover design and Editing by James Van Treese

Northwest Publishing Inc.
5949 South 350 West
Salt Lake City, UT 84107
801-266-5900

Copyright © 1993 NPI

Northwest Publishing Inc,
5949 South 350 West
Salt Lake City, Utah 84107
801-266-5900

International Copyright Secured

Reproduction in any manner, in whole or in part,
in English or in other languages, is prohibited.
All rights reserved.

ISBN #1-56901-039-0

Printed in the United States of America

To my father,
the Number One **Jack of All Trades**

Chapter One

    Alan Reiss had gone through life making lists. Some of the lists made it to paper, while others were simply committed to memory. He knew he wasn't the only one in the world making lists. But Alan believed that he had distinguished himself from most of the crowd. At age twenty-three, he had actually accomplished many of the hardest tasks on several of those lists, although the vast majority of tasks listed remained virtually untouched. He still hadn't bought that electronic keyboard and relearned how to play, or alphabetized all his cassette tapes, or read more than eleven pages of the home repair manual he had recently purchased. But he had earned a degree in civil engineering, replaced his running shoes, and learned to finger all the minor and major scales on his bass guitar.

But what Alan thought genuinely separated him from the crowd was not what he had accomplished, but rather that he still kept track of what he hadn't accomplished. For others, hundreds of small dreams and goals were lost or discarded during job promotions, changes of address, or periods of mere forgetfulness. Alan's were still on file.

It was now 7:48 A.M. on a workday. Alan recklessly slapped the sleep button on his digital clock radio for the fifth consecutive time. He stuffed his head back under the covers and knew he had only two shots left at the button. From here on in, there would be two eight-minute intervals of near bliss, framed crudely by three desperate lunges. After that, he was on his own. The manufacturer of the digital clock radio allowed only seven consecutive chances at the sleep button. Now, on the brink of dreamland, Alan wondered how that design had come about—if seven hits of the button was simply the most convenient design based on the way the available silicon chips were manufactured, or if seven hits of the button came about by a value judgment made by electronics engineers. "Look," one engineer had remarked to another, "they get seven shots and that's it. In my day, we only got three!" It didn't matter anyway. Alan was now back in dreamland, having sex with the sophisticated but earthy young woman who was once his sixth grade teacher.

Alan sat up now on his loft bed, the ceiling of his ground floor studio apartment only three inches above his skull. Inside his skull, he wrestled with a hellish tiredness which these days consumed his life, much the way intellectual and athletic achievement used to. Those things still mattered to Alan, but had clearly taken a back seat to groggy physical pain, which usually held the wheel. Intellectual and athletic achievements were mere concepts, which emerged occasionally these days as annoying back seat drivers. They were no match for the dried skin and multiple muscular tension pangs which at the moment owned him and which would continue to manipulate him for the rest of the day. Alan was angry. Somehow, numerous years of academic intensity and a four-year Ivy League education could not rescue him from the simple fact of having to drag his butt out of bed every morning and get to a little desk somewhere at a specific time. As Alan looked down from his tall loft, he knew that as soon as his feet hit the floor, the whole stupid process would begin all over again: strip, water, soap, underarm, chest, leg, hair, rinse, dry, squeeze, comb, dress, pack, slam, lock, check, walk, meet, ride, stairs, desk, Indian, paperwork, phone call, nap. . . . Alan obeyed the sneaker commercial and Just Did It.

In the shower, he thought about the contrast between ten months ago, when he had started his job as an intern engineer for the City, and today. As reality had set in, basic standards of punctuality had been thrown out the window. Whereas, on day one, he had leaped out of bed early enough to be able to start filling out forms no later than 8:45, allowing liberally for such delays as a discharged subway train and a last minute stop at the bagel place, things were different now. The trains were assumed to whiz into Manhattan, and he went to work hungry. Also, Alan knew that Sashi, his manager, had let so many 9:20 arrivals go by without saying anything that this had become "on time," for all practical purposes. Nine-twenty became a base from which Alan could build—9:25, 9:35. . . .

As Alan rinsed, something else occupied his thoughts—the hidden order and logic in his life's events that he had recently began to notice. This, like tiredness, had taken the front seat. Not the driver's side like the tiredness, but more like the passenger's side of the front seat as of late. It was the way his own actions and attitudes came back to him, sometimes within only days or minutes. Alan had long been aware of related concepts—karma, do unto others—but in his mind, those notions had always belonged to the world of wishful thinking, to the mushy thoughts of sentimentalists who hadn't read the newspaper and recognized the sterile, random reality it clearly presented each day. Now, however, Alan was taking a new look. It had started over the past year, when he was hit over the head with a few bizarre coincidences. Over the past few weeks, he had skillfully taken more control over the experiment. Mental lists of the good deeds he was planning had begun to displace mental lists of his more selfish daily tasks. Maybe this was going to be a good thing, he thought. Alan had always been reasonably compassionate and assumed it was part of a difficult, meaningless climb to nowhere in particular. The more recent idea that he would eventually be rewarded for his actions comforted him almost as much as it scared him.

Alan was dressed and ready to leave the apartment. He considered Zak, his longtime friend, who would be waiting for him two blocks away. He and Zak took the subway in together every morning. Their official meeting time had drifted from seven forty-five to eight-twenty or so. Even though they were partners in apathy, Alan sensed it was seventy-five percent his own fault. Zak was nearing his personal limit in patience and had begun to ride in on his own on certain days. But today, everything was okay, since

Alan hadn't received Zak's bail-out phone call. He looked forward to the all-knowing smile Zak would give him upon meeting, a smile that would eloquently say: "You bum."

As Alan closed the apartment door behind him, he experienced shock. There was a handwritten note taped to the outside of the door. Without taking even a second's look, he knew the note would soundly alter his life. He read it now. It was in pencil:

"Alan, I've wanted to introduce myself for a long time, but was too embarrassed in front of your friends. I have two passes to the Underground for Saturday night and thought you might like to come. Please call me Thursday night after seven at 896-1939

— Jill (the cut girl next door)"

Alan knew "cut" was really a rushed "cute," and filed the thought. His chest was tight from the overall impact. He put the note in his pocket and began walking. He had traded long looks with the young woman next door several times in the past two weeks. She appeared to be the daughter of the building owner and would disappear with a smile into her apartment after walking her tiny dog. Her looks were European with a short, straight, model's haircut. Alan was somewhat stunned this event had materialized: For every ten women he discreetly gawked at, one indiscreetly gawked back. For every ten that indiscreetly gawked back, one made an advance of some sort. Typically, once he had that concrete fact in his pocket, he could move with confidence, the kind he knew he should have possessed without such an obvious crutch.

Alan's breathing was still a little uneasy. It was hard to believe that within a few days, in all likelihood, he and Jill would be all over each other. But he couldn't actually do that right now; he hadn't gone through the formalities yet. What would they do if they passed each other in the street or in the hallway before Thursday? Look away and wait for the given time, or break it wide open then and there? Alan thought that most arrangements and patterns in life were absurd. The pattern he and Jill would go through would most likely fall into that category, he thought. They would wait out the next few days, let loose for a few weeks or months, and then reenter the dry period for whatever reason. The drought would probably be permanent between them—dwarfing any previous happiness they were able to create together. Alan would feel depressed during the drought, and wonder why he hadn't been able to bottle some of the affection when it was overflowing and take a swig later on when he really needed it.

Alan's breathing remained irregular for another, more profound reason. Yesterday afternoon, he had laid to rest the ordeal with his ex-girlfriend, Robin. The week before, she had walked out of Alan's party with a distant male friend of his and returned two hours later with flushed cheeks. His closest friends, Zak included, advised Alan to tell Robin to go to hell—she wasn't good enough for him anyway. Two days later, Alan met with Robin and made the formal break as calmly and as civilized as he could, even though on the inside his fears, desires, and rage ran wild, and even though Robin took a dozen and a half verbal cheap shots at him. He was loaded with stinging comeback lines, but released only the two or three that had some redeeming moral value. Then, on Monday morning, he had gotten up hideously late for work, albeit well rested, and walked around the corner to send six red roses to Robin's office. Alan was impressed by his own trance-like resolve to make a statement to Robin independent of any cat-and-mouse-type game and transcending any desire for sex.

Now Alan made the connection. The note on the door this Tuesday morning was the fruit of Monday's lofty thoughts and actions. He looked at Zak's wide grin.

"I was going to give you about three more minutes," Zak said.

"You mean I showed up too early again?" Alan shot back.

"That's right, you missed out on 179 seconds of valuable masturbating time."

"That's okay, I'm planning to make up for it at work," Alan quipped.

"Any new news from your cousin Rick?"

"C'mon, the man lives in a truck and smokes pot all day." Alan returned. "What sort of news are you looking for—that he switched dealers? That he has a new parking spot?"

"No, I wanna know if he's still talking about his dream house on Rockaway Beach," Zak explained, "with banana trees growing inside, and the seven female pleasure kittens. . . ."

"He's still working on that one," Alan revealed. "In fact, he's going to a New York City housing auction later this month to bid on a three-room, beat up shack out there. It's hard to believe he's planning a semi-realistic activity."

"Very realistic. What's he using for a deposit—his bong?"

"Zak, check out this note." Alan pulled the note from his pocket and shoved it in Zak's face. "Think it's real, or one of Warren's pranks?"

"It's real, Reiss, I'm almost a hundred percent sure. Anyway, if it was a prank, I would have thought of Rick, because of the pencil."

"Rick doesn't have time for pranks, Zak. He's too busy making drug runs to Lefrak City."

"Huh, so *that's* her name—Jill," Zak mused.

"Yeah. You're the perfect one for me to be showing this to, Zak. Remember that long, drawn out look she gave me on Saturday when we were carrying the table out of my apartment?"

"Yup, that's why I knew this wasn't a prank. She was definitely interested."

"Besides," Alan concluded, "no one else but us knows enough about this situation to pick such a perfect time for a prank."

"What is this 'cut' here?" Zak asked. "The 'cut' girl next door. Did she need stitches?"

"If she did, the plastic surgery was a success," Alan quipped.

"This looks good, Reiss. She's definitely hot."

As Alan and Zak walked down the steps to the subway platform, they were bumped and brushed from both sides by people rushing for the closing doors below. The E train was getting ready to pull away, jammed with commuters. Several people with coats, bags, and briefcases were on the outside, reaching into the cars through doors that had closed around their arms.

"Remember those hyper-serious safety films they used to show us in the auditorium in sixth grade?" Alan mused. "They should make one of those safety films for the subway."

"Yeah," Zak returned in a deep, serious narrator's voice meant to grab the attention of naive eleven-year-olds,

"'. . . rule number four—never stick your arm in the way of closing doors.' Then you see a guy in a trench coat being pulled by his arm down the platform and flattened on the wall at the end."

"Beautiful. I'm going to write that down as soon as I get to the office. I have a stack of stuff going back nine months. Remember 'Yuppie Death Squad?'"

"Wait," Zak added, "two stops later, the arm is still in the door."

"And the conductor is yelling over the P.A. system: 'We cannot move this train unless you let go of the doors, sir.' Beautiful. That goes down too."

"You've gotta have that doo-doo-doo-do corny, happy-go-lucky, early-sixties, school-documentary music playing in the background the whole time," Zak proceeded. "Hey, that list of yours must be like thirty pages by now. There's some great stuff in there. We probably have enough to do a movie of short sketches."

"You're right," Alan acknowledged. "As it is, though, I comb that list every week for potential stand-up material. Are you coming to watch me perform next Tuesday night?"

"I'll probably make it."

As Alan and Zak split up where Chambers Street meets West Broadway, Zak considered the early May sunlight his body was soaking up and how much of it was going to be wasted indoors, as he feigned excitement about computer software over the phone. Lately, he had been coming to grips with a grim reality—that trying to make the time in the office go fast and the time outside of the office go slow did not work. It tended to all go fast or all go slow. Lately, it had all gone fast. The first few months of 1986 had flown by, making old age seem just around the corner.

As Alan walked toward his building, he realized that he had forgotten the pattern for the aeolian mode: whole step, half step, whole step, whole step—was it half step here or whole step again—or maybe that was Dorian mode, a similar minor scale. He hated losing ground, the notion that what he thought was in the bag really wasn't, at least on a conscious level. He would make a note to check it as soon as he got home.

Now Alan caught a glimpse of his reflection in the glass doors. He looked tired, but no different from the day before: still young, fresh, and a little beefy looking, even though he was slim. He tried to reason it out. He had seen himself age in comparison to the graduation pictures of twenty-three months ago, but he had not detected any definitive aging over the span of any given day during that period. There was hope for Alan in this phenomenon. As he saw it, there were two general possibilities. The first was that he simply was not observant enough to notice the slight daily changes in his body. This didn't seem likely. Alan was very observant—he had documented hour hands moving. The other possibility was that the changes occurred not steadily but in hard-hitting bursts, just when he wasn't looking. Therein lay the hope: if there actually were periods when no aging took place, then those periods could first be studied and then manipulated into time spans lasting far longer and perhaps indefinitely.

It was a worst case scenario a few seconds after he exited the elevator on the eleventh floor. Sashi and Dick O'Malley were standing right in the hallway that led to Alan's corner. As Alan avoided eye contact, he wondered yet again how much of the avoidance was due to his hatred of their system and how much was due to genuine embarrassment. In any case, he resolved to lighten his burden.

Rich Herschlag

Now that it was May, he wouldn't have to br⸺ the next few months. He could leave a sport ja⸺ office closet overnight. He could learn to live without the backpack or maybe give it to Zak in the morning. This way, Alan could walk in looking like he had just stepped across the hall for a minute.

The unintelligible stack of papers from the day before was still on Alan's desk. The pile consisted of letters, diagrams, official forms, payment vouchers, and various other items. He received a copy of everything sent back and forth between the design consultant and the construction contractor. The project involved the rehabilitation of an unloading plant for barges carrying the City's garbage; that much Alan had gathered. Beyond that, the documents were all but impenetrable, describing points of refusal for piles whose numbers—like A7 and C4—seemed to describe locations but which could not be found on any drawing; shop drawings of things he could not visualize in three dimensions if his life depended on it; minutes of meetings that he had never attended but would have been lost at anyway. Alan considered it ironic—he was named "project coordinator" for something that seemed to function smoothly without his participation. The City hired consultants to do the real work. No one had as of yet taken Alan under his wing and shown him what this technical, bureaucratic maze was really all about. Alan's questions had rarely gotten him very far: "You mean to tell me the Dartmouth whiz can't figure this out?"

Dick O'Malley was still talking loudly in the hallway, not to Sashi anymore, but to Sal Weisel from the eighth floor.

"We don't need a change order for the formwork," Dick insisted, "we'll stack it onto item 23-A."

Jack of All Trades

"But Jones and Hanover is already going under the assumption that it *is* a change order," Sal pleaded desperately. "Whaddawe gonna tell 'em now?"

"You tell 'em they will receive payment."

Dick and Sal had learned to care, Alan thought—now perhaps he could too. What he needed was a starting point. If he could just understand one element of this mess, maybe the rest would fall like dominoes. But that wasn't going to happen yet—the first wave of sleep had just hit him, the best starting point of all. A single nonsensical thought passed through his conscious mind. Now he leaned back in his chair just enough for his head to find that comfortable but spartan position against the wall behind him. His unconscious thoughts drifted to childhood. It was fourth grade. The kids at school were making fun of Andrew for having a zucchini in his lunch box. They shouted at him: "Zucchini-head, zucchini-head. . . ." Shortly after, that became Zuck, which soon after became Zak, which then stuck for at least another decade and a half.

Alan regained consciousness before he opened his eyes. For a brief time, he did not know where he would be when he did open his eyes: summer camp in the Poconos, a dorm room in New Hampshire, the floor of his cousin's old room. No—it was definitely the office. There on the wall was a diagram of the bureaucratic channels through which a signed City contract had to go. Alan hoped no one had noticed him sleeping, and if anyone had, that they considered it brief, accidental, and productive.

In a few more minutes, Alan had gotten his bearings and had begun drafting a monthly progress report on his project. Within the department, this type of report was highly valued. It was considered to represent at least a day's work by itself. Although he understood to his satisfaction less than fifty percent of what he was writing, he knew he would turn in a moderately-to-highly praised report. He was aided by old reports, whose style he mimicked and upon whose English he improved. By the time later in the day that he handed it in with a smile to Elena, the gorgeous Equadorian secretary, the whole task would have taken him less than three hours. These spurts of productivity, though he recognized them as simply part of a game, nevertheless legitimized most of his commentary and eccentricities in the eyes of others and sometimes even in his own.

Now, with a major mundane task behind him, he resolved to buy the electronic keyboard within the next week. It would have to be one of the small ones—under eighteen inches—in order to fit into his desk drawer. With the keyboard there from now on, he could recover lost time by working out new riffs and chord progressions during lulls. The small pair of headphones he would wear would be assumed by others to lead to a Walkman—just like theirs did.

At lunch, Alan and Zak met and walked toward the center of the outdoor pavilion at the base of the World Trade Center. Situated there was a complete ring of benches, all facing outward. The ring was about one hundred-and-fifty feet in diameter, with the inside lined by marble planters and filled in with soil and plants. Sitting on the benches was the usual assortment: young urban professionals in their mid-twenties having recently traded in their argyle sweaters for three-piece suits; older young urban professionals who already owned a rehabbed condo; less celebrated office workers who just slapped a tie on over an old shirt or tried to match a new skirt with an old blouse; old men on a permanent lunch break. . . .

"Hey, I don't like all those variegated types sitting together like that," Zak let out facetiously. "It bothers me."

"*I* know," Alan suggested, "we'll make signs, put them on posts, and stick them in the dirt right behind them. Each sign will give the salary range for that bench: fifty thousand to sixty thousand, forty thousand to fifty thousand, welfare to eight thousand etc."

"And out of the blue," Zak continued, "the Salary Police will swoop down to restore order: 'Okay, you, let's see a pay stub!'"

"'But officer,'" Alan proceeded, "'I don't get paid till Friday.'"

"'Sure, that's what they all say,'" Zak responded. "'You have the right to remain silent. . . .'"

"This one makes the list," Alan noted. "I was thinking this morning that we generate a lot of material. We really *should* get serious about doing a movie of short sketches like you said. We could definitely do it. We just have to buy a good video camera or maybe rent a really good one."

"That would be good. We should look into it."

Twenty minutes later, Alan and Zak stood by the spiked iron fence that surrounded a small graveyard by a church. The headstones were visually aged. Most were crooked. In some cases, they dated back to the early 1800's.

"Okay, picture this," Alan mused, "by the year two thousand thirty, the yuppies have taken over this graveyard and gentrified it. That headstone right there will have headphones on it and a Visa Gold card for a plaque."

****

As Alan walked down the hill to the entrance of his apartment building in Queens, he spotted his cousin Rick sitting on the back steps of the row of stores whose rear faced the building. Rick had a scraggly beard that he had started growing seventeen months earlier to mark the unofficial end of his adolescence. His eyes were wild and bloodshot from the pot he had undoubtedly smoked within the past hour or two. Several feet from him was a green dumpster holding two days worth of commercial refuse. Rick often waited here for Alan here at 5:50 P.M. to intercept him on his way home from work. Alan was usually pleased to see him, but sometimes a little annoyed as well. He envied Rick somewhat for not having to wrestle with the clock in the morning, even though everyone said the price Rick paid was enormous. Alan knew that every moment of his own day had a counterpart in his cousin Rick's day. Alan often considered how Rick might have wasted the day, while he had wasted his own.

"Ayyy, Alan," Rick let loose in a gravelly, though once tender voice, "how's it goin'?"

"I've gotta take a nap, and then get up and do some writing," Alan explained, as Rick rose from the steps to follow Alan to the apartment.

"Ayyyyy, I been thinkin' about somethin'," Rick announced through damaged cilia, "you work for the City of New York, right?"

"Right."

"Well, uhhhhh . . . do you think you could get me plans of the sewer?"

"Why?" Alan asked.

"'Cause I wanna use it to smuggle drugs," Rick explained, "You know, like my own private subway system . . . eh-heh-heh." Rick's obsessed laughter reminded Alan how far his cousin had fallen in such a short time.

"I remember when your mind was merely in the gutter," Alan said as he opened the door to the apartment. "Those were the good old days."

"Hey," Rick shot back, sinking into the couch, "can you get 'em or not?"

"I can get them, but first I have a few questions for you," Alan asked calmly. "From where to where in the city do you want to go that you couldn't just take a subway or a bus or walk or drive? What if the pipes are too small along part or all of your intended route? What if they *are* large enough, but you get flooded out by a storm? How will you get in and out of the system? Through manholes? How will you lift the covers? They're a few hundred pounds, you know. And what if you're seen? Would you like me to fake you a work permit or steal a sewer worker's uniform for you?"

"Ay . . . don't bother me with any of *that*. Just get me the plans."

"Can you answer even *one* of my questions?" Alan prompted with a faintly amused smile.

"I'm gonna use a boat. . . ."

"Then you're assuming that there *will* be a flow of water in, let's say, a six foot diameter line, and that that flow—which by the way will have feces, piss, tampons, and used toilet paper in it—will be sufficient to float your craft. What if you hit a dry spot?"

"Ayyy, I'll walk the rest of the way," Rick explained.

"And what if you're suddenly flooded out? How will you breathe? How will you smoke pot?"

"I'll . . . uhhhh . . . carry an emergency oxygen tank," Rick responded in a harried tone which revealed mild discomfort from the challenge to his logic.

"And what's your intended route?" Alan continued.

"I don't know . . . lotsa places. From Forest Hills to Lefrak City. From Queens to Manhattan."

"I've got bad news for you, Rick. Sewers don't go under the river. They go *into* the river. Why don't you try the Queens-Midtown Tunnel?"

"Are you gonna help me or not?"

"I'm *gonna* help you, Rick. First, I'm gonna tie you down and make you go cold turkey for a week."

"Ay," Rick replied, giggling slightly, and pulling out a joint, "it's only pot."

Alan controlled his temper, as he had learned to do fairly well with his cousin Rick. Now Alan flipped through one of his music books and found the pattern for the aeolian mode.

"So what's up with you?" Rick asked, casually blowing out pot smoke.

"I might have a date for Saturday night. The girl next door. She left me a note."

"Ho *yeah!!*" Rick let out, punching the air with his fist, coughing, and laughing, "she's hot. You oughta be fucking her brains out in no time."

"I wouldn't bet on it," Alan responded. "It looks like she comes from an Old World family. Anyway, that's not my only goal."

"Oh man," Rick blurted out, looking at his own knees and shaking his head with marijuana-induced giddiness, "that's what you say *now*. So no more Robin?"

"No. I have no need to torture myself, or if I do, not to that extent. Robin's free to go back to the west-coast, preppie pseudo-intellectuals she spent three months bragging about."

"Ay, that's too bad in a way," Rick revealed. "I was getting used to you two being together."

"Okay, Rick, here are my plans. After my shower, I'm gonna take a nap for an hour. Then I'm gonna get up and write for like an hour and maybe go to the "Y." You can drive by around ten and maybe we'll talk some more and get something to eat."

"All right," Rick agreed. "I was gonna go see Tony now anyway."

"The guy who stole your electric guitar?"

"He's a good guy. Everybody makes mistakes. You wanna hit?"

"Okay, just one," Alan said, reaching for the joint, taking in his mandatory allotment, and giving it back.

"Ay, pretty soon we'll be going to the beach again," Rick observed as he began climbing out the window.

****

Two hours later, while Alan was working on his novel, the phone rang. The voice came over the answering machine:

"Alan, it's Jordan. If you're there, pick up. . . ."

In 1984, Alan's longtime friend Jordan had gone straight from Duke University in North Carolina to Salamon Brothers in New York. Alan's mind was now in mid-paragraph, but he made an exception and picked up.

"Hello. . . ." The beep sounded, discontinuing the recording process.

"Alan, I'm still at the office. I've got a problem. It's about Andrea. She told me her ex-boyfriend from college is coming in for the weekend and that they're just friends."

"That might be a lie, but there might be some truth in it," Alan propounded. "It's very hard for me to read these situations when I never get to meet these women. The same thing happened with Kara. You met her at the office, and it began and ended without my ever laying eyes on her, or any of our other friends ever seeing her."

"Well, I know," Jordan explained. "I'm busy with work, and when I have a relationship, it's intense. From work we either go out to do something or to Andrea's apartment or mine. There's no room for anything else."

"Maybe that's part of the problem," Alan suggested, "but I'm not even gonna get into that now. I'm just saying it's hard for me to read it. I have to go completely on what I know about you. From the sound of your voice, I'd say something *is* wrong."

"She said he's interviewing in New York because he's finishing business school," Jordan continued, "but I don't see why he can't stay in a hotel. I don't know what to do. If she's lying and she's still got something going on with this guy, she can just go fuck herself. I don't take shit from anybody, even though I've gone as far as telling her I love her. But if Andrea's telling me the truth and she's just helping him out, I'd feel terrible."

"Great. Now you *can't* win either way," Alan observed. "So . . . otherwise, how have things been going with you two?"

"Fine. We've slept together practically every night this week. But she's been making weird statements, like that we don't spend 'quality' time together. Damnit, we spend *all* our free time together."

"What is quality time," Alan stated, "the ten seconds surrounding an orgasm? Look, sounds like something's up, but I would just relax. This is another case of the Heisenberg uncertainty principle—the way observing an experiment changes or influences the actual outcome. If you're feeling insecure, those very perceptions could influence what happens with you and Andrea over the next few days. Now I'm not saying those perceptions aren't based on something real in the first place. I just don't want to see them get out of hand."

"I understand what you're saying," Jordan acknowledged, "but I can't completely suppress what I'm going through."

"I know, but how's this—I hope you have feelings towards her that are independent of her actions," Alan asserted. "If you don't, then you're only going to be a character in a story narrated by Andrea's unconscious mind. If you *do* have feelings independent of her actions, try to concentrate on those for a while."

"How can I judge her on anything other than her actions, Alan? What you're saying is absurd."

"I doubt we have time to get into this now."

"Hey, I have to go anyway. I'm meeting Andrea for dinner in fifteen minutes. Maybe we'll talk about it some more. All right, thanks, Alan. Hey, how's your cousin Rick?"

"Stoned out of his fucking mind."

Chapter Two

Thursday, at 7:23 in the evening, Alan looked at the pay phone in the hallway of the "Y." He had brought along a couple of quarters and Jill's phone number and knew that the correct time to call was arriving any moment. Alan didn't like the mental game he was playing. "After 7:00" in the note logically meant a nanosecond after 7:00 or any time after that. Now, reluctantly, Alan was balancing the notion of calling much later and seeming uninterested against the notion of calling soon after seven and appearing desperate. At 7:25, the quarter went in and dialing began. The third ring was interrupted.
"Hello?"
"Yes, could I please speak to Jill?"

"Jill? Just one minute."

Alan took the male voice on the phone to be that of Jill's older brother, a slick looking, dark haired man in his late twenties who looked like he was pulled right off the set of the "Miami Vice" series. Alan thought back on his own words: ". . . could I please speak to Jill." He was glad he had avoided saying please twice: ". . . could I please speak to Jill, please." He had heard other people make that flub, and to him it sounded moronic and overly subservient. Now he heard the brother speak something akin to Greek in the background and call a name: "Katti, Katti. . . ." How did Jill become Katti, or vice-versa?

"Hello?" Jill's voice was an American one, with only the slightest hint of ethnicity.

"Hi, this is Alan. I got your note and I'm very flattered."

"Okay," she let out with an inflection.

"And I'd like to go with you Saturday night."

"Good, I'm glad," Jill responded. "I'll knock on your door at 7:30 Saturday."

"Do you need directions to my house?" Alan quipped. Jill laughed now and quickly recovered her composure:

"Make me a map and slip it under my door."

"By the way," Alan added, "if you're hearing grunting in the background, it's because I'm calling from the "Y." I don't want you to think I'm calling from my apartment."

"Oh, now I'm disappointed."

"Okay," Alan concluded, laughing slightly, "7:30, Saturday night. I'll be ready."

"Bye."

****

Friday at 5:47 in the late afternoon, Alan walked along Queens Boulevard silently celebrating the end of another work week. But his thoughts were invaded by Robin. Getting her out of his mind was not going to be as easy as he had thought, even with his karmic experiments and a new girlfriend in the works. In fact, the imminence of his seeing Jill seemed to pound in the reality of Robin's departure. Alan understood his own integrity and how once he so much as kissed the next woman, there would be no turning back. But years of sporadic fixation on Robin—culminating with the last three months of trial and error—were ringing in his head. Foremost was a nagging remembrance of the two of them talking philosophically for hours but never being able to achieve the normal physical union. Now Alan turned the corner and walked down the hill to the entrance of his apartment building. He spotted his cousin Randy's big white truck parked down the block. Even with his keen sense of irony, Alan still could not fully believe that he had *two* cousins who had dropped out of college, smoked pot all day, and lived in a truck. For most people, one was sufficient.

"Hey, man, what's up," Alan said as he stuck his head in through the open window of the front door and looked to the rear. Inside the large, box-like step van once used to deliver milk and baked goods, he saw the customized interior that he and Randy had designed and built together three months earlier. There was a sturdy, built-up wooden floor with trap doors all over for storage. Sitting on the floor were two large foam mattresses with quilts. There was also a beanbag on the floor and loudly colored drapes hanging from the walls. Randy was reclining and holding a large hardcover book.

"I've been reading the *Bhagavad-Gita* all day," Randy answered. "I can't stop. It's the most fascinating thing I've ever laid eyes on."

"I remember reading that three years ago in college," Alan revealed. "It's kind of the Hindu Bible. It was pretty influential in my thinking."

"This is pure essence, Alan. It all makes sense. Every day for years I wonder who I am, and now I'm getting somewhere. I am not this body. I am a spirit-soul with eternal life and a definite relationship to God."

"Self-realization in a milk truck. Sounds like a good cable show."

"And my position in life," Randy continued, "is to serve the Eternal, not to live for my own material pleasure."

"I guess Club Med's out then," Alan quipped. "Seriously, the *Bhagavad-Gita* was influential for me. I always had a sense of wanting to live for a higher purpose, and that book helped me crystalize my thinking on that. Wanna come in for a while?"

"Thanks," Randy responded, "but I just want to stay here right now and absorb this."

"All right. I'm glad to see you're putting aside *Hustler* and *Swank*. The *Bhagavad-Gita's* awesome. Have you seen your brother around today?"

"Nope."

"Yeah, I know," Alan mused, "you two just pass each other on the Parkway once in a while."

****

At 7:55, Saturday night, Alan paced in his apartment and tried to ignore the twenty-five minutes that had passed since Jill was supposed to come over. A stray notion passed through Alan's mind: if there was some sort of cancellation, he would have to spend the night confronting his thoughts about Robin. It didn't matter, though, because now the doorbell was ringing. He opened the door and faced Jill from an arm's reach.

"Hi, come on in." Jill took a few steps along with Alan into the narrow, ground floor apartment. This was the first time, Alan realized, that he was allowed to take a good long look at Jill from up close. His quicker glances from farther away hadn't deceived him. She could have walked comfortably onto the set of a fashion magazine photo session. Her face was ever so slightly wider and flatter than most American models, giving Jill the exotic look Alan had recognized earlier. But the large collared leather jacket and the tight wrapped cotton pants ending above the ankle bone were what young American women were being told to wear now. Her perfume was the same as the one used by the second girl he ever felt up, summer camp 1977.

"I'm sorry I'm late," Jill began. "A friend of mine called at the last minute."

"No problem," Alan replied, "as long as you don't tell me you got caught in traffic."

"Nope," she replied, beginning to point towards the back wall of the apartment. "I see you built yourself a platform bed. It's nice."

"Thanks. I was kind of proud of the way I got it to fit right into that little alcove. As you can imagine, I need the extra space in here." Alan looked at the wooden loft bed and the couch below it and thought of the four times he had been unable to get Robin to respond—twice on the loft, twice on the couch.

"Maybe you can build one for me one of these days," Jill suggested.

"As a matter of fact, I still have the plans on file," Alan noted. "I even did calculations on its load capacity."

"And then you tested it," Jill quipped.

"Yeah." Alan noticed how Jill's voice sometimes went up slightly in pitch near the end of her sentences. It came off as a half-conscious attempt to be cute, submissive, and shy.

"Hmm," Jill let out, "I really wanted this apartment for myself."

"Does your father own or *manage* the building?" Alan asked.

"We own it," Jill answered, *"and* manage it. We used to live in Manhattan, when we first owned it a few years ago. Then my father decided he didn't like the way the supers were taking care of it, so we moved here to do it ourselves. For a couple more years, we still had a super, but my father fired the last one and decided to rent out this apartment. I tried to convince my parents to let *me* have it, but they didn't go for it."

"What's it like next door, where you *do* live," Alan inquired. "I've wondered what it's like. There aren't many windows."

"Oh, that's not really where we live," Jill revealed. "We have a duplex. We had a hole cut in the ceiling and a staircase put in running up to the upstairs apartment. That's where we live mainly. Downstairs, we keep an office and an extra living room and workshop. But the bedrooms are upstairs. My bedroom is right over your sleeping area."

"That's really weird," Alan observed. "I guess you've seen my cousin Rick crawling in through my window a couple of hundred times."

"Is that who that man with a beard is?" Jill half giggled.

"Yup. You're not satisfied with all that space up there?"

"It's nice," Jill explained, "but I want a place of my own. Where I can have some privacy. Well, we really should go."

As they walked together down the hall, Alan assumed they were walking toward a car Jill was allowed to borrow. When envisioning this date a day earlier, Alan had pictured the two of them dressed to kill, boarding a grubby subway or the beat up '76 Dodge Alan was in the process of buying. Now as the building garage door continued to roll up behind them, those fears were put to rest.

"Not bad," Alan said. He laid eyes on a sleek, grey 1984 Camaro, free of urban cuts and bruises.

"My father gave it to me, to make up for moving us to Queens. By the way, my friend Denise is coming along. I hope you don't mind. I wasn't sure if you were coming, and I had an extra pass anyway."

"No problem." He was being checked out. He could deal with it. As they pulled out of the driveway, Alan observed Jill's sense of control in the way she handled the car. They were doing forty within five seconds.

"What do you do?" Jill asked.

"All sorts of stuff. I'm working for the City of New York right now as an engineer. When I get home, I work on a novel—writing one not reading one. I'm also working on some bass riffs and developing them into songs. I'll be looking to join a hard rock band in the next few months and probably trying to flesh out my songs on guitar and keyboard."

"Sounds ambitious," Jill asserted.

"Yeah, my goal is someday to own a limousine that people can see into, but that I can't see out of." Jill laughed soundly, somewhere between polite and hearty, something like a release. The laughter was accompanied by a head turn and direct smile at Alan, who returned the smile. He was glad she had gotten the joke.

"Well, it's good that you're ambitious," Jill resumed. "My talents are also in the creative areas, and I like to think I'm ambitious too. I like to learn about all sorts of different things."

"Right, same with me," Alan agreed. "I get interested in all sorts of things, make lists on things—I'm really organized, sometimes—I work on dozens of little projects on the side. Recently, I've been practicing reading lips. So far, I can only read my own . . . in the mirror."

Jill laughed and smiled again. Alan instinctively reached for her hand, alongside the stick shift. She had begun to move for Alan's hand at almost exactly the same time and now held it sensually. Alan perceived energy flowing back and forth between the two hands, not unlike the phenomena described in the two or three holistically oriented books he had recently skimmed. Several minutes later, when they pulled up in front of Denise's house in Astoria, the hand games were put on hold.

"Denise, this is Alan." Alan shook Denise's hand and took a quick look at her as she settled into the back seat. She had an attractive Mediterranean face and thick, black shoulder length hair in curls, some of them natural, some of them not.

"Denise and I went to F.I.T. together to study fashion," Jill explained. "Actually, I'm still finishing up."

"My father's in the fashion industry," Alan noted.

"I'm really upset, Jill," Denise revealed. "Roberto hasn't called me in a week."

"Mmmmm...."

"I don't feel like I should have to be the one to call," Denise continued, "and also, he's always telling me what to do. Sometimes I hate that."

"Some people act like they own the world," Jill said.

"I act like I lease it," Alan let out.

Laughter came from both women, but more from Jill.

"Where did you go to school?" Jill asked.

"Dartmouth," Alan responded.

"That's famous, isn't it?" Denise asked.

"Especially among alumni," Alan answered.

"That must have been great," Jill asserted.

"Basically, I got into trouble there," Alan revealed.

"Really? For what?"

"For not taking them as seriously as they wanted to be taken. That seems to be part of my function in life. You know, I did things to irritate them. I set up my own department, put out my own course guide, protested my own syllabus...."

"Why did you do this?" Denise asked sincerely, missing his joke.

"I don't know," Alan said, "but some people appreciated it."

The Underground resembled a few of the trendy clubs that Alan had been dragged to over the past several years. Ironically, they were housed in a facility that had once served some useful purpose—a warehouse, a church, in this case a subway station—but had for one reason or another been surrendered and converted into an overdecorated yet sterile enclosure where two thousand young people could drop in for fifteen dollars, buy a drink for five, and get their already numb brains pounded by vacant synthesizer beats played at one hundred and ten decibels. Alan reminded himself to suppress his usual disparaging comments about this scene. Now Jill, Denise, and Alan pushed their way through throngs of mildly annoyed, slickly dressed nineteen to twenty-three-year-olds severely doused in perfume. Alan tried not to process mentally the words coming over the P.A. system: "What have you done for me *lately*. . . ." He thought instead about how at the window outside, as he had tried to pay the thirty dollars for both of them, Jill had quickly come out with a ten and the passes, but had looked confused nonetheless.

"Can I get anyone a drink?" Alan shouted.

"A screwdriver?" Jill responded.

"Oh, thank you," Denise said. ". . . Scotch and soda."

As he sifted his way toward the bar, Alan overheard the conversation of three young, well-dressed, male drug-war hopefuls: "You gotta fuck fat girls, I'm telling you. . . ."

Several young women rolled their eyes unpleasantly as Alan accidentally brushed against them. He considered how strange it was that Jill seemed to have a special attraction for the same slab of flesh that was becoming a nuisance to these untouchable females. The Euro-effeminate voice over the beat was especially loud now: "I want some-*Body*, I want some-*Body*. . . ."

Alan gently handed Jill and Denise their drinks and considered the most challenging segment of his evening now over.

"So what am I going to do about Roberto?" Denise pressed. ". . . if I call he'll think I'm desperate. . . ."

"Just do what your heart desires," Jill said solidly. "You can't accomplish anything by torturing yourself."

Denise was silent now, almost stunned. Soon, Alan and Jill moved out to the dance floor, where as a good looking couple, they mixed in reasonable well. They looked at each other and smiled as Alan did his best to move to the beat and was thankful none of his heavy metal friends would see him. When they arrived back at the outskirts of the club, Jill spoke into his ear:

"I have something to admit." At close range, her lips and tongue ever so gently touched his ear. Alan was now hard as a rock. "I've been watching you for months," she continued. "I love you in your tight sweatpants and t-shirt. I used to watch you from my window every day."

"Thanks," Alan acknowledged, "and I'll tell you something. I really like what you said to your friend before, about doing what your heart desires. I admire that, and I hate games. The truth is, you can get the most out of life simply by straight out asking for things—as long as you're sincere."

"That's the same way I've always felt," Jill confirmed.

"If you were ever to come to me for advice," Alan stated, "I would probably tell you something along the same lines."

Hand holding started again. They were both standing. Alan was easily drunk enough not to worry about rejection. He waited for a slight movement in Jill's rear shoulder and put his lips to hers. Her kisses came in rapid-fire multiples. Her tongue gave out small, close range licks that made Alan half-crazed. He had never experienced this little trick and felt sure it was a personal invention of Jill's resulting from parental repression she had almost managed to defeat.

"I'm a very traditional girl," Jill said almost whimsically, "and if we're together, everything that's mine is yours."

"What's your heritage?" Alan asked.

"Half Greek, half Bulgarian," Jill stated.

A few minutes later, Alan emerged from the men's room and began heading back towards Jill, who was waiting at their spot on the outskirts. He knew their physical contact a little while earlier must have been pleasurable for her too. The same should have been true of the after thoughts he was having at present. He needed a different perspective to make it all hit him, and now he was getting it. Alan viewed Jill through the crowd from across half the club, about ninety feet away. She was striking in appearance, the same type of woman he would have stared at in awe from afar had he for some unlikely reason come here alone. "Try to remember that while you're fooling around with her," he told himself.

Jill was talking to a young, white urban professional couple in their mid-to-late twenties.

"We just got married," the woman announced to Alan.

"And it feels great," the man followed, lifting his beer.

"Is this your honeymoon?" Alan asked.

"Our flight doesn't leave till tomorrow," the woman explained.

"They're going to Aruba," Jill added.

"Are *you* two getting married?" the man inquired.

"This is our first date," Alan replied. "It may be too early to tell."

"You should give it a try," the woman urged.

"You should," the man added. "You make a good couple."

"I need at least a day to mull it over," Alan said.

In the Camaro on the way home, after they had dropped off Denise, Jill made an observation: "It's so rare that I'm attracted to anybody like this."

"Isn't it weird living next door to each other, or . . . whatever . . . upstairs and downstairs?"

"It'll be weird, but we'll get used to it. My parents will get used to it too," Jill predicted. "I'm not walking in on the middle of a relationship, am I?"

"No," Alan replied, "not at all."

"Good. I *hate* when I do that." How many times *have* you done that, Alan thought.

"No," he continued, "it's definitely over between Robin and me. You might have seen her coming in and out of the building."

"Uh-huh," Jill acknowledged, "she was a little on the short side, dark hair, always wore nice business suits."

"Sometimes. She wore normal clothes too. We went out like six years ago, at the end of high school, and broke up a few months later. That, by the way, means she dumped me. She showed up a few months ago after getting back from Berkeley and Israel and pleaded with me to try it again."

"Well, sometimes things just don't work out," Jill mused. There was a long pause. Finally, Jill spoke: "I would imagine that if you were having sex in that apartment, everyone could hear."

"Why? Did you hear anything?"

"No. That's what I mean, Alan."

A short while later, as they locked up the Camaro in the garage, Jill brushed her hand along the inside of Alan's thigh, outside his pants, and then indicated with body language that that would be all for tonight. At the adjacent apartment doors, they kissed again.

"I still say this is weird." Alan let out.

"How do you think *I* feel?"

****

At noon the next day, Alan let Warren into the apartment. Aside from the fact that his legs were now ten inches longer, Warren looked the same at age twenty-four as he had at age eleven. His bright blue Mets baseball cap, matching blue sweatshirt, corduroys, Converse sneakers, and large framed glasses had etched a permanent image in Alan's mind. The bat slung over his shoulder with the crusty old mitt dangling from it gave the image a finishing touch.

"Ya' ready, Al?" Warren asked, fingering a softball.

"Almost. I thought you'd be over a little more towards one."

"No, *you're* the one who means one when he says noon," Warren asserted. "I really mean noon."

"I mean noon too," Alan explained. "I just don't show up then. Is Zak coming?"

"Yeah, he should be here soon."

"I had an amazing date last night."

"You did?"

"Yup. Jill, the landlord's daughter, next door."

"I guess she's looking for a super," Warren cracked.

"Hey, it looks good," Alan stated. "I have very positive feelings about it. Know what I mean?"

"You sly dog, you. It's probably just what you need to forget about that bitch Robin."

"Who? So how are *you* doing?"

"Great," Warren replied. "Have you seen what kind of year Gary Carter's been having? Eight home runs and twenty-seven ribbies already. He could be M.V.P. He was named player of the month for April."

"And he handles the pitching staff tho' well," Alan added, in a mock-gay tone.

"Yeah, that goes without saying."

Out of the corner of his right eye, Alan saw something hairy in the window near the loft. It was cousin Rick.

"Ay, folks," Rick growled, as he began to climb in through the window.

"That's okay, Rick," Alan said, "just use the window, don't bother with the door."

"Thanks," Rick grumbled, apparently unaware of the sarcasm. Rick took a seat on the loft and dangled his legs.

"How's the dream house in Rockaway Beach coming?" Warren asked, also with an air of sarcasm.

"Pretty good," Rick responded. "I'll be goin' to the auction in a couple of weeks. Then it'll be mine."

"What are you doing for the down payment?" Warren inquired, ". . . selling your hair?"

"No way, man," Rick let out, "I'm never cuttin' it. Not till the day I die."

"But on *that* day, he's going for a trim," Alan added.

"Ay, I got insurance money comin' in," Rick asserted. "It should be comin' in any day now. Five thousand dolluhs."

"I've got it," Warren interjected, "he's gonna start charging rent to all the things living in his hair."

"That accident in January, huh?" Alan proceeded with Rick. "You really think that ship's coming in?"

"Ayy, I got a lawyuh workin' on it right now," Rick explained.

"*I* know," Warren mused, still stuck at the beginning of the conversation, "he'll sneak into a bank vault from the sewer. . . ."

At that moment, the intercom buzzer rang, indicating that, most likely, Zak would be at the apartment door in a few seconds. Within two seconds, the phone also rang, and Alan reached for it.

"Hello?"

"Alan, it's Jordan."

"Hey, what's up?"

"Would you like to meet me and Andrea for dinner tomorrow night, Monday night?" In the background of Alan's consciousness, Warren and Zak were now both teasing cousin Rick, who was still accepting the abuse with stoned grace.

"Keep talking."

"At a place on 48th street we always go to," Jordan continued, "after work."

"I'll be there. Lemme grab a pen and take down the details. I'll tell you, I can't believe I'm going to meet her."

A comment of Zak's rose above the noise: ". . . what about porn movies?"

"She's interested in meeting you," Jordan stated.

Out behind the high school a short while later, they took batting practice and rotated positions. They let Rick have a couple of dozen swings. As they watched Rick take his wild cuts at the ball's arched trajectory, they sensed this would be one of the twenty or thirty images they would never forget. Rick was like a wild bagman with a stick, waving at the wind.

****

At 6:30 in the evening the next day, with the sun hanging low, invisible behind the city's skyscrapers, Alan walked into an upscale bar and grill on 48th street. He immediately spotted the woman sitting next to Jordan—a slim, compact-framed woman with straight shoulder length hair and a dainty but stern face.

"Hi, sorry I'm on time," Alan said, extending his hand to Andrea, who shook it.

"Hey, have a seat," Jordan said. "Alan, Andrea. Andrea, Alan. I already ordered us a pitcher of Sangria."

"All *right,*" Alan let out, "I was hoping for something like that. You know I'm missing my nap for this."

"After his nap," Jordan explained, "he starts his second shift."

"You're very busy, right?" Andrea asked rhetorically. "I heard you were involved in numerous endeavors."

"Yeah, the hardest one of which is keeping track of the others," Alan remarked.

"Well," she continued, "what's your book about?"

"I don't know yet, and that could prove to be a problem. I'm sorry everything coming out of my mouth is a wisecrack. It's probably because I'm so damned tired."

"Oh, I feel the same way," Andrea agreed. "Today was a disaster. The mainframe crashed and we were missing some of the back-ups. I lost five hours of work, and that pisses me off. Do you believe I'm expected to be back there at eight tonight. . . ." Alan noticed that as she spoke her voice sped up a little.

"I hate losing work," Alan stated, "much more than losing money."

"I'm sure we could find an equilibrium in there," Jordan proposed.

"I knew you were going to say that," Alan let out.

"So did I," Andrea concurred. "I'll be right back." She got up and walked towards the rest rooms. Alan waited till she was out of sight to speak:

"I like her. She's a bit frenetic, like us. What happened this weekend, with that guy?"

"We worked that out," Jordan responded. "He only slept over one night, and I was there too. The rest of the time, he's staying with another friend of theirs in the City."

"So everything's worked out now."

"Nothing we can't handle," Jordan said.

"That's cool. I have some news of my own."

"Yeah, I heard you got a note from that woman next door," Jordan revealed. "Did you call her?"

"You're a chapter behind. . . ." Andrea was now returning to the table. "I called her up last week, told her I was flattered. . . ."

"You shouldn't have said that," Jordan asserted.

"Now that time, I *really* knew you were going to say that," Alan let out. In reality, Alan had set it up and startled himself in the process.

"What's wrong with telling her he's flattered?" Andrea asked. "I think it's perfectly fine."

"It's like demeaning yourself," Jordan argued.

"No it's not," Alan argued back. "The woman had already laid herself on the line. Why should I be guarding myself?"

"That would have made *me* feel good in the same situation," Andrea put forth.

"Excuse me for a minute, okay?" Alan requested. He headed straight back to the vacant pay phone booth and dialed Zak's number.

"Hello?"

"Zak? It's me. More material. A couple of lines from Saturday night that I just remembered. I haven't had a chance to write them down. Got a pen and paper?"

"Hang on . . . yeah, go ahead."

"Okay, the first one is: 'My goal is some day to own a limousine that people can see into, but I can't see out of.'"

"Good one Reiss, good one," Zak muttered, ". . . okay, next. . . ."

"Okay, next is: 'Recently I've begun reading lips. So far, I can only read my own—in the mirror.'"

". . . 'my own in the mirror,'" Zak repeated methodically, "got it. I have a few pages of these now. Maybe I should give you the whole list before you go on tomorrow."

"Actually, what I was thinking," Alan revealed, "was that we should get together one day soon and make two sets of everything either of us has, and you keep one set on file for me."

"Like a back-up file," Zak suggested.

"Right, in case I have a fire or something in my apartment. I think of things like that all the time."

"Okay," Zak concluded, "then I guess I'll see you tomorrow."

"Wait a second, I just thought of something. Could you throw in one more for me? Just a stray one: 'Sorry I'm on time.'"

****

Tuesday night at 9:30, Warren, Zak, and Tom sat alongside Alan in the rear of the Comic Strip nightclub and waited for Alan to go on. He was fifth among twelve relative newcomers to be looked over on this night by the management. Tom Ginotti, who sat to Alan's immediate left, was—like Warren and Zak—a longtime friend. Tom was slightly underweight, genteel, bordering on shy. Over the years, Tom's friends had dissected every physical and behavioral aspect of him and turned it into a routine. Even his name, Tom Ginotti, had been worked over during an unusually lean two-month period three years earlier and was now "Yotti," or "the Yotti."

"Is Jordan coming?" Zak asked.

"He's getting laid," Warren said, "and the Yotti's editing the highlight film."

"Oh, oh *man,*" Zak said in a voice mocking the Yotti, putting his bent middle finger to his forehead in the fashion of an exasperated eggheaded schoolteacher. The Yotti had done something like this several years earlier and dropped it as soon as it became part of the running routine. "Oh *man,*" Zak continued in the mock-Yotti voice, "do you think I can work out a cable deal with this thing?"

"Sure, Yotti," Warren explained, "it can be part of a special called 'Yotti's World,' or the 'Wide World of Yotti,' with spliced-in scenes of the Yotti alphabetizing his record collection."

"Just the Grateful Dead albums will fill a half-hour," Zak quipped.

"I always wondered how someone like the Yotti got involved with the Dead," Warren mused. "The most adventurous thing the Yotti's done since 1969 is gargle Camomile tea."

"I got stoned from it, man," Zak remarked in his Yotti voice. "I put the 'Skull and Bones' album ahead of

'Shakedown Street,' man. It was emotionally devastating, man."

"Hey, man," Warren quipped in a Yotti voice, "stop saying 'man' after everything . . . man."

"All right, guys," the Yotti himself said, sounding just like the imitations, "that's enough for now."

"Yotti," Alan said, "how does it feel to be talked about right in front of you, like a ninety year-old, senile man?"

"I thought they were talking about a different Yotti, man," Warren answered in Yotti's place.

"Yeah," the Yotti himself acknowledged, "it gets on my nerves sometimes."

"Man," Zak added, without hesitation.

"We do that to my cousin Rick a lot, too," Alan explained.

"That's different," Warren explained, "the Yotti *knows* we're talking about him."

"I think you're up soon," the Yotti observed. "What do you have planned for tonight?"

"Sick jokes," Alan stated, getting a surprisingly full laugh from the Yotti. They overheard the tail end of the fourth comedian's routine: "Yeah, I'm really good in bed, until someone else gets under the covers with me. . . ."

Alan went on a few minutes later, after being introduced by the MC. As Alan grabbed the mike, he utilized a few of the relaxation techniques he had compiled over the past several months: take full, easy breaths; make quick eye contact with a few people around the room; pretend everyone in the audience is the Yotti. . . .

"My longtime girlfriend just blew me off," Alan began. "You always get the same thing when you're being blown off—code language. Like: 'I don't want to see *anyone* right now.' Translation: 'I don't want to see *you* right now.'"

The considerable laughter of recognition around the room put Alan more at ease as he continued:

"Or how about: 'I think we should see other people.' Translation: 'I think *I* should *fuck* other men.' Or how about: 'Let's cool it off for awhile.' Translation: 'Let's make it *ice cold* for eternity.'"

The laughter around the room put Alan more at ease. He inhaled deeply, looked quickly into the Yotti's eyes as if he were taking a toke on a confidence joint, and continued:

"Or you're walking down the street with her, and she'll point at some other woman and say: 'Oh, isn't *she* cute?' Translation: 'I'll give you a one week's grace period to find someone else, asshole.'"

An attractive woman in her mid twenties, about halfway toward the back, was laughing hysterically. Alan recalled something from his notes: "Interact with audience."

"Is that one *you've* used recently?" Alan asked, directing himself to the young woman.

"No," she giggled forth, "not recently."

"Translation," Alan quipped, "'. . . last Wednesday.'"

This comeback got the most profound, thorough burst of laughter so far. Perceived as a genuinely spontaneous comeback, it made Alan a heavyweight and helped legitimize whatever was to follow. He was also pleased that he was remembering to execute other details, like using a slightly high-pitched voice for the "statement" and a lower voice for the "translation."

"Here's a classic," Alan continued, "'Let's be friends.' 'What's that? Let's be friends?' 'Yes, let's be friends.' 'Okay, what are we going to talk about in our new friendship—how you've ruined my life?'" He paused for the next wave of laughter and then resumed: "What do I tell her?: 'Yeah, I've been crying a lot lately and jerking off.' 'Oh really, tell me about it, I'm really sympathetic—wait a second, I've got someone on the other line.' That reminds me of another classic: 'I think it'll be best for both of us.' Translation: 'It's gonna suck for you—but I'm getting laid tomorrow night.'"

Alan paused, looked at someone who might have been a talent scout, and went on: "So anyway, I was dumped and I had to deal with it. And I was desperate for a while. How desperate was I? Ever have this experience? You suddenly smell your ex-girlfriend's perfume, you get a hard-on, you wheel around, and you realize it's emanating from a sixty-eight year-old lady shopping for poultry! . . . So you ask for her number, but she's already off to the dairy section. Yeah, I was desperate for a while. I figured I'd try the personal ad section, what the hell. You've seen those ads, right? They use their own code language in there, with initials, like 'GBM seeks SJF.' That's an easy one, right? 'Gay black male seeks single Jewish female. That's a common one.'" Alan pointed to an interracial couple in the front. "I think this couple over here got together using that one. I understand he was a little pissed when he found out you weren't Jewish."

This one brought the house down. Alan reflected on his near perfect lisp on the word "pissed" and told himself to make a note of it. He continued his routine: "Yeah, that's a standard one. One I saw on the same page was: 'OSSEWM seeks TTBFSK.' Pretty obvious, right? That's: 'Obese, syphilitic, seventy-eight-year-old white man seeks twenty-two-year-old blonde, female sex kitten, for wild times on my adjustable bed.' And get this—no mention of how many speeds on the adjustable bed. So I blew that off, but I was still desperate. I met this girl on a bus, started talking to her, and I figured she was pretty smart, an intellectual. She started confiding in me. She told me, 'Alan, I tend to look for my father in relationships.' I said, 'Hey, babe, don't look for your father in relationships. Look for him around the house. Like in the garage, or your parents' bedroom. And when you find him, don't be coy, be direct. Tell him you've had your eye on him for quite some time. Tell him you don't know what it is, but he reminds you a bit of your ex-boyfriends.'"

Alan's performance lasted just under fifteen minutes. He felt reasonably good as he walked back towards his friends' table. He didn't want to soak it all in right now, preferring to save some of the memory for sometime later, after a flop of some sort—in stand-up or in anything else.

"Excellent, Al," Zak said.

"Did you get it all on tape?" Alan inquired.

"Yeah," Zak assured.

Alan reached for the hand-held tape recorder with condenser mike, rewound more than half way, and pressed his ear up against the small speaker as he hit "play" and adjusted the volume. He listened: ". . . suck for you, but I'm getting laid tomorrow night."

"A little trebly," Alan noted to Zak. "I'll have to equalize it out."

Chapter Three

The following evening, Wednesday, Alan's cousin Randy crawled through the apartment window and began discussing the *Bhagavad-Gita*.

"Remember that talk we had about reincarnation?" Randy asked. "I've understood that truth unconsciously for years, and this book is hitting the nail on the head for me. I've already read and reread it. When I think about it, I realize that I've always existed, and always will exist."

"I wonder if your parking tickets will carry over to your next lifetime," Alan quipped.

"Be serious for a minute," Randy said, toking on a joint, "you have the same belief, don't you?"

"Sure I do," Alan acknowledged, "I believe that I'm more than just a clump of chemicals. Actually, part of the reason my beliefs took that turn is because of my scientific observations. It's a scientific fact that of the atoms contained in my entire body—say, five years ago—not a single one is contained in my body right now."

"Right."

"And," Alan continued, "of the atoms I have in my body right now, not a single one will be present in my body five years from now. Yet somehow I'll still consider myself to be the same person and still call myself Alan Reiss, just like everyone else will. So obviously, there is some other element that constitutes me, other than matter itself. I suppose that would be the 'soul.'"

"Uh-huh," Randy agreed, "and since that soul is maintained throughout a lifetime, throughout all the surrounding bodily changes, we have no reason to assume it didn't exist before the formation of that body, or that it won't continue to exist after that body disintegrates."

"That's true," Alan asserted, "that does follow logically, but I have to admit, that's where—although I have an abstract understanding of the concept—the argument gets a little murky for me. What actually is the 'soul' then? Where is it? Can I catch it in a jar after someone dies?"

"Just because the mechanics of the process are beyond our conception at this point is no reason to doubt the validity of the process," Randy observed. "But what the *Bhagavad-Gita* teaches is how to get out of or transcend the process of birth, death, and rebirth. Listen to this: 'A man should not hate any living creature. Let him be friendly and compassionate to all. He must free himself from the delusion of "I" and "mine." He must accept pleasure and pain with equal tranquility. He must be forgiving, ever-contented, self-controlled, united constantly with Me in meditation. His resolve must be unshakable. He must be dedicated to me in intellect and in mind. Such a devotee is dear to Me. He neither molests his fellow men, nor allows himself to become disturbed by the world. He is no longer swayed by joy and envy, anxiety and fear. Therefore, he is dear to me. He is pure, and independent of the body's desire. He is able to deal with the unexpected; prepared for everything, unperturbed by anything. He is neither vain nor anxious about the results of his actions. . . .'"

"Sure. No problem." Alan quipped.

"I got my copy from some Hare Krishnas I met on the street," Randy said, "around Union Square."

"I recently had a talk with one of those guys," Alan revealed, "on Chambers Street. He was a bit more sane than anyone would have had me believe, even though his head was shaved like a cue ball with a pony tail."

"Well, I'm finally reading something that really makes sense to me," Randy stated, "not like that existentialist crap I was into a few months ago."

"Do you have any thoughts on how you're going to support yourself over the next few years?" Alan inquired.

"I don't want to punch numbers and program all day for Moody's again, okay?" Randy shot back.

"I'm the last person in the world to tell you to do something you dislike just to be like everybody else," Alan explained. "I'm simply calling to your attention the fact that there's a material side to life as well as a spiritual side. I'm not concerned with your leaving Amherst or Rick's leaving Emory. I'm not concerned with various aspects of prestige the way some of our relatives might be. When people ask me about you guys, I tell them I'm proud: my cousins have dropped out of some of the finest institutions in the country."

"As far as money goes," Randy explained, "I was thinking of becoming a private distributor of pay phones. But mainly, I want to get out of this dreadful cycle of birth and death."

****

Thursday, after work, Alan walked toward the South Street Seaport, where he and Jill had arranged to meet. For the past several days, Jill had been leaving him cute little notes in his doorway and mailbox. They said things like: ". . . been thinking of you all day—the girl next door," ". . . here's a card that reminded me of you," ". . . I'll meet you near your work." Alan acknowledged to himself that the cards were thoughtful, but he had larger issues on his mind concerning the young romance. Unlike couples separated by a physical distance of even a mile or two, Alan and Jill had no standard excuse for not having gotten together every night since the first date. Alan understood it was probably neither his fault nor hers, but due rather to a vague sense of her parents lurking about.

After a long, drawn out stalemate with Robin, Alan recognized that his body's demands for immediate gratification were particularly strong now, and that was not ideal for adjusting to this new situation. Now, in the middle of the well kept outdoor pavilion of the South Street Seaport, with hundreds of young urban professionals going about their business on all sides, Alan walked up to Jill and kissed her neatly on her closed, ready lips.

Upstairs, at a small table for two overlooking the large atrium of a massive drinking establishment, Alan remarked on the environment:

"My friend Zak and I were here a couple of times over this past winter. We couldn't believe what a yuppie hangout it was. We actually saw some guy showing off his pay stub to some woman he was trying to impress. I think she demanded to see his W-2 form, though."

"Zak. . . ." Jill inquired. "Is that your friend I see a lot, kind of tall, blond, sort of handsome, but with this big nose?"

"Yup, that's him. Everybody was just trying to impress everybody else. We were having such a crappy time that we decided to turn it around and have some fun."

"Really?" Jill asked, flatly. "How?"

"I took my wool hat," Alan explained, "and pulled it down completely over my head. Zak walked me around and introduced me as the 'Masked Mogul,' fighting warmth and sincerity wherever they rear their ugly heads. About half-way through, we changed my name to 'The Unknown Yuppie.' You wouldn't believe the response we got. People actually spoke to us and got the joke, left and right."

"Hmmmm," Jill let out innocently.

"Yeah," Alan continued, "and there was an unexpected return. A lot of the women were going crazy trying to get me to take off the mask or trying to take it off themselves. They couldn't stand not knowing. They were saying things like: 'Nice ass—I wonder if his face is as hot.'"

"Can I ask you something?" Jill said with little emotion, but apparently wrestling with the confusion of conflicting feelings. "Haven't you ever gone some place, dressed up, maybe tried to impress someone? . . ."

"I know what you're saying," Alan jumped in immediately, "that my friend and I were being pretentious. That we're really not above the rest of the people there." Jill's head nodded slightly, while Alan paused and continued. "Well, I considered that, even at the time, and I knew that part of the joke was on ourselves. That's at the core of most humor, the notion that the one conveying the criticism is flawed too. Of *course,* somewhere in our minds, Zak and I shared the wishes of other people there. How else could we have so accurately tuned into the minds of the crowd with our prank?"

"Hm-hm, I see. Okay."

"Very few people were insulted by what we did," Alan continued. "For the most part, people were—I don't know exactly how to express this—relieved. Relieved that someone else recognized or shared their plight."

"I guess I'm surprised to hear someone from a school like Dartmouth doing something like that."

"Hey," Alan quipped, "did you ever hear the rumors about Dartmouth men and sheep?"

"My parents are going away in a few weeks," Jill stated, "to Greece. They'll be gone for most of June."

"I'm looking forward to that trip," Alan said, "even though I'm not going on it."

"It's gonna be good," Jill stated. She reached for his hand across the table. *"How* good?" Alan wondered silently. He asked himself why it was necessary to wait for the parents' departure instead of simply going away themselves for a day or two. He knew he should have been asking Jill this question. At least, he thought, her mind was on the same thing his was, or perceived what his mind was on. And at least she demonstrated some character by challenging his "masked mogul" routine, even though it was a weak challenge.

"After we left here that night," Alan resumed, "Zak and I walked by a heavy duty yuppie restaurant right outside with enormous windows. A couple that looked like the Trumps was eating by one of those windows, so we stepped up and put our faces to the glass, so that our noses, cheeks, and chins were all deformed. We stayed there for two full minutes."

Jill had parked the car outside and had to make a seven o'clock class on 26th Street. She drove Alan to the subway stop and gave him an inner-thigh job on the way. Alan got out of the car and walked away, aching.

At 9:52 that night, Alan was curled up in a sleeping bag on the floor of his apartment taking a nap of an unplanned length. He had lost track of the evening and hoped perhaps he could regroup his thoughts in a dream. Alan looked back on his life and understood that from time to time he had made himself sleep on the floor when he was both unhappy with the way things were going and when he held himself partially responsible as well. The mess on the floor symbolized the mess outside the door.

Now, outside the door, there was a knock, then a ring of the bell, then another knock. Alan got up in a daze. Through the eyepiece in the door, he could see that it was a distressed Robin, with her head down. He opened the door immediately. Robin was fighting back tears and stormed past Alan into the apartment. She collapsed on the couch, beneath the loft.

"I hate her, I *hate* her," she half screamed, half moaned.

"Your mother, right?" Alan observed. "You don't hate her. You resent her."

"No, I *hate* her," Robin yelled. "Don't you tell me I resent her. I've heard enough of that psychological *bullshit*. I hate her. I hate her guts!"

"I guess you do."

"I'm *glad* this happened, I'm *glad* it happened," Robin continued, pausing only for the brief gasps that accompanied her crying. "When I came home from work, I just wanted to be alone. I just wanted to look at my mail, go upstairs, take my bath, and go to my room to write, Alan. But she started right in on me. She went through my mail and then asked me all these questions about work. I said: 'Mom, I really just want to be left alone now, okay?' Then she snapped, Alan. She told me: 'When are you going to take stock of your life? When are you going to move ahead?' So I said it, Alan, I just said it: 'Mom, when are you going to stop blaming me for the fact that you never had a real career yourself?!!' I don't even remember what happened after that. There was so much screaming, and then my father jumped in and said: 'When are you two going for counseling? Why do you do this to your mother?' I'm *glad* I did it. I'm *glad*. I've taken this shit for so many years, she can rot for all I care. That's it, I'm going to California tomorrow."

"Hang on," Alan advised, "don't go flying across the continent yet. You definitely need a couple days to think. You're more than welcome to stay here. Hey, you already have the keys." A look of gratitude swept over Robin's face as she responded:

"You're so nice, Alan. I don't even deserve you as a friend. I can't believe you would do that for me."

"Well, you can't be too surprised by it," Alan asserted, "considering that you came here in the first place." Alan paused for a moment to focus his thoughts. He felt immature and immoral for having loathed Robin, for having been disgusted with her, for having mimicked her in front of his friends. That's right, he thought, this was her true self, the one desperately and openly appealing to him for help—not the one playing soccer with his brain, leaving parties with his distant friends, speaking in a contrived, callous voice. It was easy to see that true self now, her face flushed from tears. Why couldn't he see it when she was wrecking his life?

"I just don't know if I should stay here," Robin wondered aloud. "I feel like I'm imposing on you. I know you have your own problems, I know that . . . with your job."

"Have a sense of proportion, okay?" Alan urged. "What great inconvenience is this going to cause me for a night or two? I can still watch 'Odd Couple' reruns and play my bass. Compare my small, almost non-existent inconvenience against what you're going through right now. I couldn't live with myself unless I offered you whatever help I could give."

"It's more than that," Robing explained. "I don't see how anything's going to be resolved. I'm a mess now, right? Let's say I find a way out of this, and my mother's off my back, I have my own place. I know I'll still get depressed over something else then . . . anyway, there are so many things. So now I'm looking ahead at the hard road immediately in front of me, and I'm thinking—why *bother?* Why *even bother?*"

"Don't try to swallow your whole life in one breath," Alan stated firmly. "You *think* you know exactly how you'll feel when certain alleged problems are solved, but you really don't know how you'll feel. As a matter of fact, that attitude is an indication of the depth of your problem. You're so far removed from the real solution, you assume that the solution is ultimately fictitious."

"Okay, then what do I do?" Robin demanded, a bit angrily.

"You mean what do you do right now?" Alan asked rhetorically. "Good. That's the question you ought to be asking, instead of pronouncing a belief in futility. Think about where you're going to stay after you decide to leave here."

"You know what I need?" Robin stated. "I need to take a walk by myself for awhile. I'll be back before you go to sleep."

"Okay, that's cool," Alan concurred. Now Robin stood up and wiped a tear from her cheek. She walked gracefully toward Alan and put her arms around him.

"Thank you so much," she offered. "I don't know where I would have gone without you." She kissed his neck platonically and rested her head against the upper part of his chest.

"Just realize that this explosion came for a good reason," Alan explained. Alan looked up at the windows and was glad the blinds were closed.

While Robin was gone, Alan lazily picked out riffs on his bass and tried to digest what had happened. He resolved almost immediately that he wouldn't fool around with Robin if the opportunity came up. This was difficult for him. His few get-togethers with Jill, as alluring as she was, did not hold a candle to his years of matching wits, opinions, and despair with Robin. But he couldn't let himself succumb to the trap, even if she came back and dropped all her clothes. The karmic laws, assuming he was interpreting them correctly, had to be followed. Since his kind, forgiving, non-sexual behavior with Robin had brought him Jill, anything less than continuing along that high road would spell disaster. Aside from the immediate negative effects such a fall would bring, it seemed to be an abuse of the Boss's energy. What kind of life would that be anyway, Alan considered—being pulled like a cheap magnet from one opportunity to another for immediate satisfaction?

On a more obviously practical note, Alan's thoughts turned to Jill and the possibility that she had seen Robin coming, going, or anytime in between. The way to handle this he thought was to head it off at the pass—to bring it up with Jill before she got a chance to mention it or wonder about it too long. Whatever small risk that plan of action involved would be worth it, in light of the fact that Alan was doing the right thing.

His thoughts proceeded, now to still more base aspects of the situation. He recalled wondering, in the weeks just past, if Robin had quickly acquired a "sexual partner," as she liked to call it. Alan had wondered if some anonymous yuppie with a penis had stumbled into the right place at the right time and squeezed more physical gratification out of Robin in one or two nights than he had gotten over a period of years. Now, however, Alan felt guilty for having reduced Robin's life to a cheap sexual adventure. Obviously that had little to do with anything. She had serious problems to work out with her parents. Yet at the same time, he believed Robin was entirely capable of having wild, meaningless sex with a stranger on one day and showing up the next day like a poor waif at the doorstep of someone else more suitable to fulfill her other needs—whatever they happened to be at the moment. And now that he thought back on what Robin had said just thirty minutes earlier about her not wanting to "impose," it made him sick. She happily imposed on twenty-eight year old stock brokers who also had to get up for work the next morning. And they imposed on her. The phone rang. Alan grabbed it.

"Hello?"

"Hello, this is Robin's father." With the first syllable, Alan recognized the hoarse voice of Sheldon Feld, the man responsible for bringing Robin into this world and molding her into the combat machine she had become. He was a man who didn't have to wait for the afterlife for *his* consequence. Usually, it came by breakfast. He was a sharp lawyer, with hundreds upon hundreds of wins under his belt, none of them worth a damn thing in the long run. Alan had once, several years before, been upstairs in Robin's room getting a small handful of tit, while downstairs, the big lawyer counselled a young black couple preparing to sue someone. "Remember, ya' gotta limp in the courtroom," he boomed, "ya' gotta use everything ya' got. Lemme see ya' limp. Walk." Now over the phone, Sheldon's voice had plummeted from New-York-cocky to New-York-drained. Sheldon was now at the mercy of someone who had physically done more to his daughter than he would ever do, yet less than the strangers had done.

"Listen, is Robin there?" Sheldon asked meekly. "I know it's late. I'm sorry ta' bother you."

"Yes, she is here, and it's not late at all."

"Robin's a very intelligent girl, but she's got a lot to learn," Sheldon let out without preface, "and I hope she can learn what she needs to know without getting hurt. I couldn't stand it if any harm came to her. . . ."

"She's fine," Alan interjected. "She came over for a while to talk it out and now she's stepped outside for a few minutes to get some air."

"You know, you're really wonderful," Sheldon asserted. "You must be a really good friend for Robin to come over when she was in such pain, Alan. I'd like to meet you sometime."

Alan recognized the absurdity of the situation. Sheldon didn't know he was Alan Reiss, the same Alan that had gone out with his daughter at the end of high school and unwittingly prompted her to use the word "love." As Robin had explained recently, she didn't want her parents to know she was "seeing" Alan again. He was a bad influence on her—bohemian in his own unusual way, getting Robin to do disruptive things like looking into herself and doing what was right, even when it was inconvenient. So Alan Reiss became known around the house as Alan Garber, a young Wall Street vulture going for his MBA and his JAP, a safe bet for the acquisitive young woman carefully balancing upscale dinners with sexual encounters in the name of decency. The real Alan wondered if the brilliant Sheldon could be so stupid as to think Robin would come running in desperation to someone with these characteristics.

"I'll tell you," Alan explained, "Robin is angry with herself. I wouldn't worry about what she thinks of her parents. I wish I knew exactly *why* she was so angry with herself, but I will tell you this much—she works very hard to get other people angry at her too. That way, she doesn't feel so alone."

"Oh, you're so smart," Sheldon said in absolute earnest. "It's scary how well you know Robin."

"What did you mean when you said Robin had a lot to learn?" Alan asked.

"Well, she's not making the most of her time," Sheldon responded confidently. "She needs more of a plan in life."

"My impression," Alan asserted, "is that she's trying to avoid having a plan 'merely for the sake of having one,' and I applaud her for that. It would be convenient for her to do the law school or business school dance and hear people say nice things about her. But in reality, the time she's supposedly wasting now is more valuable than the time she'll be spending once she's already adopted some 'plan.'"

"I just want her to be happy," Sheldon let out.

"Some people think happiness is the absence of distress," Alan mused. "I call that numbness."

"You're right, you're right. I know I'm keeping you. Can you do me a favor and ask her to call her mother and father?"

"Sure."

A short while later, Robin returned and walked confidently into Alan's small apartment.

"Do you have a *plan?*" Alan prompted.

"As a matter of fact, I *do,*" Robin responded. "I bought the paper and I'm going to move into a hotel in Manhattan that rents rooms on a weekly basis. I'll be closer to work, and I can have some time to think while I save some money. Can I use your phone?"

"No problem." Robin opened to the classified section and carefully dialed a number.

"Hello," she began, "do you rent rooms on a weekly basis?"

****

On Friday evening, cousin Rick walked Alan over to Gene's apartment. Gene was a local heavy metal guitarist who sold pot for a living. According to Rick, Gene was looking to form a band around his original music, and Alan might be the right bassist.

"Ay, don't be surprised at all the kids runnin' around," Rick warned. "He's got three of 'em."

"In a studio apartment?" Alan asked. "How did the situation get so out of hand?"

"Ay, he likes it," Rick explained. "He can keep an eye on 'em in there."

On the sixth floor of the building, the door opened roughly one third of the way. The man Alan assumed to be Gene stood in the crack. He was about five-feet-eight, mid-to-late twenties, with long dark brown hair breaking on his shoulders, and a five o'clock shadow covering his face.

"Ay, Gene," Rick began, "this is my cousin, Alan."

Alan extended his hand in the standard handshake style and found the position quickly rearranged by Gene, who preferred the musician's interlocking-thumb shake.

"Alan plays bass," Rick continued.

"I'm no John Paul Jones yet," Alan added. "I picked it up in college. What I really need is more time to practice. Not just copying songs, but fundamentals."

"I'll check it out some time," Gene said dryly, breaking his silence.

"Could I get a nickel bag?" Rick interjected as he whipped out a five dollar bill. With a somewhat resigned look on his face, Gene disappeared behind the door and closed it. Twenty seconds later, he reemerged with a rolled up piece of tin foil which he handed to Rick.

"This neighborhood's going downhill," Gene noted during the transaction. "The fucking crack dealers are moving in. What kind of place is this gonna be to bring up kids?"

Alan looked past Gene in the doorway and saw there was a whole world back there. Little kids were running around and getting into minor skirmishes. A woman about Gene's age in tights was darting back and forth between the stove and a table while holding a frying pan. Burned grease was coming off the pan in columns and reaching Alan's nostrils. Farther back in the room was a music store's worth of equipment pushed up against a wall and corner. Quickly, Alan identified two guitars, a keyboard, a digital sampler, a four-track recorder, a reverb unit, and a patch bay. On the wall above the equipment was a large color poster of Ozzy Osbourne, looking painted and puffy, like he'd just returned from the Betty Ford Clinic.

"It would be great if I could listen to some of your original stuff," Alan stated.

"I'd invite you guys in," Gene said flatly, "but we're gonna have dinner in a few minutes. Give me a blank tape some time and I'll let you have a few songs."

"Okay, I'll definitely come by one of the next few days."

"Ay," Rick let out, sniffing the contents of the tin foil package, "this is good shit."

When Alan and Rick appeared in front of Alan's building a few minutes later, cousin Randy was waiting outside.

"All *right,*" Alan explained, "I finally have the two of you in the same place at the same time. Your truck or mine?" The three took various seats in Alan's apartment. Rick began to roll a joint on the coffee table.

"We just got back from Gene's," Alan explained. "Man, would I like to go on tour or something this summer. Getting out of bed around two P.M. is perfect for me."

"You're gonna have to really practice," Rick remarked, as he let out a lung full of pot smoke. "Gene's really good."

"I'll be able to do it, no question." Alan contended. "It's just a matter of being able to hear the notes correctly and then striving to play them back the same way. I know I'm hearing them correctly—now I simply have to put some time in. That applies to even the most complex bass lines you could find. Just give me a few months. I'm good at playing catch-up ball."

"Ay, the house auction is comin' up next week," Rick stated. "Pretty soon I'll have my own place. I'll be set for life."

"What about your *next* life?" Randy let out. "Have you thought about *that?*"

"Hey, lay off," Alan shot back. "When Rick even knows what he's doing next Tuesday, I'll be ecstatic."

"Setting yourself up in a nice house and thinking you're set for life isn't the answer," Randy continued. "That's nothing more than creating an illusion of security and comfort."

"It's no illusion," Rick argued, taking a hit from the joint. "I'm gonna have a big sky roof there, with light comin' in and a pool and banana trees and lotsa girls runnin' around pleasin' me n' shit."

"Of course," Randy explained. "You have a limited, gross material conception of heaven, and you think you can attain this heaven by physical manipulation of your material environment."

"Bingo," Alan said, wryly.

"But what you unconsciously desire," Randy proceeded, "is not attainable on this earth."

"Not even in Queens?" Alan remarked.

"Ay, I don't believe in any of this reincarnation bullshit," Rick barked, coughing out a burst of pot smoke. "When I die, I'll be in the ground, man, or maybe in the real heaven."

"No you won't," Randy asserted, "you'll be right back in a womb, maybe even the womb of a pig."

"Sounds like those frat parties you used to go to, Rick," Alan remarked. A knock came on the window, and Jordan appeared.

"Hey, I can't believe it," Alan boomed, "seeing you around on a weekend."

"Andrea won't be back from her parents' till Sunday," Jordan revealed as he climbed down into the apartment. "Hey Rick, I'm glad you guys are here, too. I've been thinking about your predicament."

"Ay, what's up, Jordan?" cousin Rick let out.

"You guys still aren't working, right?" Jordan postulated.

"I know you think that's what it looks like. . . ." Alan stated, smirking.

"Well that upsets me," Jordan proceeded. "I've known you guys for a long time, and I know how smart you are and how productive you could be. It hurts me to see you guys stoned all the time."

"I've got plans," Rick contended. "We were just talkin' about the house I'm buyin' at the auction next week."

"The one in Rockaway Beach, right?" Jordan acknowledged. "Alan showed me a picture of it a few weeks ago. Is this a realistic plan? How are you paying for it?"

"I should be getting five thousand in insurance money this week for my accident," Rick answered.

"The upset price for the house is only fifteen hundred," Alan explained, "and you only need ten percent down, as long as you promise to bring the house up to code and make it your primary residence for at least three years. So let's say the place gets bid up to forty thousand. Four thousand will cover the down payment, and the City will automatically arrange a low interest loan for the rest."

"I'm glad to see you're taking some initiative, Rick," Jordan noted, "but I hope you're not counting your chickens. What if the house is bid up to seventy thousand?"

"For that piece of shit?" Randy quipped.

"Rick's starting a savings plan, Jordan," Alan explained. "Between now and this Thursday, no pot and no Seven Eleven nachos."

"You don't need pot to get through life," Jordan pronounced. "I'll tell you what—I'll make up a list right now of ten things to do instead of smoking pot. And all of them will be fun and beneficial with no harmful side effects." Jordan found a pen and pad and disappeared into the bathroom—unofficially the study. Rick took big hits from his joint and flipped through the lone *Playboy* magazine in Alan's apartment, a two year-old issue, put out about the time Alan noticed that most Playmates of the Month now had more recent birth dates than his. To Alan, the printed dates looked like typos.

"Hey, babe," Rick shouted at a picture in front of his face, "wanna go to Rockaway Beach?"

"How're you doin' in there, Jordan?" Alan let out.

"Done," Jordan said proudly, emerging, list in hand. He dropped the piece of paper in Rick's lap, over the centerfold. "I tried to be well rounded in my selections."

Cousin Rick, in his prematurely gravelly voice, read the items aloud: "Swim one hundred laps, take a course in financial strategies, read a novel, remove a girl's bra, learn how to tune up a car, learn a song on the guitar. . . ."

"Not bad, huh?" Jordan asked rhetorically. "There's nothing so terrible in there."

"I like this 'remove a girl's bra' part," Rick said with a sheepish grin, "especially when I'm stoned."

****

A little after 3:00 P.M. on Saturday, Alan walked down East 22nd Street and entered the residential hotel Robin had checked into. The tiled lobby smelled of stored-up elderly perspiration. A lady in her seventies head-bobbed her way across the floor and complained: "I told them about the door two weeks ago." Alan had the sudden impression that she had first come to the hotel when she was Robin's age and never gotten the breaks she had planned on. Meanwhile, an elderly man in a buttoned down shirt stared out the glass doors and mumbled. Alan stood at the elevator door, took sparse breaths, and rooted for the light to move down faster.

Alan knocked on room 1727, but there was no answer. He remembered Robin had told him that she might be sunning herself on the roof. Alan walked down the hall and pushed on a door that looked like it could have led to an incinerator room. Instead, it opened up onto a tarred building ledge, about six feet wide, with a parapet wall around the perimeter. Robin sat in a low beach chair and held a notebook in her hand. At her feet was a typewriter. She wore large, dark sunglasses that hid most of her face as she looked up at Alan.

"Hi, I'm really glad you're here," Robin said. "This place gives me the chills."

"I can't see why," Alan tossed off.

"Here, I want you to look at my resume and tell me what you think," she said as she handed him a typed page. "I've decided that I'm going to be a success."

"And *this* is where it all began," Alan quipped.

As he skimmed through details of her accomplishments on various collegiate journals, he glanced back down at Robin and tried to figure out why the sympathy he was feeling for her was so limited. Part of it was because she had done such a good job of bringing sunny California to this desolate roof top. Part of it was because she should have moved in with him a long time ago, dropped her psychotic attitude swings, and avoided this entire attention-getting scene.

"Looks good," Alan stated. "Care if I mark this one up?"

"Okay."

"It's fine," he continued. "I just want to chop these full sentences into phrases to be consistent with the rest of the resume."

"It's really nice of you to come and visit me."

"No problem."

"I know now that I want to be a writer and an editor, Alan. I'll eventually wind up living in San Francisco or L.A., but I think I'll stay in New York for awhile. Obviously I can't stay in this dump too long. I'm already checking ads for apartments. . . ."

"This is a lot like looking back at myself almost two years ago," Alan interjected. "I went down to Atlantic City two weeks after vacation, with no planning involved, and wound up with a room that looked a bit like what I think your room here must look like. When I saw the room, I experienced an overwhelming sinking, choked-up feeling inside. I knew that sensation was temporary, just like the situation itself, but that knowledge didn't lessen the sensation at all. What *did* help was resolving to have a bold, warlike attitude about the situation. I told myself that I'd narrate my own thoughts and actions, as in a movie or novel. That made everything a hell of a lot easier. And I knew I'd spend as much time outside that cubicle as possible. I think the woman next door was a prostitute. At least that's what it sounded like. There were guys walking in and out every hour or so."

"Why don't we go back to my room for a minute so you can finish your retrospective?" Robin asked. "I have to get some more paper for my resume."

A minute later, Robin opened the door to room 1727 and walked in just ahead of Alan.

"Same size as mine was," Alan observed, "nine by six. I think it's a standard for these dives. But your walls are a newer shade of green than mine were. And your window shade looks reasonably clean. My window had about eight different layers of shades and curtains in it. I was afraid to touch any of it, 'cause I thought there were things living between the layers."

"I had to spray in here for roaches," Robin explained, "that's why it smells so bad. They were all over the place. I've gotten so little sleep in the last two days."

"I don't think it's only the room," Alan suggested. "You're probably avoiding some troubling dreams about your parents and yourself."

"But," Robin let out somewhat tentatively, "aren't you glad I'm finally out of there. Now . . . you can come into the City and spend the night. . . ."

"Yeah, I'm glad," Alan responded flatly.

"I'm invited to a party in Manhattan tonight. We could go together."

"Actually, I already had plans for tonight," Alan responded. "Sorry, I would like to have gone."

"Are you seeing someone?"

"Sort of," Alan responded.

"Who is she?"

"She's the daughter of my landlord. I met her recently."

"What's she like?" Robin pressed.

"She's nice. She's American, our age, half Greek, half Bulgarian in descent. She's a fashion design student."

"I suppose she's beautiful," Robin stated. Alan was silent and looked around the room.

"Call her and tell her you're feeling sick," Robin suggested, "that always works. . . ."

"You know I don't pull shit like that."

At 6:00, Alan and Robin were in a bar two blocks away from Robin's S.O.R.

"You know," Robin related, "in the last two days, I've spoken to my mother over the phone a lot. I think mom and I are becoming friends."

"Great." There were long gaps of silence in the discussion. After three lost minutes, Robin now resumed:

"Are you sure you have to meet this woman tonight?"

"Yeah. As a matter of fact, I should use the pay phone over there in a minute and call her."

"Is she prettier than I am?"

"You're both very pretty in different ways," Alan explained. As he walked over to the phone, he considered how Robin had uncharacteristically deprecated herself, playing the spurned woman. Alan knew it would be followed by a reaction from Robin. She was intelligent. None of the imbalance was escaping her. She was sitting here, observing herself exposed, faintly pleading, being turned down. For Robin, it was all good material for mulling over and brooding on for the next few days. She wouldn't be able to digest and absorb it like most people. She would have to spit it back up half digested, having absorbed little if any of the important nutrients out of the incident. Alan knew there were no freebies with Robin. Nothing went unanswered.

As Alan began to dial, he considered further what an impossible event had just occurred. As recently as a few weeks ago, something like this was pure fantasy—Robin literally saying: "Please pick *me*." And of course, now Alan couldn't do what he wanted to do with Robin and maintain his moral standards at the same time. He understood that it always worked this way. He recognized that everything he wanted would one day indeed be presented to him, but only after he had overcome the moral circumstances surrounding the original desire. This, he thought, was the unfair, frustrating system of the universe—almost frustrating enough to make him fuck Robin's brains out tonight.

Chapter Four

At his desk Monday morning at 9:43, Alan was blown away by tiredness and at how little he had to show for another weekend gone by. Not even the prospect of a ten minute nap in the men's room was comforting now. Alan began writing out his thoughts:

> I can't sit down and do the kind
> of work I want to do
> I can't lie down and get
> the kind of rest I need
> I'm juggling things and the balls
> are in the air ninety-five percent of the time
> And in my hands only five percent

> I don't want to live dreading Monday
> and longing for Friday
> I don't want to pray for some days
> to go fast and others to go slow
> While time, overall, speeds by,
> marked only by my wanting
> I don't want to be groggy
> during my work, or delinquent
> I want to salvage my twenties,
> the tail end of my childhood
> I want to help people for a living,
> instead of making myself miserable,
> giving them what they think they want
> I want credit for the work I've done so far,
> The kind of credit where someone with authority
> says: "Go ahead, do whatever you want for
> the rest of your life. Your creativity and
> good will can carry the day."
> I know that person with authority
> is me
> (time sheets are due)

The phone in Alan's apartment rang Tuesday morning at 8:17. Alan had exhausted the sleep button feature over ten minutes earlier. It was Warren's voice on the phone:

"Al, ya' godda' help me out. My asshole's on fire."

"Another busy weekend, huh?" Alan groaned.

"Who was your doctor when *you* had hemorrhoids?"

"I had about five of them," Alan explained. "They all sucked. But there was a guy on Queens Boulevard that was recommended to me that I never used. He might be good."

"Okay, I need you to pick me up and drive me over to his office. My Dad's at work and my mother has classes. I can barely make it to the bathroom."

"All right," Alan agreed, "I didn't really want to go to work this morning anyway. I'm going to give you his phone number, okay?"

"Arggghh. . . ." Warren let out.

"I know you can't make it to the bathroom," Alan said. "Can you hold a pen?"

"Yeah . . . wait a second . . . okay. . . ."

"His name's Dr. Habib. The number's 275-4595. You give him a call while I'm on my way over and see if he'll take you right away."

"Okay," Warren said, apparently between flare-ups, "ring me and I'll come down."

"And one more thing," Alan advised, "make sure to see if he takes your kind of insurance. These guys charge an arm and an anus."

As Alan drove over, he considered the number of sick or personal days he had remaining for the year. It was something like three or four, but he had lost track. He would have to take an exact inventory of it. That task was already on a list somewhere. Two minutes before he left his apartment, he had called in sick. He knew which number to call to get the most lenient secretary, who would pass the message on to more stern people a half hour later while Warren was getting probed. That way Alan could avoid their immediate reactions.

Warren emerged from the building wearing his Mets cap. He moaned as he slid down into the passenger's seat.

"You don't know what this is like. . . ."

"I could write a *book* about what this is like, Warren," Alan exclaimed. "I went through that hell for two months, as if I were feeling the pain of a needle back there, stretched from the usual two seconds to hours on end, to the point where you can't believe the body could permit such prolonged pain. I could write chapters on it: Chapter 1—ice cubes and other drastic measures, Chapter 2—six positions for relief, Chapter 3—the Preparation H myth, Chapter 4—sitz bath tips, Chapter 5—basic bullet biting, Chapter 6—piles, and piles of bills. . . ."

"These asshole doctors are really that bad?" Warren asked.

"Usually. They like to violate as many orifices as they can. I still have half a bottle of Cleocin 100 in my medicine cabinet. If you get frustrated with this futile process, I'll give you some of that. In fact, I'll give you some of it today, regardless. That shit'll knock out you *and* your piles."

"But wasn't that last guy you went to okay?" Warren inquired. "Wasn't he the one that *prescribed* the Cleocin?"

"Yeah, he did the job, but he was outrageously expensive. It was five hundred dollars just to walk in the door. Some guy off the street walked into the office by accident and they nailed him for five hundred too. Anyway, that proctologist was a last resort. That's for when you're squirming around the floor of your apartment, hoping for death. My parents hooked me up with him. He doesn't even take insurance—of any kind. He's the same guy that does Woody Allen's asshole."

"What else did he do besides prescribe an antibiotic?"

"He did everything," Alan responded. "After an enema or two, he told me to lie face down on this slanted board. Before I knew it, I was rising and rotating, with my ass sticking way out in the air. He took a long, clear probing tube and jammed it way up my butt, so he could look around my intestines on a video screen. Meanwhile, he had four or five other patients waiting around in other rooms. I kept wondering if he could get their assholes on other channels."

"He oughta go commercial," Warren quipped, "sell air time to Anusol and Preparation H."

"It'll happen," Alan said. "In six months, Donald Trump will buy him out and rename the place. But let me tell you the strangest part of that whole experience. Suddenly, while I was up there with my ass in the air, I was sure I had taken a shit spontaneously and I started apologizing profusely. But all that had happened was he had pulled the probe out. What an incredible simulation!"

"Well, I'm willing to go through any sort of humiliation," Warren related, "as long as this agony stops."

"Which brings me to an important point," Alan asserted. "Tell me if you've observed this so far. When you're lying on the floor in all that pain, looking for a position for relief, in amazement that you have to go through this, thinking about the sick days this is rapidly consuming, thinking about all the things you had planned for the next few days of your tightly scheduled little life and how those plans are all getting shot to hell, don't you find a sort of strange boost or feeling of relaxation sweep over you for a few moments? It's the knowledge that all this happened and you're life really hasn't fallen apart after all. Nothing's really changed during that time, even though you've been invaded and beaten down. You realize you can waltz right back into your life whenever you feel up to it. And maybe you'll return with a new feeling of security because of that knowledge. In that sense, the illness actually serves a purpose."

"Reiss, you just went through a stop sign."

At the doctor's office, Alan sat in the outside waiting room, and read *Sports Illustrated,* while Warren sat on the padded, papered patient's table inside. He wore a long, loose fitting white gown over his naked body. He glanced at his normal clothes, crumpled up in the corner. Warren, with his right index finger, held a gauze pad to the spot on his left arm where Dr. Habib had taken blood two minutes earlier.

"Are you homosexual?" Dr. Habib asked.

"No," Warren grunted.

"I'm sorry, I must ask these things for your sake." Dr. Habib was Arab-looking, balding, a bit plump, in his early forties. Now he turned toward Warren and held a Q-tip between two fingers.

"Would you stand up please?" Dr. Habib asked politely.

Warren stood up facing the doctor.

"I must ask to see your penis," Dr. Habib stated. Within three seconds the whole nightmare had transpired. Dr. Habib held Warren's penis with his left hand and with his right drove the cotton swab about an inch up Warren's urethra. Warren was speechless except for a pathetic little yelp. He thought back to his conversation in the car with Alan and now understood an additional unexpected bonus of his suffering—that its duration and intensity had been so great as to render a crude invasion of even this great magnitude almost innocuous.

"I am sorry for the pain," Dr. Habib let out. "This is necessary for a series of tests."

In the outside waiting room, Alan kept picturing Warren inside, getting invaded from every angle while still wearing the Mets cap. Now Warren appeared, cap still on head, and walked over to where Alan was sitting.

"He shoved a Q-tip up my dick," Warren whispered.

"He did? I hate that. That's totally unnecessary. It's just a way to tack seventy-five bucks onto the bill." Several minutes later, Alan overheard a dispute developing at the receptionist's window.

"I called you up fifteen minutes before I came here and asked if you accepted GHI, and you said 'yes,'" Warren attested.

"Who did you speak to?" the nurse-receptionist shot back nastily. "It wasn't *me* you spoke to. I know it wasn't *me.*" She was in her early-to-mid-thirties, slim, and angular looking.

"I don't care *who* I spoke to," Warren complained loudly, "it was the phone number of this office and the woman who answered said you accepted GHI. I wouldn't have come here otherwise."

"You might have gotten the central office," the nurse-receptionist explained, exuding stress. "We have five doctors in this building."

"Whose problem is *that?*"

"Well, you'll have to pay by cash or check."

"I don't have a cash or check on me!"

"I'm sorry but. . . ."

"Hey," Alan let out, stepping up to the window, "the guy just had a Q-tip rammed up his penis—how 'bout giving him a fucking break."

"That is irrelevant to paying the bill. . . ."

"Give it up," Alan said. "We're out of here. Send him a bill and pray we don't turn you in."

The nurse-receptionist was dumbfounded as the door was slammed.

"How's your asshole?" Alan asked outside.

"Almost bearable. Every once in awhile it simmers down. So you're gonna drop me off, right?"

"No," Alan retorted, "I'm gonna sit here and watch your sorry ass hobble home at a half mile an hour."

"Well, wait a second," Warren remembered, staring at the small piece of paper he held in his right hand, "he just gave me a referral to see another guy, a specialist." Alan put his foot on the gas and they pulled away.

"Really?" Alan let out.

"Yeah, Dr. Kelvin. The guy's on 72nd Road, just a few blocks from here."

"Gimme that," Alan said grabbing the note from Warren's hand, crumpling it up and tossing it out the window in one cool motion.

"Hey," Warren reacted.

"Forget about that piece of paper and the quack that filled it out," Alan cut loose. "Don't you know that this referral shit is a racket? Don't you know that this specialist will just penetrate a few more orifices and slap you with another bill?"

"Okay then, what do I do?" Warren demanded.

"We're driving over to my house right now to get the Cleocin 100 I told you about before. If you'd like, we can buy a sitz bath too—believe me, you wouldn't want to borrow mine. Be glad. You'll be out like a light the rest of the day, while your ass takes care of itself."

"All right," Warren submitted. "What are *you* doing the rest of the day? Going into work?"

"What is it, 11:00 already?" Alan asked rhetorically. "No, even though that would represent a valiant effort in reality, it would be met with snide remarks and bad attitudes at the office. The office is shot for the day. It's better to write it off and give it a fresh start tomorrow."

"What are you going to do, then," Warren inquired, "watch a little 'Gilligan's Island'?"

"Nope. I'm going keyboard shopping. I'll probably try Sam Ash, on Queens Boulevard."

"Actually, that's sounds interesting," Warren mused. "I'd go but. . . ."

"I know, 'you'd be a pain in the ass.'"

"Exactly," Warren agreed with a slight laugh. "Let me mention something, though. In the future, even if you think you have all the answers, I'd appreciate if you didn't take something like that out of my hand and throw it out the window. It's my asshole. I'd like to be the one to make decisions for it."

"Hey, I *know* who that referal guy was, Warren. I've been to him. I still owe him money."

At Sam Ash Music, Alan pawed a few of the larger keyboards before working his way to the drawer-sized ones, from which he would choose one to buy. To the left and right of him, messing with the gear, were keyboard enthusiasts—some of the same people he had seen the last time he walked into the store, about two months earlier. In fact, they were playing the same melody lines as last time, except perhaps in a different selection from the tone bank. All of the unrelated riffs in different tones from all directions, colliding in the middle of the room near Alan's head, made the place feel like a loonie bin. As if they were just now, finally getting close to making a purchase, some of the players would look up and comment to friends or long-haired salesmen. Alan noticed that most of their playing was one-handed and recalled how difficult it was as a child student to play competently with both hands. Meanwhile, the long-haired employees tromped up and down the aisles screaming serial numbers and "don't fool with that button." They were thoroughly absorbed in one of only a handful of sales jobs they could conceivably have gotten in New York or anywhere else.

Alan now moved down to the smallest keyboards, in the thirty-nine to sixty-nine dollar range. He considered how many millions of these high-tech toys, small and large, were being consumed in the U.S. every year, now that the silicon revolution had fully impacted music and made the gadgets so readily available. Alan tried to comprehend how few of them actually fell into the hands of someone with the self-discipline of a good pianist. Like pianos in homes all over the country, they would sit idle, though as compared to pianos they were more amenable to being thrown into the closet when the time came. Now Alan looked at a small Casio for fifty-nine dollars that had received a mediocre rating from *Consumer Reports* magazine. Bingo—that was the one. Just to make sure, he pulled out his tape measure. Seventeen inches—perfect. The day had been turned around, he thought, as it was possible to turn around almost any day. It was good that Warren had woken up with a flaming anus.

****

"Sal was looking for you," Ben Stolich said as Alan walked toward his desk at 9:33 Wednesday morning.

"Uh-huh," Alan said, sitting down and slipping his new keyboard out of a plastic bag and into his top drawer. Ben was a city planner, about three years older than Alan. Ben was articulate and, Alan thought, functioned somewhere in the vicinity of his own wavelength. Alan wondered why Ben hadn't lost his mind yet. "What time was he looking for me?" Alan asked.

"Nine," Ben replied, ". . . maybe five after."

"Sure, there was a chance in hell I'd be here," Alan remarked. Alan now recalled that last week, Dick O'Malley had explained that starting sometime this week, Alan would be assigned to Sal Weisel. Alan had hoped it would never actually materialize, but now it had. Coming in at 9:20 or 9:30 wouldn't fly with Sal Weisel. Not with Sal Weisel who, unlike many, did not bald gracefully but rather exhibited a randomly located missing follicle for every pleasant thought he had crushed. Wiry and nearing forty, Sal Weisel was quickly shedding any remnant of boyhood that didn't relate directly to churning out progress reports and combing through invoices. Looking for Alan at the unlikely 9:05 was, in effect, his first statement of authority to Alan. His second came now:

"Where were you?"

"When?"

"Half an hour ago."

"On a train, dreading this moment."

"Do you have a problem commuting?" Sal prompted.

"You know how bad the subways are."

"That's beside the point," Sal shot back, pointing in various directions. "I do it, Ben does it, Sashi does it, *she* does it. You have to be here at a certain time."

"We're not talking about much time, are we? You know, I usually stay here half an hour later than everyone else."

"It's not fair to everyone else. Anyway, it's not an issue. When you're working for me, that's the way it is. I don't know what Sashi's policy is. . . ."

"Yeah, he's real loose. He hands out crack in the morning...."

"Just get here on time. Here's some things to familiarize yourself with," Sal said, plopping down a stack of overflowing folders. "We're going to work out a drainage plan for haul road number three at Fresh Kills, Staten Island."

"Right," Alan concurred, "Sashi told me. I came up with some good ideas for that over the weekend, just thinking about it a little. I think a swale alongside the road is the way to go...."

"Before you get into any of that," Sal cautioned sternly, "you know we're probably getting a consultant to do the actual design work. You and I will be dealing with the consultant. Right now, you should just be familiarizing yourself with the site and design issues."

"Why should we get a consultant?" Alan questioned. "For this piddling job? You and I can have this whole thing designed and buildable in two weeks flat. It'll take *twice* that long just to *find* a consultant, who we'll just baby sit for anyway."

"It's not definite yet. Just familiarize yourself with the issues." Sal turned and walked away.

Alan put on the headphones leading to the keyboard and began finding the notes to "96 Tears," by ? and the Mysterians, circa 1964. He considered whether the thoughts in his head would be any different when the clock radio went off tomorrow morning, now that Sal Weisel was formally part of his life. But now an even more uncomfortable recollection swept through Alan's mind. Tomorrow was the City Housing auction. He had heard through the grapevine that Rick's insurance money came in on Monday, just in time. Uncannily, in the immediate aftermath of Sal's harangue, Alan would have to find a way to disappear for four hours or so in the middle of the day tomorrow. Now he had Zak on the phone: "Zak, you ready?"

"Yeah."

"'Where were you half an hour ago?' '. . . On a train, dreading this moment.'"

****

In the early evening, Alan left open the door to his apartment slightly open for cousin Rick, who had just rang the buzzer and would be appearing any moment. In the meantime, Alan dashed back over to his bass guitar on the floor to continue working out a riff. Cousin Rick walked through the door with a brand new cowboy Stetson sitting on his head, framing the inconsistently grown fuzz on his face. He had on big leather cowboy boots, a vest to match, and a huge drugged-out, shit-eating grin. He took a few long, overconfident strides towards Alan and glanced down at him. Alan looked up. Now cousin Rick spoke:

"Here's ya' money." Rick whipped out three crisp hundred dollar bills from a wallet and tossed them around the room gratuitously in various directions.

"We're even."

"No we're not, you asshole," Alan let out. "When I lent you that money—five and ten bucks at a time—*I* didn't throw it around for *you* to pick up like a dog, and I don't want it returned that way."

"Ay, I didn't mean anything by it," Rick grumbled. "I thought it was kind of cool."

"Then *you* pick it up."

"Ayy, whaddaya think o' my new Stetson? A hundred and fifty bucks. I got it today."

"I thought you just got the check on Monday." Alan inquired. "Did your parents front you the cash?"

"Some of it," Rick explained. "The rest I got from other people. I got about two thousand on me right now." Cousin Rick paused for a brief spurt of inexplicably delirious laughter and continued. "That oughta be enough for tomorrow."

"Well, call me tomorrow when you get into the City," Alan advised. "I'll come down and meet you and walk over to the auction with you. You know, I'm bidding on a property myself. That attached brick house on 145th Street in Queens. The upset price is only twenty-five hundred, but you can be sure it'll go for quite a bit more. I have two thousand in my checking, so I can go up to twenty thousand on a bid. We'll see. . . ."

"Yeah, I can't believe by tomorrow I'll have my house," Rick mused, barely hearing Alan's words. ". . . I'll be fuckin' pretty girls in no time."

"On the floor of that one-story shack on Thursby Avenue?" Alan asked.

"Yeah," cousin Rick retorted, ". . . on the floor, in the bathtub, ina' hallway. . . ."

"I hate to burst your bubble for the thousand and first time," Alan explained, "but there are quite a few things that have to happen before you move in there, even assuming you *do* win the bid. First, you have to get a temporary Certificate of Occupancy from the Department of Buildings. That could take as much as six months with the City's red tape. That place is probably trashed inside. You'll have to bring the place up to code before you can get a permanent Certificate of Occupancy. There's plumbing, electric, fire safety . . . I still don't know where you're going to get the money to follow through on all these things. . . ."

"Ahh, screw that," cousin Rick asserted, now sucking on a joint beneath his Stetson. "Once I make that down payment, that fucking place is *mine!*" Rick pounded on his chest.

"Bullshit. Read the rule book. The place is padlocked. You don't get the key unless you've met certain. . . ."

"I don't even know if I'm gonna keep that same house on the land," Rick mused loudly, now blowing out smoke. "I think I might level the whole fucking place and start over. I'm gonna get stones from Maine, from this quarry I know, an' build my own little castle. I'll be three blocks from the beach."

"Rockaway Beach," Alan repeated. "I guess that's where you're gonna pick up all those girls."

"Some of 'em. I'll get 'em from all over New York. I'll give 'em their own room. Man, they'll fuckin' worship me."

"The only girls you're gonna be picking up are drug addicts, except worse than yourself."

"We'll see . . . I'll tell you what," Rick began.

"It's not that I don't wish you luck," Alan assured him. At that moment, Jordan came through the window dressed in his work clothes—an expensive, dark, three-piece pinstriped suit. Jordan's face was red.

"It's over between me and Andrea," Jordan sulked. "We had a big fight. I don't want to go home."

"Rick'll get you a girlfriend," Alan offered.

"Ay, you oughta come to the auction with us tomorrow," cousin Rick suggested, ". . . you got lotsa money. You could buy a whole fuckin' block."

"Excuse me, what happened?" Alan asked.

"I could probably kill someone right now if I had the chance," Jordan said, putting his fist through a plaster wall separating the living room area from the bathroom.

"Hey, hey!" Alan screamed. "Don't do that shit in here. Right now I don't care if ten yuppie airheads dumped you—don't ever do that again!"

"I'm sorry, okay?" Jordan grunted, pulling a twenty from his wallet and letting it fall to the coffee table.

"Buy plaster, patch, paint. . . ," Alan thought.

"Andrea told me she needed a couple of weeks alone," Jordan revealed, "and I'll tell you, this time, I could see right through it."

"Hey, I've got it. Why don't you start seeing someone else immediately," Alan suggested, "without even a minute in between to be by yourself and digest what happened? Do what I did."

"Do what *she* did," Jordan shot back.

"Are you certain that's what happened?" Alan asked.

"Let's put it this way—it wouldn't surprise me."

"Because I was just kidding," Alan explained. "My situation hit me over the head out of nowhere. A lot of women, in particular, can't stomach that situation—having a string of weeks by yourself, where it's only your own ugly thoughts and 'Honeymooner' re-runs on the tube. So they overlap—start one thing before the last one's completely dead. I'll never have to resort to that, because I've had years alone to get used to it. . . ."

"What you need is a good whore," cousin Rick directed to Jordan. "Juan an' me are goin' to this Spanish place in the City tonight . . . only twenty-five bucks. Man, with your money, you could have the whole fuckin' place!"

"I think I'll pass," Jordan stated scowling.

"You'll be missin' out. . . ." Jordan grabbed a wine cooler out of Alan's refrigerator. Two months earlier, Jordan had brought over the very same wine cooler along with five others still sitting there. He was the only one who drank them. The phone rang, and Alan picked it up before the second ring began.

"Hello. . . ."

"Hello . . . Alan?" It was Randy's voice, tentative in its tone. In the background on Randy's end, Alan heard reverberating voices and footsteps. In the background of his own apartment, he heard the conversation between Jordan and cousin Rick pick up again:

"When are you going to cut your hair?"

"Ay, Sampson wouldn't cut *his* hair, an' I'm not cuttin' *mine*. Tomorrow's the biggest day of my life. . . ."

"What's going on?" Alan spoke into the phone.

"Well," Randy said, "I joined the Hare Krishnas."

"Keep talking. . . ."

"Well," Randy continued, "I have to surrender all my attachments."

"What about the truck?"

"That too," Randy explained. "At the moment, I still have it. It's in the parking lot across the street. But I'll have to give it up. I'll probably let the temple sell it or keep it for their own purposes. I have to give up all material attachments in order to advance to Godhead. That includes attachment to family."

"Really? How does this phone call fit into that scheme?"

"Well," Randy explained, "I'm calling out of courtesy. I'm calling my parents, too. I know it sounds weird, but what I'm doing is necessary. It's ultimately for everyone's benefit. You can visit the temple if you want."

"Do you have a phone number? I have a pen. . . ."

"4-5-9 . . . 8-7-7-3," Randy conveyed. "You should come to the temple . . . not so much to see me. To get out of the cycle of birth and death."

"This is too bizarre," Alan said. "I can't even begin to react to it."

"That's only temporary."

"When's a good time to call?"

"Between seven and nine P.M."

"Are you bald yet?"

"Yup."

"Okay," Alan said, "I'll call you. Okay? Bye." Alan put down the receiver.

"Hey Rick, your brother just joined the Hare Krishnas."

"Hoo man," Rick said, laughing, dribbling beer from his lower lip.

"How sick. He joined a cult," Jordan pronounced.

"Ay," cousin Rick mused, wiping his foamy chin, "I heard they got some hot girls over there. He'll be gettin' laid every night!"

****

Thursday morning held some pleasant surprises for Alan. For no apparent reason, he had slept almost perfectly and would now get to work, play keyboard, and conceive comedy ideas at maximum efficiency. By ten, he had discovered that Sal Weisel had called in sick. Getting out of the office would be cake. At ten-thirty, Jill made a rare call to the office, to remind Alan that her parents were leaving Sunday afternoon.

By noon, Alan had not only gotten through about half the folders Sal had given him but had also made a list of key design issues. Now he got up and approached Elena. "Um, I'm taking a few personal hours this afternoon."

"Don't worry," she said with a knock-out smile, "I won't tell Sal."

Alan met cousin Rick across the street, in front of City Hall. With Rick was Juan, a longtime friend from the neighborhood, known mostly for his drumming. Juan had straight, shoulder length black hair, stood about five-foot seven, and was moderately shy. Cousin Rick was attired in his Stetson and other newly acquired cowboy gear.

"Ay, Alan, we fucked two hot Spanish prostitutes last night," Rick bragged. "You shoulda' come with us. I woulda' treated."

"Oh boy," Alan let out sarcastically. "So you did this shit too, Juan?"

"He got the hottest one," Rick revealed, "an' now he's buyin' a house. . . ."

"I felt kinda' strange about it," Juan leaked out. "I probably won't do it again for a long time."

"I'm goin' back tonight," cousin' Rick said.

"Still have all your money?" Alan inquired.

"Two thousand and change," Rick stated, pounding the front pocket of his jeans. "Let's go."

"I slipped out of work for about fifteen minutes this morning to go to the bank," Alan recounted. "I have a money order for fifteen hundred and another thousand in cash. There's seventy-eight bucks left in my checking right now."

At the large pavilion outside the One Police Plaza auditorium, the line was nearly two city blocks long. Most people on the line were at least in their thirties and looked like they would be filling their new houses with kids. The sun beat down on Alan, Rick, and Juan.

"This sucks," Rick complained. "If someone else gets my house, I'll kill 'em."

"The line's starting to move," Alan offered. "Don't worry. I don't think the auditorium's even half full yet."

"Ay, I'll take two hundred bucks out and *buy* someone's spot," Rick bragged

"Why don't you sell *your* spot for five bucks first and defray the cost?" Alan suggested.

"Just forget it and stay here," Juan advised, taking the whole thing too seriously.

"How much money did you bring, Juan?" Rick asked.

"About eleven hundred in cash," Juan replied. "I saw something I liked on 203rd Street in Queens."

"I heard you've been jamming with Gene," Alan stated. "How's that going?"

"Pretty good," Juan replied. "You should join us sometime."

"Where do you play?"

"My house," Juan explained, "in the afternoon."

"Which reminds me," cousin Rick said, "I got your blank tape back from Gene. He put a whole bunch o' songs on it, so you can start practicing." Rick pulled a cassette tape out of his jean pocket and handed it to Alan.

"Thanks a lot," Alan offered, "I appreciate it. Now when did you say you were practicing, Juan? In the afternoon? What days?"

"Weekdays, like around one," Juan stated.

"Shit," Alan let out, "that'll be impossible for me. Did you ever consider practicing on week nights or weekends?"

"Well, Gene makes most of his money at night, so he has to stay home. Weekends is possible, I guess, but Gene is usually doing stuff with his kids."

"Okay, I'll be cashing in a few vacation days soon," Alan said, "so why don't we try it out for a day or two."

"Yeah, sure," Juan agreed, "give him or me a call." A minute went by with little said. The line moved forward a few feet.

"You know," Alan observed, "being out here, just standing around being bored, really allows you to understand how much raw time is really expended in the office. From this vantage point, it's almost frightening. What happened back at the office these past few minutes while we groped for topics? Someone read a page and a half? Someone else put a stack of papers in order—now onto the next task? It's almost inconceivable to think I'm going right back into it tomorrow."

"Hey, it's Zak," cousin Rick blurted out. Zak's wide grin appeared, and some brief hand shaking and hand slapping occurred.

"I knew I would find you guys on this line," Zak explained.

"Ay, are you buyin' a house?" Rick inquired.

"Yeah, sure," Zak kidded, "right next to yours, so I can turn you into the cops."

"And get some left over action from his dancing girls," Juan added.

"Did you sneak out of work or something, Zak?" Alan asked.

"Actually, I got laid off of work a few minutes ago," Zak explained.

"Holy shit," Alan exclaimed, "any specific reason?"

"We're a small company," Zak deliberated, almost as if he were repeating verbatim what was said to him moments before. "Originally, when they created my position, they anticipated being able to generate enough sales through it to allow the software development people to concentrate solely on what they were doing, such that the position would more than pay for itself. And that would allow the principals of the firm to look into new areas. But since growth in the software market has slowed somewhat, it hasn't worked out that way. So, in essence, my position is being phased out."

"They fired you, huh?" cousin Rick blurted out.

"Yeah," Zak conceded.

"Hey," Juan observed, "now you can hang out all day and smoke pot like Rick."

"My advice to you is to spend six to eight months carefully revising your resume," Alan reeled off.

"Like last time," Zak agreed.

"There's always unemployment insurance," Juan counseled.

"Or you could get into an accident and sue someone, like Rick did," Alan added. "Damn it, it's gonna suck not going in together and hanging out making fun of things. Make sure you get another job around this area."

"Actually, they'll be paying me for a few more weeks," Zak affirmed, "and I'll still be in for at least another week to wrap some things up. Believe it or not, I have to get back in a few minutes. I just came out here to walk around for awhile and think."

"Randy joined the Krishnas," Juan asserted.

"You're kidding!" Zak said.

"Nope, just happened," Juan reiterated. "I heard he shaved his head."

"What about the truck, Zak asked?"

"I guess *you* can live in it now that you're unemployed," Alan asserted. "Hey," Alan continued, looking down the long line, "it's not so bad in the Krishnas. I heard they play softball against other cults. They beat the Moonies five-three last Friday, with two runs in the ninth. Write this stuff down when you get back to the office."

"You're right, it's *not* so bad," Zak continued. "You get married at Madison Square Garden."

"I think you're thinking of the Moonies in that case," Alan noted, suddenly understanding why he had been looking down the line. "They did that a few years back. They married like two thousand couples in a row. They formed two long lines—one with brides, one with grooms. I don't even think those people knew who they were going to be paired up with until they got to the altar."

"Imagine the fear that must run through their minds," Zak mused.

"Yeah," Alan agreed, "you count back four hundred and ninety-three places and realize you're lined up with the fat girl with the mustache. Then it's like: 'Hey, wanna cut in fronta me?' to the guy behind you."

At 3:15 P.M., Alan, cousin Rick, and Juan made it through the doors of the auditorium. "Parcel one-twenty-nine," they heard the speaker announce, conveying the fact that their properties hadn't yet been put up for bid. The room held about fifteen hundred people. It was packed, alternately quiet and loud every minute or so, and tense. A few people trickled out and a few trickled in, with the body of the assembly largely intact. At least half the people in the room evidently hadn't been born in the U.S., yet few people looked as weathered and wayward as cousin Rick. The speaker was middle-aged, astute, enervated, a bit overwhelmed by the property-hungry masses. He spoke: "If you are no longer bidding on property, we kindly ask you to please leave. There are still many people trying to get in." On the floor below the podium and stage was a long fold-out desk with three City employees behind it processing bids and dealing with the "winners." Alan, cousin Rick, and Juan managed to squeeze into three vacated seats in the fourteenth row. They sat and observed the next bid.

"I remind you," the speaker announced, "that if the purchase price is less than two hundred and fifty dollars, the full amount of the purchase price will be required as the deposit. If the purchase price is over twenty-five hundred and the building has been designated by HPO for ownership occupancy, the deposit shall be ten percent of the purchase price. Please be prepared to pay the cashier immediately after a successful bid. If you do not make the required deposit, you property will be *re-bid*. All right, we continue . . . parcel one-thirty-two—160-14, 107th Avenue in Queens, upset price two thousand dollars. Do I hear more. . . ."

"Ten thousand," the voices began, ". . . fifteen thousand . . . seventeen thousand . . . twenty-five thousand. . . ." Seamstresses taking a rare day off from the sweatshop jumped up and down in place, burning off nervous energy. To the best of their ability under the seating constraints, entire families hovered around Daddy, who shouted out multiples of five thousand. Real estate pros and speculators appeared interspersed in the crowd, although theoretically, they were not allowed to bid on the properties with an owner-occupancy requirement.

"Thirty-five thousand. . . ," the bids continued, "forty thousand . . . forty-two thousand . . . forty-five thousand . . . seventy thousand."

"The dream house in Rockaway Beach is looking worse every second," Alan said to cousin Rick, whose face had turned pale.

"How do you like that asshole?" Juan asserted. ". . . bidding seventy thousand just to blow everyone else away?"

"He should be shot," Rick stated, "but no one's gonna bid seventy thousand on *my* house."

"Why, 'cause it's such a piece of shit?" Alan snapped.

"Sold for one hundred forty-five thousand. . . ."

"I don't get it," Alan said, "that house was a fucking shack when we drove by it. *Tell* me that guy in the Ralph Lauren suit is actually going to move into that neighborhood and fight the crack dealers!"

"He has to have at least fourteen thousand dollars in cash on him," Juan observed. "This is a great place for muggers to hang out."

"Hear that, Rick?" Alan quipped. "You still have a chance." Rick was near silent until his parcel, 147, came up.

"Upset price three thousand. . . ."

"Six thousand . . . eight thousand . . . nine thousand. . . ."

"Twelve thousand," Alan shouted. "Sorry, Rick," he said calmly, "I just wanted to hear what my voice sounded like in an auction."

"Sixteen thousand . . . eighteen thousand. . . ."

"Nineteen thousand," cousin Rick shouted, marking his first positive participation in a public function in two years. He received a brief acknowledgement from the speaker.

"Twenty-three thousand . . . twenty-seven thousand. . . ."

"Ay Alan, could you loan me two thousand dollars?"

"Sure. What the hell."

"Forty thousand," cousin Rick shouted, receiving acknowledgement once again.

"Forty-five thousand, fifty thousand, fifty-three thousand. . . ." Within half a minute more, a Latino family of five or so had won the bid at one hundred twelve thousand and now skipped down the aisle.

"Shit. Fuckin' assholes," cousin Rick muttered.

"Boy are they going to be surprised when they move in and find Rick sitting in the middle of the dining room floor, smoking a joint and opening up a can of peas," Alan mused.

At 5:30 P.M., Alan, cousin Rick, and Juan sat on a bench in front of City Hall. None of the three had become real estate owners. Cousin Rick had bought a thirty-two ounce beer with some of the money left over. Alan now took a swig from it and passed it on to Juan.

"I don't intend to get down about this," Alan let out. "I made a mental list of the good things that happened today: my crotchety, pain-in-the-ass supervisor was out today, I got a nice call from Jill in the morning, we generated some good material when Zak came by. . . ."

"That's a good way of looking at things," Juan noted.

"Right, and one more thing," Alan continued. "I'm going to take this tape home and learn every song on it, note for note." Now, for the first time, Alan took a closer look at the tape and read to himself the song tittles written on it: "Minds of War," "Sanity on the Rag," "Roll Call for the Reaper. . . ."

"Good," Juan asserted, "the faster you learn them, the faster we can get moving." Still between swigs, cousin Rick sat there frowning.

"And I have yet another thing to add," Alan said. "I don't even look at the auction itself as being a negative entity, although it's understandable that we view it as a temporary setback. But you have to realize the nature of events and progressions in this world. A few months ago, you didn't even realize that things such as public home auctions existed. You went from not knowing it, to knowing it, to expecting a house of your own—very rapidly—and then onto physically pursuing it. And you didn't get it on your first try. Okay, that's three steps forward, one step back—a far better rate of progress than exists throughout most of the world, at any given time."

"But I heard people got houses for very little money," Juan noted. "What the fuck happened?"

"I think about three years ago," Alan conjectured, "when the City started this program and it wasn't at all well known, people *were* getting property for very little—probably the ten or twenty thousand that we were expecting. But obviously, word spread, and the competition went up. But the point is, there are other auctions and sales, around here and all over the country. Now that we're aware of that and have actually gone through the process of bidding, we're far closer to getting what we want than you would ever imagine."

"I really wanted that house on Thursby," cousin Rick pronounced, releasing a small belch on the last syllable.

"*I* know," Juan suggested, "set off a bunch of explosions around the house and scare them off."

"I'll find out about some other government auctions for you," Alan continued. "Look at it this way, Rick. You're walking around with over four thousand dollars now. You can use that money to pull yourself out of the rut you're in. Why don't you take art classes again, buy yourself some supplies, maybe venture into commercial art? Get yourself a personal computer and start learning about that."

"Well, I, uh, also got my health to worry about," cousin Rick noted. "I gotta use some of the money to go back to the chiropractor, for my back. And my parents want me to pick up some of the payments on my truck."

"That sounds reasonable," Alan said. "They've been handling that for over a year, right?"

"Yeah," cousin Rick concluded, leaning back, "I guess I could pick up a few payments."

"A glimmer of generosity in the face of defeat," Alan stated. "That's admirable."

Chapter Five

"Okay, Xenos! I'll do it later!" Jill called to her older brother, who was at the front end of the apartment. "Please leave," Jill whispered for only Alan to hear, in reference to her brother. "I know he's doing this just to keep tabs on me."

"Take it easy," Alan replied. He was hardly taking it easy himself. His erection pushed out strongly against his jeans. They sat fully clothed on Jill's bed, with legs touching as they watched television. Xenos, supposedly getting ready for some sort of date himself, had popped his head into the bedroom three times in the last half hour. This made four: "All right, Katti, I'll be back a little later."

"Okay, *okay*. . . ." Half a minute later, they heard the front door close.

"This pisses me off, you know?" Jill offered. "I *know* my parents told Xenos to keep an eye on me while they were gone, especially with you around. And get this—he and I are supposed to be managing the building while they're away. So I can manage a building, but I can't take care of myself."

"I think they think you can take care of yourself," Alan suggested, "but not in the way they want you to."

"But getting Xenos to watch me is sort of a low blow. I feel like I've had enough of him sometimes, you know? When I was little, he was always bigger than me. And he would hold me down and torture me . . . not let me breathe for twenty seconds."

"That's terrible," Alan asserted. He quickly counted the women he had gone out with who had an older brother that had tortured them in one way or another: one, two, three, four, five . . . five. Alan considered it unlikely that he could remain entirely unscathed by such experiences, even though they weren't his own.

"Anyway," Jill concluded, "I'm twenty-three, and I don't need his shit. I've put up with it for two weeks already. He's twenty-eight. He should get out of the house and get his own apartment. I wouldn't mind getting *my* own apartment."

"I have *my* own apartment," Alan quipped. There was no reply from Jill—ten seconds of silence. They both focused on the television again, which teased the brain:

"We have great sex. Sex isn't the problem," the thirty-ish female actress deliberated. "The problem is communication."

Jill reached casually for the crotch of Alan's jeans. Less than five seconds after Alan had begun to absorb some of the pleasure through the fabric of his pants, Jill's tiny, ribboned Yorkshire Terrier jumped up onto the bed and got in the way.

"Hello, Fu-fu," Jill said with forced glee, as she began stroking the dog with the same hand that moments before stroked Alan. Alan put forth a staunch grin of acceptance while boiling with disgust inside. Jill continued actively petting the dog all over and under its pint sized body. The dog waddled, panted, and drooled all over everything. "As soon as he sees body contact," Jill explained glibly, "he goes crazy."

"Uh-huh," Alan acknowledged, as he watched body contact on the screen. "Thirty more minutes of this shit, and I'm out of here," he thought, "no matter what the consequences." Now Jill's right hand resumed feeling Alan's penis through his jeans, while her left took care of the dog. Alan resented the possibility of even the faintest vibration of ecstasy emanating from the dog and travelling up through Jill's one arm, across her body, down her other arm, and into his own genitalia.

"Yes, Fu-fu," Jill encouraged. Now Fu-fu climbed over Jill's lap and onto Alan's. Alan tried to stay planted. "He likes you," Jill explained, "pet him." Alan gave the dog a brief superficial scratch on the top of the head to avoid the drool below. Alan thought: "Wash right hand, blot out mental image of Jill with dog, be verbal about resentment." Now Fu-fu, more or less giving up on Alan, straddled Jill's right thigh and began humping furiously.

"Come on, come on," Jill encouraged. "That's it. That's it. It's coming." In seconds, the dog's frenzy increased exponentially, until it suddenly stopped altogether.

The dog wheezed, shrugged, shook its head, and walked off the bed. Jill got up and walked to the bathroom. Alan watched the screen. "That was the best I've ever had," the woman revealed. Amid mild nausea and awareness that thirty minutes had not yet elapsed, Alan had become anxious when he considered that Jill might not return to her previous position alongside him. But within three minutes, she did. Her hands smelled of Camay soap. The wet spot on the leg of her jeans had widened. Within another two minutes, her hand was back over his crotch, then under his pants. Alan leaned over to kiss her lips, which, he recalled, had emerged basically unscathed from the dog affair. Suddenly, Fu-fu was back on the bed.

"Okay, enough of this shit," Alan let out.

"All right. Let's go to your apartment," Jill stated without affect.

On his couch downstairs, Alan covered as much area on Jill's body as he could with his hands, arms, and head, to contrast himself from the dog. Jill had taken off all her clothes promptly, as if to take a shower after gym class. Alan had followed. Even with a flurry of penetrating kisses, Alan couldn't even begin to make up for the waiting and frustration. He noticed how tired he was; not a clear tired, but rather a disordered tired from a backlog of missed sleep, due most recently to his anxious early awakening that morning. Now his skin felt a little tight and dry and his mind, directly behind his eyes, a bit clogged. He considered why he was never fully primed to enjoy fooling around on the few occasions it was stretched out in front of him.

Jill moved around beneath him, half in spontaneity, half in predetermined patterns. Now she stopped. "I don't have any birth control," she stated softly.

"Great," Alan sighed, "'cause I don't either. I guess we shouldn't have intercourse then."

"Oh, I would never have sex without birth control," Jill agreed.

"Right. Well, I guess that's that," Alan remarked stoically.

"There's still a lot we can do," Jill offered.

"That's true."

Now relaxed, Jill resumed action, sitting up for a moment and entering a more familiar routine. Alan took the opportunity to study how different Jill looked naked. He realized now how much thinking and planning went into the selection of Jill's clothes. Her clothes hugged and hung loosely on her straight body in exactly the right places, like out of a Macy's catalogue. Without the clothes, her body was narrow, flat, athletic, attractive, but probably too plain for Jill's own liking. In what he assumed was a rare, valorous attitude, Alan appreciated the intimacy her nakedness represented.

"I've only had sex . . . full sex, twice," Jill revealed in a mildly confessional tone, "and both times it hurt . . . One time, it wasn't even complete . . . and it's going to hurt again."

"No it won't."

"I used to think sleeping with someone was wrong," Jill explained, "unless you were married to him."

"And even then. . . ," Alan quipped.

"But now I don't think it's wrong if you *love* that person."

"I'm impressed," Alan stated sincerely. "Your standard—your original standard—is a noble one, and your substitute standard's not so bad either. I walk around this planet with pretty much the same standard and the same substitute. There's a problem in actually living up to the 'marriage first,' thing. There are so many moral standards to try to measure up to, I just figured I'd let that one slide a little, and concentrate on the 'no-lie,' 'no-cheat,' and now for me, the 'no-meat' standards."

"That's right, you're a vegetarian," Jill stated.

"That gives you an idea of how high in difficulty I rank the non-intercourse-before-marriage standard—ahead of virtually all the Ten Commandments, of which, I should note, it isn't one."

"It's hard to be like that," Jill elaborated, "when your friends aren't like that and the people you go out with aren't like that."

"Your mind and body aren't even like that," Alan added. "It would be an uphill battle on ice all the way, and you might even scare off your soul mate in the process! So in the end, what's the point of adhering to it? I guess that when you finally get married, you can say: 'Whew, I made it,' like a runner at the end of a marathon. And I guess there would be no sordid, jealousy-inducing 'past experience' stories, told or untold, hovering over your marriage. No great advantage other than that, so I've let it slide down a notch." With that, Alan returned his tongue to the middle of Jill's flat abdomen.

"I've been thinking about it," Jill continued, "because Denise has been going over to this guy's house on her block and having sex with him. She thinks he's in the Mafia."

"At least he's not unemployed."

"She keeps calling me and asking me what to do," Jill revealed.

"Well, tell her—hold out for thirty percent of the movie rights or a piece of his turf. No offense," Alan predicted, "but she'll just continue until she's either bored, scared, confused, or some sufficient combination of the three."

Now she rolled on her side and looked away. "Did your ex-girlfriend go back to Israel?" Jill asked succinctly.

"Go back to Israel?" Alan repeated a bit bemused. "I didn't know she *had* any plans to go back. I don't really keep in touch with her. I think she's living in Manhattan and planning to go to law school. I don't really know."

"And how's your cousin?" Jill asked, as if to minimize the strategic importance of her previous question.

"My cousin? Which one? One's walking around with four thousand dollars in insurance money and the other one just joined the Krishnas. I guess I should be thankful they're not the same person. Then he'd be out four thousand bucks."

"Randy joined the Krishnas?" Jill mused. "What a family." There were loud clicks from heels against the pavement just outside, in front of the glass lobby doors. They were obviously from a woman's shoes.

"My brother'll be back soon," Jill observed. "We'd better finish up."

****

Tuesday morning at 9:45, Sal Weisel hovered over Alan's desk and scowled downward as if he were waiting for some sort of explanation. After five seconds, Sal spoke: "So what have you done so far?"

"A lot," Alan replied. "I calculated the runoff for the entire surrounding landfill area based on a twenty-year storm, and I sized a swale along the haul road accordingly.

We can run the swale into a culvert under the road at this end and into. . . ."

"Wait a second," Sal interrupted, "that's not what I asked you to do. You were supposed to familiarize yourself with the design issues."

"I did," Alan shot back, "and it didn't take long. I went through all this stuff. And then I followed through with a quick design, to put us in the ballpark."

"That's a waste of time," Sal pontificated. "We're gonna be giving this whole thing over to a consultant, like I said."

"Wait a second," Alan responded adamantly, "I'm not going to be penalized for working efficiently. Let me ask you something. At that moment in time that I finished going through and absorbing those folders, what should I have done—twiddled my thumbs? I went ahead and produced something."

"You should have told me and I would have given you something else to do. We're gonna have to write a scope of design services for this thing. You could have been working on that."

"I also could have lied to you and said I wasn't finished going through the folders," Alan retorted. "And even if I *were* to start writing a scope of services, don't you think that it would be about five times as thorough and accurate if we tried a rough design first?"

"No. If you wanna do that, you can do it on your own time."

"Yeah, it *is* always a toss-up between that and getting laid," Alan shot back. Alan scanned Sal's face for a reaction, positive or negative, but there was none—only the same look of sour, bottled up disgust coupled with the steadfast determination to have someone else, anyone else but himself, express it instead.

"Just get started on that scope of services," Sal uttered in a gruff tone that only he considered to be one of moderation. "This is critical."

"Like a car crash victim?" Alan asked, as Sal disappeared into the hallway. This got a modest outburst of laughter from Elena, who had dealt with similar treatment from Sal and who had had the same phrase slung at her. Before Alan could start swapping Sal stories with her, she was taking another phone call. Alan quickly considered the three or four other people within earshot and ventured over to Ben's desk. Alan looked down at Ben and spoke: "What's he got up his ass?"

"Who, Sal?" Ben asked rhetorically. "Eh, Sal's okay. He's under a lot of pressure. The I.G.'s office has been looking into some of our contracts."

"The I.G. is *always* looking into some of our contracts," Alan returned, "that's their job. That's the pressure you're referring to? Big fucking deal. No one's about to be fired, and he knows that. I can't imagine what kind of 'pressure' would make me act that way. Hey, I'm more respectful to people minutes after learning a relative died."

"Well," Ben reeled off, "sometimes you have to deal with this. It goes with the job."

"Not *my* job." Within seconds, Alan had Zak on the phone.

"You're lucky you got me in," Zak pointed out. "I'm only working a few hours today."

"Your lame duck status will make it easier for you to meet me downstairs in five minutes," Alan returned.

"Is it that asshole again?" Zak surmised.

"Yup. I'll meet you at the usual corner of the park. Bring a notebook."

At 10:50 A.M., Alan and Zak stood at the outskirts of the park. It was sunny and warm, virtually beach weather. Alan swiped a couple of leaves off a tree as he spoke: "I think I'm gonna hit him."

"Definitely get him to hit you first," Zak offered.

"Have you ever dealt with someone who's completely up your ass every step of the way? It slightly stifles creativity, know what I mean? His every other sentence begins with the phrase: 'I thought I told you. . . .'"

"Did you have it out with him? Zak questioned.

"Not really. I got off some good one-liners, but I didn't go all out—I'm still holding back for some reason. God only knows why. I mean, I can get another fucking job if it comes down to that. I don't have to put up with this asshole. Well, at least there was some benefit. Supervisor says: 'You can do that on your own time.' Other guy says back: 'Yeah, it's always a toss-up between that and getting laid.'"

"That's pretty good," Zak observed as he began jotting down the lines. "Next."

"Yeah. Supervisor says: 'This is critical.' Other guy goes: 'Like a car crash victim?'"

"Got it. Like a car crash victim."

"What gets me almost as much is this guy Ben," Alan revealed. "I would have thought he would be pretty cool, but he bends over backwards to make excuses for that moron."

"I hate that," Zak confirmed. "I've had people in my office who will never acknowledge, at least not to your face, how bad someone else is. I think that's the way they stay sane."

"I know, and it's pathetic. That's a very narrow form of sanity. And the amazing thing is, an asshole supervisor can always rely on the fact that there'll be two or three wimps voluntarily grinding out excuses for him. I wonder if he knows who he's dealing with now . . . if he's even vaguely aware of the challenge he's taking on."

"So," Zak inquired, "taking the rest of the day off?"

"No. I've gotta go back up there. We need more material."

Alan settled back into his desk around 11:10. He put on his headphones and started working out a chord progression, but quickly heard something he didn't like: "Sal was looking for you," Elena said.

"Really?" Alan returned, removing his headphones.

"Yeah. Isn't that nice?" Elena mused.

A few minutes later, Sal was back in the flesh: "Where were you at 11:00?"

"Mars."

"When you're working for me," Sal shot back without a flinch, "I need to know where you are at all times. Where were you for twenty minutes?"

"The bathroom. It was more like twenty-five," Alan remarked.

"Do you have a medical problem?"

"Yes. I have three weeks to live. And I'd prefer to spend that time in the bathroom."

"I want you to show me what you've done at the end of the day," Sal tossed off, as he walked out the door. A minute later, Alan had Zak on the phone:

"Zak . . . we got it."

****

Cousin Rick climbed through Alan's window in the early evening. His tall Stetson hit the top of the window frame and fell to the sill. Rick swiped it up and hit the apartment floor hard with his feet. Alan noticed his cousin was in the same t-shirt and jeans he had worn to the auction, where he had last seen him.

"What's up, Sampson?" Alan inquired.

"A lot of bad shit, some good shit," Rick replied. "I got my locker ripped off at the 'Y'. Some fuckin' asshole picked the lock. Musta' been when I was swimmin'. He got four hundred bucks in cash."

"Holy shit. Anything else?"

"A watch I just bought. It was worth only about forty. They left my clothes, but I'll still kill that motherfucker if I ever find 'em."

"Well thank God you didn't have the whole four thousand in there," Alan observed.

"Yeah, well, I woulda' had about six hundred stolen," cousin Rick explained, "if I hadn't a' just come from the whorehouse."

"You *did* go back there, huh?"

"I fucked every girl in there, some o' them twice," cousin Rick explained. "You wouldn't o' believed how hot they were. For half an hour, I had two o' them at the same time—one suckin' my cock and the other givin' me a massage. Then I fucked one, while I had my face between the other one's titties."

"That's more sex than I've had throughout the whole 1980's," Alan stated flatly. "You must be doing something right."

"Ay, just give the word and I'll take you there."

"I'll keep it in mind," Alan said, "the same way I keep suicide in mind. I hope you used a rubber, or should I say—rubbers."

"They *made* me use a rubber," cousin Rick recalled, "all except one."

"The one with the death wish. . . ."

"She was cool. . . ."

"You fucking mean to tell me you had sex with a prostitute without wearing a rubber?" Alan demanded. "One out of every two prostitutes is carrying AIDS, and still more are carrying other strains of diseases. I should fucking slam you against the wall. Are you out of your mind?"

"One time's not gonna hurt," Rick insisted.

"It's more than one time," Alan asserted. "I've been keeping a mental list of how many times you've gone. How about the time you went with Juan last week? Did you use a rubber then?"

"Uh . . . no."

"That's two," Alan exclaimed. "How about the one in the cab this past January? Did you use a rubber with her?"

"No. . . ."

"That's three. And there was the one near the Lincoln Tunnel just before Christmas. Those are kamikaze hookers on that block. There's no way you were protected that time either, right?"

"I don't think so. I don't remembuh."

"Well, I *do* remember," Alan deliberated, "because somebody's gotta keep track of your life, if not you. So four times in all since you dropped out of school. I was able to get the corresponding dates right too—how do you like that? And I'm encouraging you to tell me about any other ones you've done, even if you have to put yourself into a drug-induced stupor to remember. Oh, I forgot—you already *are* in a drug-induced stupor."

"Those four are it, okay?" cousin Rick let out, now apparently rattled from Alan's badgering.

"Well you better get yourself an AIDS test, buddy," Alan advised stridently. "Let's calculate your odds, off the top of our heads. One in two prostitutes carries it. So, one-half to the fourth is one-sixteenth. In other words, there is a fifteen in sixteen chance you've been exposed to the virus at least once. Let's pray that you have an incredibly strong immune system."

"First of all, I know I don't have it," Rick insisted half-heartedly. "And I *will* get an AIDS test."

"No you won't," Alan shot back. "You don't have the frame of mind or organizational resources to arrange for anything like that. Face it, you're not going to be combing through the Yellow Pages for a clinic, making a call, getting an appointment, going in. That's just another fleeting idea, quickly merging with the oblivion of the rest of your life."

"I'll get the test."

"Bullshit. You know, you can go ahead and think I'm an asshole for grilling you and busting your chops. And you can think I'm insane for keeping track of all these things, like the number of times you've potentially been exposed to the HIV virus, but I think it's probably the only sane policy. Some people have given me shit about that tendency from day one, but I think it's great. If you don't put your mind—not all of it, just some of it—to keeping track of the events in your life, then how can you possibly learn and move forward? Some people hate my methods because (A), although they know the methods are legitimate, they think it's too late in the game for them to start, or (B), they simply don't want to experience the initial pain of starting to put together the whole picture, or (C), they want to believe they're entitled to an effortless life. I'm not telling anybody to drown themselves in personal statistics and grind their lives to an analytical halt. I'm only strongly recommending a reasonable effort. Without some sort of direction for the future and conscious absorption of the past, all that's left is an endless string of mood-driven reactions to whatever is thrown your way."

"All right," cousin Rick acknowledged, "but what has this got to do with me? Did I ever criticize you for keeping track of things?"

"No, not at all—and thank you. But it hurts someone like me to observe someone like you. Let me explain by analogy what you're like. You're like this guy who gets a speeding ticket one day, for twenty-five bucks. He doesn't pay it or deal with it. When they take his license away, he continues driving anyway. Hey—so far, the story isn't very hypothetical. Okay, then, when he's caught driving without a license, he takes a swing at the cop. He's arrested, convicted, and jailed. In jail, he has a problem. He likes to do drugs to forget about prison, but the inmate who sells to him wants too much money. So he gets into a fight with the pusher and gets thrown into solitary confinement. And so on . . . all seemingly over a speeding ticket that was never dealt with. Instead of keeping track of a small string of easily solvable problems at hand, the problems are reacted to. It bothers me that you're like a piece of dust floating in space, with no past or future."

"Oh yeah?" cousin Rick contended. "If I don't do any planning or thinking, then how was I smart enough to keep *this* in the truck instead of in the 'Y' locker?" Cousin Rick pulled out a large bag of marijuana. "Three ounces for five hundred dollars. I've been smokin' round the clock . . . heh, heh, heh. . . ." Cousin Rick's laughter was near delirious and brought the phrase "end stage" to Alan's mind.

"Do me a favor," Alan remarked, "crawl back out that fucking window."

****

Alan was working on his novel at 9:16 P.M. when the phone rang. Now that Alan was becoming overwhelmed with various problems and concerns, he worked on the book only sporadically. And now that he worked on the book only sporadically, virtually the first half hour of the writing session was devoted to refamiliarizing himself with his own project—story line development, thematic and stylistic consistency, rereading the work to insure against redundant character development and dialogue. Alan considered that if his typical session was an hour-and-a-half, the refamiliarization process consumed roughly one third of it. Sometimes it was only ten percent, other times as much as half. Alan mentally filed away this ratio and labelled it "the disturbance factor," an indirect measure of his personal turmoil. Alan grabbed the phone on the fourth ring, just barely preempting the answering machine. "Hello."

"Hello, Alan." It was Robin's voice, highly charged with avoiding any discussion of her real intentions or recent past. "How would you like to meet me at my apartment Thursday night and go out for dinner?"

"Okay, sure. How about 8:00, so I can come home, change, relax, and take the subway back in? You moved, right? Where are you, 31st Street?"

"That's right—213 East 31st, apartment 2C. Do you have my phone number?"

"Yup."

"Okay then," Robin confirmed, "eight o'clock. I'm looking forward to it. I haven't seen you in awhile."

****

Thursday at 8:10, when Alan walked through Robin's apartment front door, he was greeted by a well rehearsed, swift, closed-lipped kiss on the mouth. Behind Robin, he saw a one-room studio apartment neatly crammed with the artifacts of the artistic, intellectual, athletic superman who had sublet the place to Robin. There were woven wall hangings, ceramic pots and mugs, textbooks on finance, photography, real estate, and a bicycle rack without the bicycle. There was a framed photograph of what appeared to be a girlfriend, rather than a sister. It looked amazingly similar to Robin.

"What do you think?" Robin announced, putting her hands in the air proudly, as if she had only minutes before finished redecorating. "Isn't it fantastic?"

"Yeah, I really love what he's done with the place," Alan said.

"Bill was so nice, Alan," Robin continued in a gleeful frenzy. "He let me have it for only four hundred a month with no security, and I love what he did with it, and I love my view. He is so nice, and so . . . so good looking. If he weren't going away for the summer, we would have had an *affair,* Alan."

"Well, he can always fax you his semen," Alan quipped.

"And do you know how *close* I am to work," Robin continued, without a pause to digest or react to Alan's remark. "*Seven blocks!* I can get up and enjoy my morning, have my coffee, read the paper. And I *love* my walk to work. It's changed my thinking."

"That's the best news I ever heard."

Fifteen minutes later, they sat face to face at a small table in a Mexican restaurant on 26th Street. "So Alan, tell me about the girl from next door." Robin's face was perfectly poised. Sure, Alan thought, she had everything together now. He recalled how just a few minutes earlier, on the way over to the restaurant, Robin had insisted they walk arm in arm. Once in position, Robin had kept her interlocked arm as stiff as possible.

"Jill?" Alan returned. "There's nothing to say really."

"Oh, come on Alan, I assume you've slept with her."

"Well . . . I . . . well . . . you could say that. . . ."

"Good, Alan, because I'd like to tell you about my sex life." Here was the reaction still due from weeks before. There would be no stopping it. "I've been seeing this lawyer," Robin continued, "and it is so great, Alan. I mean, it is so casual. He'll get home from work around ten and call me up. And I'll go over there, or he'll come over to my apartment, and then, Alan, we'll have *good sex*. Believe me, it's the best sex I've ever had. We're completely uninhibited. . . ." Even though Alan recognized the words as an attack, he couldn't quell the sickening feeling that gripped his stomach. Robin was relentless:

"There's no game playing, and I like that. But can I confide in you? Something's been bothering me. He's told me he wants to start seeing me on a more serious basis, and I don't know if I want that. Things are great the way they are, and I don't really know if he's my type in the long run.

But Alan, should I feel guilty for wanting to keep things the way they are? I need your opinion."

"My opinion? Okay, here's my opinion. You are transparent and disgusting."

"What?" Robin objected. "I'm not *allowed* to discuss my sex life? You discuss *yours!*"

"Bullshit," Alan said calmly but sternly, "you pulled that out of me so you could have an excuse to brag about your exploits."

"Are we angry Alan? We need to talk."

"Okay, Dr. fucking Ruth, I'll start. Don't ever call me again. Don't ever ring my bell. Don't ever write. Don't tell me about your fictitious yuppie friend. . . ."

"He's not fictitious."

"*You're* fictitious. Who would believe the shit you do?"

"Well, you know what you are, Alan?" Robin said, now for the first time revealing a small dose of controlled anger. "You're a *loser,* Alan. You go from an Ivy League college to working for the City—in a civil service position. You're . . . you're wasting your time writing a book that will never be published. You keep track of everything on lists, while life passes you by."

"You know," Alan said, "I never realized how jealous you were."

"I'm not finished. Your *friends* are *losers* too, Alan. Warren's a loser. He wears a Mets cap like a ten-year-old. Your cousin Rick is a *loser.* He lives in a truck, smokes pot all day, and fantasizes out loud. He'll be dead before he's thirty, Alan. And I heard your other cousin joined the Hare Krishnas. Alan, I'm not even going to touch *that* one. And Zak . . . well, anyone twenty-three years old and named after a vegetable is a *loser,* Alan. Jordan is a *winner* though, Alan. At least he's making *money.*"

"Nice sense of values, Robin."

"Juan is a *loser.* Ha—he lives with his mother and sells hot dogs for a living. And Tom Ginotti is a *loser.* He thinks everything you do is great, and that's *pathetic,* Alan."

"Wanna see what a winner is?" Alan stated as he stood up. He held out a twenty dollar bill, released it, and watched it float down to the table. "That's a trick I learned from my loser cousin. Bon appetite." He turned and walked away. "Fine. Fine!" he heard Robin say as he exited. Alan began walking in a downtown direction, to virtually eliminate any possibility of running into Robin again in a few minutes. The nausea remained in his stomach and now the full pain of the mental imagery began to set in. Alan saw the sleepless night that separated him from the morning. As he walked, he felt the complete absence of any spring in his legs.

Within five minutes, Alan had resolved to recover. He began compiling a plan of action, in list form: call Jill, call Jordan, consider Robin's motivations, forget Robin, run five miles a day, start lifting weights again, write at least two pages a day, look into getting a different job. He knew the first four items on the list would have to be performed with the wound still throbbing heavily. He spotted a pay phone on the corner of 19th and Second Avenue.

"Hello. . . ."

"Hi, Jill . . . I'm glad you picked up."

"Where are you?"

"In Manhattan. I had dinner in the city tonight. Remember what we talked about a few days ago, and I didn't give you a response?"

"Yes. . . ."

"Well, I just wanted to finish it," Alan explained. ". . . I love you."

"I'm glad."

"I'll call you when I get back from work tomorrow, okay?"

"Okay," Jill responded. "My parents are coming home on Wednesday, you know."

"I know. I'll talk to you tomorrow, okay?"

"Okay. Bye." Alan dropped another quarter into the phone several seconds later. "Hello. . . ."

"Hello, it's Alan. Is Jordan there?"

"Just a minute. I'll get him." It was Jordan's mother.

"Hey, what's up?" came Jordan's voice.

"Congratulations."

"For what?" Jordan asked.

"For being the only winner on Robin's list. Everyone else on the list was a loser, including myself."

"Robin's psychotic. I don't know why you still talk to her."

"I did worse than that," Alan explained. "I went out to dinner with her—actually a third of a dinner, for the price of a whole one. But I had no intention of doing anything with her, even if I had felt like it and if the opportunity had arisen. You know me. She presented this as a chance to see how she had put herself back together from a few weeks ago, and I wanted to wish her well, I'm not kidding. But she set me up. Right off the bat, she started telling me how she was fucking some lawyer."

"That is sick."

"And I'll bet you it was fictitious," Alan continued. "But whether it was or wasn't didn't really matter."

"You *took* this shit?"

"No, I told her to fuck off. I'll give you all the details later. How 'bout if I sack out at you place tonight? I'll admit it—I'm a little shaken, and I don't like the idea of staring at my own four walls tonight."

"Okay," Jordan agreed. "I'm sorry this didn't end neatly for you, but it needed to happen. At least you weren't sucked all the way in—into doing something stupid."

"Gee thanks." As Alan walked toward the 23rd Street subway, he considered Robin's motivations. No one who was satisfied, sexually or otherwise, could possibly have done what she did. The stud lawyer was most likely fictitious, but even if he wasn't, he was just another pawn in the sick chess game in her mind. That's right. She had set the whole thing up tonight, solely to injure Alan, because in her own confused, malicious way, she still wanted a piece of him. "Hey," Alan thought, "forget Robin."

Chapter Six

Friday evening at 7:00, Alan looked out of the blinds in his apartment window and saw Jill, moderately well dressed, walking up the service entrance ramp with her brother and his girlfriend. The sounds of the apartment door next door being closed and locked only moments before had prepared him for this. Alan was angry, but he refrained from calling out to Jill as her ankles passed a foot or two from his windows. He let them go. Twice since coming home from work, he had called and gotten her brother, who took a message both times: "Katti . . . call Alan. . . ." No doubt Jill had received the messages and most likely had actually been there both times, waving and frowning in the background. Now the fears started flying loose in Alan's head. Jill hadn't responded to his phone call last night the way he wanted her to. Maybe she didn't want to hear it. Could this be his cruel fate—Jill cuts him off just as Robin's done twisting the knife? He didn't deserve it. He had never intended to have sex with Robin and hadn't. But what about the fact that the meeting itself was a secret from Jill?

There wasn't going to be any writing tonight. The anxious pangs were coming in intervals too close for that. Instead, doing some bass guitar drills and organizing papers would serve to fill the time mindlessly enough. But now, an octave of the way through a two-octave, G-major scale drill, cousin Rick pushed his way through the blinds.

"Hey," cousin Rick let out as he made his way down, "whatcha doin'?"

"Losing my mind," Alan replied.

"Hey, I ran into Jordan as he was comin' outa' the subway. He told me what Robin did to you . . . toldja she was gettin' fucked up the ass by some lawyer or something. . . ."

"The rectal part is purely your own embellishment," Alan remarked, "but you got the general idea. I blew her off, Rick. If I cared, I would've shot her. I guess she was disappointed."

"I know she's a bitch," cousin Rick conceded, "but I still think you two were a good couple in a way. Uh, not the way you are with Jill. Something's missing with her. I'm gonna miss seein' Robin around."

"Hey, call her yourself if you like her so much," Alan quipped sarcastically.

"You know," cousin Rick stated, scratching his scraggly beard, "I think I will . . . yeah."

"Great. This'll probably be the first advice of mine you ever actually take."

"Well, I uh, need some real advice on a couple of things," cousin Rick revealed. "I been really down and frustrated. I need these x-rays for the insurance company and . . . my chiropractor has them, but he . . . uh . . . won't release them . . . cuz he says I owe him forty-five dollars."

"Do you?"

"No. And that shouldn't have anything to do with it anyway. I want my fuckin' x-rays!"

"I thought you already *got* your insurance money," Alan inquired.

"I could still get another ten thousand, but they need to see those fuckin' x-rays."

"How much money do you have left?"

"Nineteen hundred."

"Take forty-five out and just pay him."

"No fuckin' way," cousin Rick insisted. "I've already paid him. Anyway, that's not my main problem."

"You're kidding," Alan said, keeping a straight face.

"My main problem is Randy. I've been thinking about him being in the Krishnas, and the more I think about it, the more I know I have to get him out of there. Even if I have to storm the fuckin' place."

"You won't get him out by force," Alan asserted. "I heard they have the place guarded. And even if you did manage to yank him out that way, without understanding his real reasons for being there you can't hope to have even the slightest effect on him."

"Oh yeah? Once I get him outa' there, I'm gonna de-program him."

"Start with yourself."

"You'll see," cousin Rick pronounced, "there'll be no stoppin' me."

"Before you do anything stupid," Alan offered, "I'm thinking of visiting him at the temple next week, just to talk to him. You can come with me, if you promise—no violence."

"I'll think about it."

At 10:20, Alan saw Jill through the blinds, being dropped off from her brother's car and walking toward the front entrance. She made an effort not to glance in his direction. After hearing the door close next door and then feet on the ceiling, Alan dialed.

"Hello. . . ."

"Jill, we have to talk."

"I know. . . ."

"Why didn't you call me tonight?"

"Well, there's something bothering me." Now Alan's stomach tightened and turned.

"I don't see any reason for anything to bother you. Not with me."

"Well," Jill continued, "how serious do you take this relationship?"

"Serious. Very seriously."

"Do you ever think about marriage?"

"Yes . . . yes I do. But I think it's a little early to be talking about that."

"I don't," Jill shot back, firmly, yet uneasily. "I don't like to waste time. If a relationship's not going anywhere, I don't see any reason to continue it."

"I hope that's not an ultimatum," Alan stated.

"No, it's not. It's just the way I feel."

"Uh-huh," Alan replied, "that's the way you feel about the *issue*. How do you feel about *me?*"

"Well . . . I *told* you I loved you. . . ."

"And I told you the same thing," Alan asserted, "and let me tell you something else. I hope our relationship *does* become a marriage. I wouldn't be with you unless I considered that a possibility. But . . . it feels weird to be discussing it. I remember playing in little league like it was yesterday."

"You're not getting any younger."

"The same can be said of a little leaguer. But I guess he could only *dream* of making love to someone like you."

"That's been the case for you too so far, ay?" Jill quipped, her voice now much more light and soothing than a minute earlier.

"True. But at least my dreams are wet." Jill broke out in controlled laughter now, calmed down quickly, and continued:

"Well, I'm very glad you feel the way you do. I really am. But I worry. . . ."

"About my prison record? Look, I made a lot of good connections in that cell."

"No, stop, I worry that you'll leave me for someone smarter and more educated than me."

"Don't be ridiculous," Alan shot back.

"I know you're more articulate than I am, and I can't help thinking that makes you uncomfortable."

"Please, don't even start this. You're very smart, and you think very logically. In fact, we think a lot alike . . . I think. And if you ever have the compulsion to learn a thousand or so new words, I'll dig out my old S.A.T. review book for you. Anything else?"

"Well . . . one more thing." Jill conceded. "My mother always planned that I marry a Greek man . . . but that's not important to me. The fact that you're Jewish is fine with me. But how do you feel about marrying out of your religion?"

"That should be the absolute last of your problems," Alan asserted. "My parents voted me most likely out of the whole family to marry a black woman because they know none of that shit means a thing to me. And if it happened, they'd all be afraid to even mention it to me, because they know I'd go crazy on them."

"Well," Jill conceded, "I don't know about you, but I feel a whole lot better now. I feel great."

"Me too."

"And listen," Jill explained, "I don't mean to scare you off with all this marriage talk. You know what? You know where I get most of that? From my parents."

"Scared? Me? I look great in a tux."

"I'm coming down."

While awaiting the ring of the bell, Alan considered what Jill would look like when she was much older. His mind quickly guided her body through its twenties and thirties with little change in her sleek appearance. Beyond that, his mind met a roadblock. It could not take her past forty-eight or so, where a significant change in hair style and attire seemed to be needed. The bell rang. Alan opened the door and kissed Jill on the lips.

"Could I have a beer?" Jill asked, wide eyed.

"You've come to the right place," Alan said, opening the refrigerator and pulling out a Michelob.

"I'll admit it," Jill said, "I've had three glasses of wine already tonight. But I know better than to ask you for wine."

Alan turned on the television set and sat next to Jill on the couch. Immediately, she flung her leg over his. A commercial for hair weaves came on. "Would you ever buy a hair piece?" Jill asked.

"Sure, but not for myself."

"I'm not saying you need one," Jill continued, "I'm just interested on where you stand."

"Actually, I'm waiting for the Supreme Court decision to be handed down. But you know what I find really curious?"

"What?"

"That." On the television screen, a thirty-ish man, allegedly wearing a hair weave, took a short, careful, well rehearsed dive into a swimming pool. "That they always show a guy jumping into a pool to test his hair weave," Alan continued. "If they really wanna demonstrate something, why don't they show him having sex, with his girlfriend ripping away at his hair in a frenzy?"

"Ha, ha, ha. . . ." Jill laughed loudly. "That's right. They should do it in a swimming pool." She flung herself face up on Alan's lap. "My brother won't be home till something like four. They went to an all night dance club."

Five minutes later, Alan sat up and looked down at Jill's bright, slightly out of focus eyes and naked upper body. He reached over to a drawer and pulled out a condom.

"I'm glad you remembered," Jill said.

"It was first on my list," Alan returned.

"But . . . remember what I told you . . . I don't want it to hurt."

"Well, here's the key, Jill. We're not even going to have intercourse. Unless you reach a point where you can't avoid having it."

A half hour later, Alan lay alongside Jill on the couch. Having seen her over a major hurdle, he felt as much like a parent and friend as a lover. He wondered if he had missed something as a result. At least he had been present at close to full mental capacity, having not been excessively drunk or tired. Even so, he knew ninety percent of the pleasure would emerge from looking back on it. Fortunately, Robin had popped into his head only once or twice.

"I can't believe it," Jill let out. "I just can't believe it."

"Well, now that you feel so good," Alan began, "can I ask you a question? Why does everyone in your family call you Katti? Is that your middle name?"

"No. I remind my mother of her aunt, who I never met. *She* was Katti. It just kind of stuck. Call me Jill, okay?" A gravelly voice came through the blinds:

"Ay, Alan, you in there?"

"Yeah, Rick. Whatever you do, don't come in. Come back in an hour."

"Okay," cousin Rick replied. "I can wait. I got some weed left in the truck."

****

On the following Thursday night, Alan sat with Jill and her parents in their apartment.

"Why are you a vegetarian?" Jill's mother asked.

"For a lot of reasons, Mrs. Piros." Jill's mother was only in her mid-forties, perhaps at one time extraordinarily attractive. Now, she dyed her hair an unlikely red and wore horn-rimmed glasses reminiscent of the early nineteen-sixties. His Balkan accent was noticeable.

"What reasons are those?" Jill's mother proceeded.

"Before I tell you any of them," Alan said, "let me tell you that it makes me uncomfortable to explain this to anyone other than another vegetarian. People react as if I'm trying to prove I'm better than they are, but that's the furthest thing from the truth."

"No, I really want to know," Mrs. Piros insisted. "I'm curious."

"Okay," Alan began, "first of all, there's the moral reason or group of reasons. I don't like to see animals killed. I wouldn't do it myself, and so I don't want to have anything to do with their slaughter."

"But they don't know what's happening to them," Jill's mother argued.

"That's simply untrue," Alan objected. "Do you think Fu-fu would know what was happening to him? A cow is several times smarter than a dog."

"That's right, Mom," Jill chimed in. "I'm going to become a vegetarian like Alan some day. I couldn't bear the thought of anything happening to Fu-fu. And I'm sure there are people who love farm animals the same way."

"But this is what certain animals are here for—to eat," Jill's mother said, directing her words at Alan. "Do you think you're a better person than me because of that?"

""No," Alan quipped, "not because of that."

"Okay, okay, Lalia," Mr. Piros interjected, "leave him alone, he's a nice boy." Mr. Piros was about ten years his wife's senior, average in size but solidly built, with the piercing stare of someone thwarted many times before finally receiving his piece of the pie. His Balkan accent was thick: "We talk about something else."

"It's just that Katti told me he is a vegetarian," Jill's mother continued, "and I did not know what I should make!"

"Don't even worry about that," Alan stated.

"You know," Jill's mother continued, "here it is easy to be a vegetarian. We have everything in this country. In Greece, you could not do it."

"You're going to miss Katti, Alan?" Jill's father asked.

"Very much," Alan replied.

"When she comes back," he continued, "we will have a nice dinner again."

"I'm excited," Jill let out. "I haven't been to Greece in three years."

****

On Monday morning, Alan sat at his desk and stared at a pile of paperwork waiting to be done. Jill's plane had left on Saturday afternoon. Alan felt emptier than he had expected to. He had no way of reaching Jill in Europe or Greece. He would have to wait for a postcard or phone call. Waiting was one of Alan's least favorite things in life, but he was now fighting back with a long list of things to do in the interim: "continue to lift weights (three times a week), resume running (three miles a day), continue looking for a different job, write Jill a letter in advance, for when a mailing address becomes available, become platonic friends with two new women, write two pages a day of novel, learn four new songs on keyboard. . . ."

Alan was distracted from compiling the list. With Zak no longer working downtown, the nature of going to work had changed. In addition, Randy's joining the temple had now begun to sink in. Alan wondered if he would ever see him again in a normal context. Now Alan jotted down two more items on his new list: "visit Randy at temple, call Zak at new office. . . ."

"Alan, pick up on seven," Elena called out.

"Okay, thank you," Alan returned. "Hello?"

"Alan, it's Jordan."

"Hey, what's up?"

"I was thinking of visiting Randy at that Hare Krishna temple," Jordan explained. "How do you feel about going today?"

"Holy shit," Alan responded, "that's amazing. You're not going to believe this, but I was just putting visiting Randy down on my list, at the exact moment you called."

"I've been known to do a few psychic things in my time," Jordan mused, "even though I think all of that is a bunch of bullshit."

"Leaving aside the possibility of God's existence," Alan inquired, "don't you think human beings can communicate, at least accidentally, through some sort of extrasensory means?"

"No."

"So you think we're less powerful than a cheap AM radio," Alan asserted. "Okay. Save your ideas for when we visit the temple. How about meeting at your house at 6:00 and then we drive over?"

"Sure," Jordan replied. "Hopefully, we'll leave with your cousin Randy in the back seat."

"Don't bet on it. And we're not bringing Rick. He's gonna go crazy in there or pull some stunt. You know it."

"Okay. . . ."

"Wait a second," Alan said. "I have to go. I'll just see you at your house, six o'clock. . . ."

"Cool." Alan watched Sal Weisel walk into the area and over towards the desk. Sal wore his usual dour expression:

"Are you finished with the scope of services?" Sal pressed.

"Almost," Alan responded. "Another half day to a day."

"Wait a second," Sal objected, "why is it taking so long?"

"I'm translating my work into seven languages."

"Don't get funny," Sal warned. "I don't mind telling you, this is critical."

"I mind hearing it."

"It was supposed to be done by Friday."

"Let's look at the facts for a second," Alan proposed. "This is the third draft of it. I finished the first draft well over three weeks ago. The only reason a second draft exists and a third draft is going to exist is that you asked for them. You changed what you wanted included and even had me go into some specifications for which there was no prototype."

"I may have changed some things," Sal argued, "but that doesn't change the fact that you told me 'Friday.' If you're a professional, you deliver it when you say you're gonna deliver it."

"Oh, don't give me that shit," Alan shot back. "This professional has been doing about five other things on the side for Sashi and another two for Ben."

"Then you should have told me Tuesday," Sal concluded.

"Okay, I'll be finished the second Wednesday in October, 1994. Am I covered now?"

"I expect to have it tomorrow morning," Sal stated as he turned and walked out the door.

"Alan, pick up on seven," Elena called out once more.

"Thank you. Hello?"

"Reiss—Warren. Coming to my show Friday night?"

"What show?"

"I'm in this play on 48th Street, with my theater group. We've been in rehearsal for two months. It's sort of an updated Shakespeare thing."

"I don't think I'm doing anything," Alan said. "Sounds good. I'll probably be there."

"Well, you really should order tickets in advance. It's a small theater. Should I order them for you?"

"No, I'll take care of it," Alan asserted. "Is there a number to call?"

"Yeah . . . okay . . . 212 . . . 463-9095. Ask for Peg."

"How much are they?"

"Fifteen apiece."

"You sure I can't just show up?"

"No. I wouldn't chance it. You've gotta see this."

"Okay, okay, I'll take care of it. By the way, how's your asshole?"

"Never better. Thanks for the Cleocin."

****

At 7:00 P.M. that night, Alan and Jordan sat upstairs in a large, barren room inside the temple with Randy and Radha, the man Randy had introduced as his friend. Radha appeared to be in his mid-thirties. Thin-rimmed glasses framed his clean shaven head and genteel features. Randy was shaved bald as well, except for a little swatch of hair in the back. The temple had at one time been a synagogue, as indicated by a Jewish star still remaining on the exterior facade of the building. Inside, the air was permeated by the smell of incense and industrial cleaning fluid. In the room upstairs, a distance of roughly ten to fifteen feet separated each person from any of the others. This configuration seemed to point the way to a forum of sorts. Alan proceeded:

"So how do you like it here, Randy?"

"It's good," Randy responded carefully. "I've been getting up at 4:00 in the morning with everyone else to chant my rounds."

"Why not get up at 4:00 and bicycle?" Jordan inquired hastily.

"That would defeat the whole purpose," Radha interjected calmly. "The purpose is to surrender yourself to God—or Krishna—and give up all your attachments to material things and to the thousands of activities we're always engaged in. And especially the results of those activities. Face it—we're always running around worried about a thousand little things and a thousand little problems. And every time we solve one problem, another one pops up. This is the nature of life in the material world. But in reality—spiritual reality—the only thing we should be concerned with is serving God. And the best way to do that in this day and age is to chant his holy names."

"Wait a second," Jordan interceded, "even if we assume God exists, which I seriously doubt, and even if we assume that the most important thing is to serve Him, which I don't see why He would even need, how does sitting around chanting accomplish anything?"

"The Hare Krishna mantra we chant is a transcendental sound," Randy stated. "It might be just a bunch of words to you, but on a spiritual level, it awakens Krishna, seated at the center of your heart. And once He is awakened, you become ecstatic."

"And that's because you then know you've begun a one-way trip to Krishna," Radha added, "and out of the dreadful cycle of birth and death."

"Wait a second," Jordan demanded. "Randy, how do you know that chanting those words accomplishes that, or that any of what you told me isn't something someone just made up? I was taught to be scientific and not accept anything until it's proven."

"This is a false objection," Radha insisted. "You simply wish to believe that everything you think you know is a proven fact. But that simply isn't the case. The sciences that you believe in rest on fundamental principles that have never been verified to you. You simply take it on authority."

"Oh yeah?" Jordan challenged. "Give me an example."

"Simple enough," Radha replied. "In chemistry, you're told that the basic elements of matter are the proton, neutron, and electron. What personal experience do you have of any of these?"

"I've read about the scientists who performed experiments," Jordan deliberated. "In those experiments, the only possible explanation for the results was the existence of those particles."

"But do you see my point?" Radha explained. "You did not have the experience yourself. You still accepted it on authority. And I'm not saying it is wrong to accept something on authority. In this life, we do not have the time to verify everything ourselves. Will you check the road for weak points with your feet before you ride over it with your car? No. You accept the competence of the road engineer who supervised the construction and simply use the road to get where you are going."

"You might think you know what the best way is to enjoy your life," Randy added, "but actually, you're just engaging in mental speculation."

Radha continued: "You can speculate forever on the purpose of life and merely go around in circles. But you need to accept the foundation of what I'm saying on authority—and then practice the chanting, abstinence, vegetarianism, and other guidelines in order to receive results on a personal level. Only then will you become convinced."

"Do you feel any difference?" Alan asked Randy.

"Absolutely," Randy replied. I feel an inner joy, and I feel the difference in my mind and body. Could you get up at 4:00 in the morning and chant some nonsense from work? No. But I've been granted Krishna's mercy, and with that comes newfound spiritual energy."

"Then why not use that energy to do something useful," Jordan insisted, "like find a job?"

"This is fundamentally what you don't understand," Radha explained. "Krishna is the tree and you are a branch. You are always trying to water the branches and getting nowhere. To get any growth, you must learn to water the roots. Krishna is the Supreme Enjoyer. You may enjoy as an offshoot of His enjoyment. You are going around thinking you are the master of this or that. But your true identity is as His servant."

"Excuse me," Jordan let out, "you have no idea what I'm going around thinking. We just disagree, okay? But if what you said were true, why can't Randy chant and be a vegetarian in his own home?"

"He can," Radha responded. "There are different levels of spiritual pursuit, just as there are different levels of everything. A correspondence course may be good, but living on the campus may be better. Each individual chooses. Randy is here by his own choice."

"He's here because he's depressed and gave up," Jordan shot back.

"Actually, I gave up very little," Randy quipped.

"Here at the temple," Radha asserted, "we don't pay much attention to why someone came. What's important is why they stay."

"Something you said did ring a bell," Alan submitted. "You were talking about hundreds of activities and hundreds of problems, and unending complications. I've experienced some of that myself and tried to cope with it in my own way. A few years ago, I recognized that I had dozens of different ambitions, but only a few decades in which to realize them. And at the same time, I experienced continual setbacks. Juggling everything in my mind became too difficult and painful, so I began making lists, if for nothing else than to clear things out of my mind and come back to them later."

"This is a perfect example," Radha pronounced. "I used to wander myself, and in the 60's, I experimented with hallucinogens. You're an intelligent man, but you've come up against the wall of material satisfaction, which is a strong illusion. But you can take your intelligence and your same sense of thoroughness and apply them to serving God. *Then* you'll get satisfaction. And you don't have to give up what you're doing now. Just dedicate your efforts to Krishna. What do you do?"

"How do I earn my living? I'm a landfill engineer. I work with garbage."

"Fine. That is a useful service. People need sanitation. Dedicate your efforts to God. Chant at home. And try giving up meat."

"I'm already a vegetarian," Alan said. "Sure, okay, I may take you up on that. But let me get a couple things off my chest. First, Randy told me he had to give up his attachments to his family. I don't see the logic. . . ."

"Oh no," Radha explained. "No. Bhakta Randy misunderstood at first."

"That was like my first week here," Randy continued. "I was jumping the gun on everything. No, I can still talk to my family. The attachment I must surrender is that of my family pride."

"Why do you have to go around begging for money for this place?" Jordan blurted out.

"We've never taken the hypocritical stance that there are no material needs in our present condition," Radha stated. "We simply distribute literature and receive donations."

"I've read about this cult," Jordan exclaimed, "and. . . ."

"We are not a *cult,*" Radha insisted. "We have to be going now. Evening rounds begin in less than ten minutes downstairs. Thank you for visiting. You might see things differently at some date in the future." He stared at Jordan.

"I doubt it," Jordan returned. After a perfunctory exchange of handshakes, Randy and Radha moved out the door.

"I'll call you next week," Alan shouted to Randy.

"How could you lend any credence to what they're saying?" Jordan remarked. "You fucking amaze me."

"My goal might not be exactly the same as yours," Alan explained. "And your aggressive approach probably won't do *shit* for *your* goal."

"Rick's plan to storm-troop this place is looking better every minute."

Chapter Seven

Wednesday afternoon in the office the following week, Alan breathed a little easier, having handed draft number three into a grimacing Sal. Now he picked up the phone on seven.

"Hello."

"Alan . . . Warren. Did you call?"

"For the tickets? Yeah, once. The line was busy."

"See?" Warren blurted out. "It might sell out. The only guaranteed shows were last weekend and this Friday night. Should I do it for you?"

"No, no. I'll take care of it. I'll call back. Just relax, okay?"

"Well, you should get in touch with Zak," Warren recommended. "He's going Friday night, so maybe you can both try."

"All right. I meant to call him anyway."

"Hey, I saw your cousin Rick at the 'Y.' He kept talking about going to the chiropractor's office to get his x-rays and about rescuing Randy from the Krishnas."

"Yeah, he's been on a real tear lately—at least in his own mind."

"Hey," Warren offered, "he sounded pretty serious. But then again, he sounded serious about building a dream house in Rockaway Beach with dancing girls and banana trees."

"You have a point there. Although I don't know what it is. Okay, let me call Zak."

"Okay, bye."

Three minutes later, Alan had Zak on the phone. "Has Warren been bugging you about those tickets?" Alan asked.

"Oh man, Reiss . . . he's been driving me crazy. 'Did you call? Did you call?' I'm not gonna call. This is like . . . off-off-off-off Broadway—like in the Hudson River."

"I know," Alan agreed. "It's an opportunity for him to prance around on stage and take a lot of bows, like in grade school and high school. Are you going Friday?"

"Yeah. I guess so," Zak replied. "Wanna meet and go together? I'll drive."

"Sure, Zak. You know, I really miss hanging out with you down here. Where are you now, 57th Street?"

"Yeah. Working for the Virginia Slims tennis tournament."

"What exactly do you do for them?"

"Basically sell tickets," Zak explained, "at group rates, to companies and organizations. I'll tell you, I've been here two weeks and it sucks so far. It's all commission. I've made less than a hundred bucks so far."

"It sounds like you'd do better scalping tickets in the street."

"I may try that soon."

"Listen," Alan advised, "quit. Tell 'em you've found a job that pays better—flipping burgers at McDonalds."

****

Friday evening at 7:45, Alan and Zak parked Zak's car on 46th Street toward the extreme West Side and began walking through the drizzling rain toward the little theater on 48th near Seventh Avenue.

"I think it started around 7:30," Zak said, half giggling.

"So fuck it—we're late," Alan exclaimed. "We'll slip in unnoticed. Who cares already?"

"Yeah," Zak agreed. "I think he called me four times this week. I got sick of it."

"And after all that, we didn't buy tickets in advance. And why should we have? Frankly, I wasn't a hundred percent set on going."

Alan and Zak were mildly confused as they approached the doorway of the theater. They were sure they had the correct address, but the edifice looked like a semi-abandoned warehouse. They proceeded inside, down a small hallway, where they came face to face with an attractive woman in her twenties behind a desk. From behind a double door, they heard laughter and applause and saw a thin sliver of show. It seemed to be Warren prancing around, passing by the crack for an instant, like one frame of a movie.

"Are you here for the show?" the woman asked.

"Yup," Zak replied.

"I'm sorry," she explained, "all the tickets were sold."

"Oh, shit," Alan muttered.

"Your best bet was to pre-pay for tickets," she continued.

"I tried calling," Alan replied. "The line was busy."

As Alan and Zak drifted back down the hallway, they scanned a bulletin board crammed with black and white head shots of the actors and actresses in the cast. Warren was noticeably hamming it up in his shot, although in a somewhat serious vein. Most of the cast were in their twenties or thirties, with one notable exception—a precocious bespectacled lad of about ten, named Phillip Geller.

"What do we do now?" Alan asked.

"Go eat at Hurley's, across from Rockefeller Center."

At Hurley's, Alan and Zak got a table in the back and ordered fries, beer, and mozzarella sticks.

"Warren's gonna be so pissed off," Zak said. "I don't even wanna think about it."

"What's he gonna do—at the worst? Stop inviting you to his shows?"

"No," Zak replied, "give us a long 'I told you so' speech."

"Ask him questions about his asshole. That'll shut him up."

"Hey, I saw your cousin at the 'Y.'"

"Let me guess—he was complaining about the chiropractor for holding onto his x-rays that he needs for the insurance company."

"Yeah, he was," Zak acknowledged. "How did you know? But that wasn't the main thing occupying him. You know that yoga instructor—Candy?"

"Uh-huh—the one whose class he took just to be around her and who he thinks he's gonna fuck?"

"Yup," Zak replied, "she was there and he kept hanging on her and then telling me and Warren how he was going to have sex with her while she's in the 'frog' position."

"Yeah, right," Alan barked, "did you ever take a look at her? She's so slim and beautiful he should consider himself lucky to even exchange a few words with her. Unfortunately for her, she's one of those terminally nice people trained from birth to interact cheerfully with even the dregs of society. But I'll tell you—inside, her flesh is probably crawling. She probably looks at him and thinks he's the Wolfman."

"You know what he did last week, don't you?" Zak revealed. "He went to Candy's doorstep in Flushing and left her a Nestle's Crunch bar. And the week before, he left her a roll of Lifesavers."

"Oh God, please—no more. This is my own flesh and blood we're talking about. So how's that crappy commission job of yours going?"

"I'm thinking of quitting next week," Zak replied. "You know my asshole boss, when I'm on the phone, walks up to me, points at the receiver, and says: 'Personal or business?'"

"Tell him business—your hookers went to the wrong address."

"I think I'll give him two weeks' notice," Zak mused. "I'll tell him: 'You know something? Fourteen days ago, I decided to quit this fucking job—bye.'"

"Beautiful. Beautiful. Hey, I just had a brainstorm. We went to Warren's play after all. All we have to do is head back over there in a little while, mill around with the crowd when they let out, and tell Warren it was the best show we ever saw. He'll be so involved with himself, he won't even remember not seeing us."

"Hoo-hoo...," Zak was beet red with laugher now, but struggled to continue: "You know what? Let's call Yotti before we go back. He saw the show last week."

"Perfect."

A little after 9:00, down the block from the theater, Alan dialed the pay phone. "Hello...."

"Yotti, it's Alan. Listen, what can you tell me about 'Hamlet and Eggs,' Warren's play? Zak and I are standing outside the theater. We didn't see the show, but we're gonna try to convince Warren we did."

"Well . . . okay . . . let's see . . . it was like Hamlet, but set in modern times . . . New York, 1980's."

"Uh-huh, keep going."

"Hamlet was a big corporate executive. A lot of it was musical. Some of it was funny."

"Was Warren Hamlet?"

"No, I forgot the name of his character—he was the ghost, Hamlet's father."

"Well what was the most outstanding aspect of the show?" Alan asked. "The most memorable?"

"Oh, the little kid," Yotti replied, "he was funny. Oh, and Warren . . . he came out in drag for one scene. That was hysterical."

"What about . . . oh shit, it's letting out now. We have to go. Thanks Yotti." Alan and Zak walked briskly down the block, towards the swelling crowd. "Just remember," Alan said, "the little kid was great. And Warren came out in drag." Now they mingled and waited. Within two minutes, Warren had emerged.

"Well, whadya think?"

"Warren, congratulations. I think it's the best show I've seen this year," Alan exclaimed, extending his hand.

"Yeah. Great, great," Zak added.

"Thanks. No problem getting tickets?"

"None at all," Zak stated.

"I'm glad you told us to buy tickets in advance, though," Alan added. "It was packed in there."

"See—I *told* you. Hey, you know, I looked around a couple of times and didn't see you."

"Oh, we were way in the back," Zak explained.

"*Way* in the back," Alan added. "Hey, the little kid was great. I really enjoyed his performance."

"Phil Geller?" Warren replied. "Yeah, he was okay. What did you think of me?"

"Oh, when you came out in drag—that was the show-stopper," Zak asserted.

"Yeah, and I liked the whole concept of moving Shakespeare to modern times. Really clever."

"Thanks," Warren acknowledged. "I helped rework some of the lines."

"Well, we have Zak's car a few blocks away," Alan suggested. "How about celebrating your show with a few drinks at the bar of your choice—on us?"

"Okay by me," Warren said. "I know this bar where a lot of the cast is going."

"All right," Zak remarked. "You know, that little kid was really great."

"Wasn't he?" Alan quipped.

****

The following Thursday, Alan sat at his desk and lifted his body four inches off of the chair by use of his arms. He had missed weight lifting the past two nights and was making up for it now as best he could.

"Alan, pick up on eleven."

"Thanks. Hello."

"Reiss . . . Zak. Guess where I'm calling you from?"

"Um . . . not your office?"

"Right," Zak confirmed with a measure of abandon. "I quit on Monday. I didn't even bother to go in. I just called my asshole boss, Raymond, from home. I told him: 'Hey, listen, I'm feeling a little sick today . . . so I won't be coming in ever again.'"

"Beautiful," Alan let out, "that's one for the list."

"Wait," Zak continued, now almost giddy with laughter, "there's more. He says: 'Well, I can't believe this. I thought we were very honest with you.' I said: 'You were. Now I'm returning the favor.'"

"Zak, baby, you've really progressed. I'm gonna start keeping lists for *you*."

"Listen, he gets all huffy and says: 'Two weeks notice would have been the decent thing to do. How come you didn't tell me on Friday?' 'Because I didn't have a crushing hangover on Friday,' I said."

"Zak, you're a fucking pro. How much did you wind up making there again?"

"Get this—exactly one hundred and seven dollars."

"Hey, don't spend it all in one place."

"And listen to this," Zak continued, "he asks me: 'Was it the money?'"

"And you told him: 'Yeah, I had a hard time finding a decent apartment in the twenty-five dollar a month range.'"

"That would have been a good one," Zak replied, "but what I told him was just as good. I said: 'Was it the money? No. I just couldn't take the pressure of getting out of bed every morning.'"

"Zak, man, that's it! This performance will never be equaled! I might as well hang it up now. So what did he say after that?"

"He said: 'Well, I'm very disappointed in you, but you really let *yourself* down. This could have been a great opportunity for you.'"

"Yeah, to go on welfare."

"Right," Zak continued, "'. . . a great opportunity for you. Many of our employees have gone on to major sales positions.'"

"Yeah, in addition to receiving a lucrative commission, many of our employees have gone on to other jobs after being fired."

"He's so full of shit anyway," Zak exclaimed. "In the few weeks I was there, the most anyone took in was three hundred. I know that for a fact."

"Why do they stay?" Alan remarked. "To gather humorous material, like us?"

"That's gotta be it," Zak replied. "Okay, finally, when he's done complaining about me, he mopes: 'Now we're going to have to look for another applicant.'"

"Tell him: 'Look, I have a couple of friends who might be interested.'"

"That's a good one," Zak acknowledged, "but I said, 'So, can I consider this to be my exit interview?'"

"You're a fucking god, Zak. I'll tell ya', this was a great day for the list. I'm gonna have to write down all the stuff you said, plus all the stuff I added, as soon as we get off. I might even borrow some of this stuff for when *I* quit."

"Be my guest. So, I forgot to ask you—have you heard from Jill at all?"

"No. Not even a post card so far," Alan sighed. "But look, it's the halfway point. She's been gone roughly two weeks and she'll be back in just over another two weeks. I think it takes ten days for a letter to get overseas anyway. I'm not gonna sweat it or anything."

"Oh, no, I was just asking," Zak explained. "From what you've said and from what I've seen, she's very serious about you, right?"

"That's right. I don't really know her whole motivation though. She might feel she has to think about marriage simply because she had sex and enjoyed it. Remember, her parents are old fashioned. Her mother's a bitch. I don't know."

"Hey, Reiss, I've literally been laughing all week from the prank we pulled on Warren. You think he suspected even the slightest thing?"

"Nope."

"Well," Zak pressed playfully, "when do you think we'll tell him?"

"When we're eighty," Alan replied. "About the same time we'll tell him about the 'Yotti' prank. He hasn't found out about that one yet."

"Which one do you think was funnier?" Zak asked.

"It's close," Alan answered. "I'll have to think about it. Oh, guess what? I just found out I'm going to be making a field trip into Queens at least once a week, starting next week—for my job. I even get a New York City Department of Sanitation car. So I might be dropping by in the middle of the day."

"That's great."

"Yeah," Alan remarked, "you'll recognize me. I'll be the one driving the big white truck with two Italians chasing it. Listen, Zak, I have one more idea. I'm gonna start calling your job in various voices and ask: 'Is Zak there? I'd like to order two hundred tickets.'"

"Hysterical," Zak concurred, "but they know me as Andrew Brinkman."

"Whatever. Listen, could you do me a favor?"

"What?"

"Could you keep getting hired and fired as much as possible?"

****

As Alan walked down the hall to his apartment that evening, his thoughts drifted to Jill. He considered how little logic and rational proportion there was to the worry and the fear that went on in the relationships between men and women. When they were together constantly, just a day or even an hour unaccounted for was cause for concern. But now, completely separated in time and space for weeks, thousands of miles, the worry was minimal. Things were expected to hang together on just an idea, even though there was more than enough room for an entirely separate relationship to begin, peak, and fall apart within that same interim—a story within a story. And perhaps the story within, at least while it was being lived, would be more important to the participants than the story without; just like the dream, while dreamt, was more important to the dreamer than the reality which he temporarily fled.

Alan himself felt concerned and confused at the same time. As of late, he had experienced sudden, unexplainable pangs of anxiety. He wondered if he was being victimized by infidelity at those moments. On one hand, he hoped he wasn't. On the other hand, he hoped he lived in a world where such a phenomenon was possible. Now as he opened his mailbox, he spotted a postcard showing a small Greek island. It was from Jill: "Been missing you a lot. Went to Corfu, had a great time. Then went island hopping for a few days. Great fun. You'd love my friends here. Looking forward to seeing you. Love, Jill." Alan felt a bit better.

As he opened the door to his apartment, he spotted his answering machine flashing. Two short pulses meant two messages. He flicked the playback switch. First, he heard two distinct voices fast and backwards, the first lower than the second. Now the forward play kicked in:

"Alan, are you there? Are you home? This is Jill. Wait, maybe you're still at work. I'm not sure what time it is there. Okay, I miss you. I'll try again. Bye."

"Alan, this is your uncle Mort. I have some very upsetting news to tell you. Your genius cousin Rick is in jail. He wouldn't leave the chiropractor's office, so the cops came for him. Don't bother calling us till at least 7:00, because we're going to see a lawyer now and won't be home. If you want to try and see him, he's at the 112th Precinct here in Forest Hills, but they may not let you do that. Please call us later, Alan."

"Shit," Alan exclaimed. Within thirty seconds, he had Jordan on the phone.

"Hello?"

"Jordan, my fucking cousin Rick is in jail for holding a sit-in in the chiropractor's office."

"Holy shit."

"Why don't I pick you up at your house in five minutes, and we'll drive over to the 112th Precinct together?"

"Okay, just ring the bell in the lobby," Jordan advised. "No, just honk, I'll be right down. What the hell happened?"

"I don't know any more than you do. See ya' in five minutes."

Eight minutes later, as Alan sat waiting in his '76 Dodge Aspen on Jordan's one-way street, a grey '84 Trans-Am pulled up directly behind him and started honking. Startled, Alan began yelling within the confines of his own vehicle: "Come on, asshole, you have fifteen fucking feet on my right to pass." Alan motioned with his right arm and rolled his eyes in disgust. The honking continued for roughly half a minute, until the Trans Am made the move to the right and passed slowly. With his reluctant peripheral vision, Alan observed the driver, who was still honking—thirties, white, mid-sized, pudgy, with a bushy mustache. The Trans-Am rolled forward. Now Jordan appeared in front of Alan's windshield and entered on the passenger's side.

"I can't believe this," Jordan let out.

"It's my fucking cousin. Believe it."

"You know I stayed home sick today for the first time in four months. I never come home this early. You're lucky you got me in."

"I *feel* lucky," Alan quipped. "Wait a second. No. Tell me this isn't happening." He spotted the Trans Am seventy feet up the block, poised smack in the middle of the street in a blatantly combative stance—no room to pass on either side. "Okay, you fat motherfucker, you just bought yourself a month on the fat farm," Alan yelled. He jumped out of the car and ran towards the Trans Am, with Jordan three steps behind. The window on the driver's side was already rolled down.

"Good move, asshole," Alan said forcefully. "Now I'm going to slap your fat body all over Queens. Any other problems you'd like to solve today?"

"You're gonna touch *me,* you piece of shit?"

"That's right. Just open the door, step outside, and collect your reward, you fat faggot. You had plenty of room to pass, you waste of flesh."

"Hey, fuck you, you kike," the driver blurted out. Jordan kicked the door before the last syllable was out, and shouted:

"You wanna *die,* motherfucker?!"

"Fuck you," the driver returned. "You're lucky I don't have time for this shit now."

"Yeah, you've proved *that,*" Alan shot back. The Trans-Am peeled out and screeched. Alan kicked it on its way and screamed: "My cousin's in jail. You wanna fuck with me?"

"What was that all about?" Jordan asked.

"When I tell you, you're gonna wish you had hit him."

"I do anyway."

Seven minutes later, Alan and Jordan pulled up in front of the 112th Precinct and parked. As they walked in, a scraggly, disheveled white man perhaps in his forties stumbled down the hallway toward them and out the door. "I don't want to see your sorry ass in here for a month," a two-hundred-and-seventy pound cop yelled from behind the desk.

"That's Rick in fifteen years," Jordan commented.

"That's him *now,*" Alan stated. They approached the desk and solicited a look from the desk officer: "Fucking guy won't stay out of here . . . can I do somethin' for ya'?"

"Yes," Alan began, "my cousin, Rick Reiss, was arrested and taken here today. I'd like to see him or talk to him if it's at all possible."

"You'll have to call central booking," the officer explained. "We don't handle that. That's a separate function in this same building."

"Okay, well how do I call central booking?"

"That phone right over there." The officer pointed to an internally wired phone on the hallway wall. "Hit one-one and wait for someone to pick up. If you dial him from outside, the number is 268-0255."

"All right, thanks." Alan walked toward the phone.

"Excuse me," Jordan asked the officer, "you can't take care of it even though it's in the same building?"

"It's done separately," the cop stated flatly.

"The line's busy," Alan called out to the officer.

"Keep trying, that's all I can tell ya'," came his response.

"I've actually tried twice," Alan informed Jordan.

"We'll wait and try again in five minutes," Jordan suggested.

"Okay."

"Hey, I ran into Zak at the 'Y.' He told me about Warren's play."

"Look, do me a favor and don't tell anyone else," Alan requested. "I really don't want it getting back to him."

"It was fucking hysterical. . . ."

"I know," Alan acknowledged, "but he would most likely take it the wrong way. He'd be furious."

"But it wasn't your intention to do it from the outset," Jordan argued.

"Of course not," Alan agreed, "but that would hardly matter. I could argue that we did it to protect him from blowing up, but that would hardly matter either. So just don't mention it to anybody, okay?"

"Okay, *okay*. I never told him about the 'Yotti' prank, so why would I tell him about this one?" Jordan pointed out. "In fact, I don't think anyone ever fully explained the Yotti prank to *me.*"

"The Valentine's Day Massacre?" Alan began. "We did that one for a good reason—almost. Warren kept complaining to me and Zak about how the Yotti kept calling him up to get together. Yotti would call and say: 'Warren, I don't have anything to do Saturday night. What are you doing?' Which is fine, right? But Warren complained about it . . . like the Yotti was asking him out on a date or something. He felt uncomfortable. But that was a ridiculous overreaction, we thought. Yotti's not gay. He's gone out with women. He's just incredibly shy. A helluva nice guy."

"But Warren wouldn't even speak to him anymore, right?" Jordan asked.

"Not only that," Alan continued, "but he tried to get us to exclude the Yotti from *our* plans, too, and that's what pissed us off. So we bought a sappy Valentine's Day card for Warren and signed it 'Tom'—you know, Yotti, and left it at Warren's door. The card was like: 'Friends are for life

... and in my life, you are a friend. . . .' Just androgynous enough to make Warren wonder—sitting right there on the fence."

"That's too funny. . . ."

"But that's only the *Reader's Digest* version of the story. We didn't want to just mail it. That would have been too easy. Instead, we waited for the perfect time to drop it off, so that we would be beyond suspicion. And lo and behold, that opportunity arose. It was Sunday, two days before Valentine's Day, at the 'Y.' I was there. Zak was there, Warren was there, Billy Kramer was there, *you* were even there, although you weren't too aware of what was going on. Rick was there—he's *never* aware of what's going on. Anyway, that was the opportunity. I hung out downstairs with Warren and you guys and finished my workout early. I biked back to my apartment like a madman, got the card, put it in my knapsack, biked the mile and a half over to Warren's building, and walked in. I knew the doorman was gonna ask me who I was there to see, so I was prepared to say 'Jon Sanders,' cause he lives there too. But I had perfect luck. The doorman wasn't even there at the moment, so I walked right in, ran up four flights of stairs, left the card leaning against the door, and left. I biked back to my apartment using a route I know Warren never takes when he walks back from the 'Y'—Queens Boulevard, just to make sure we wouldn't run into each other."

"Uh-huh."

"But here's the ultimate turn of events," Alan continued. "When I got back to my apartment, I'm like . . . 'whew, that's over with,' and figured I'd walk up the block to do some food shopping at Seven-Eleven. And when I came out of the Seven-Eleven ten minutes later with a bag full of groceries in my hand, who do I see walking into my building?"

"Warren."

"Right—Warren," Alan exclaimed. "I couldn't have planned it or dreamt it any better. He had come directly to my place from the 'Y' just to shoot the shit. And what did he talk about? The Yotti. He was like: 'Oh, I'm glad I got you in. The Yotti gives me the creeps.' And I'm like: 'Come on, you're being too hard on him.'"

"And then his mind was blown when he found that card back at his door," Jordan stated.

"Oh yeah, man, the shit hit the fan. I wasn't around that night. I was with Robin. Warren called Zak and tells him to meet him at the Irish Pub off of Queens Boulevard—he has something he has to discuss with him. It's urgent. Zak brings Billy Kramer along and tells him everything beforehand. When Warren walks into the bar, he looks like a fucking zombie. He sits down and says: 'Guys, order another pitcher. I don't know how to tell you this, but the Yotti gave me a Valentine's card.'"

"Did Zak and Billy crack up?" Jordan asked.

"Yeah, they couldn't hold it in," Alan explained. "But fortunately, they turned the laughter into an asset. They expressed it as their amazement that Yotti would do something so bizarre. They're like, 'Warren, we can't believe this shit!' And Warren's like: 'Yup. I knew something was strange. It's all those phone calls. I've analyzed it a hundred times. It couldn't be a prank by Reiss—he went shopping after he left the 'Y.' And you guys were with me the whole time.' He just kept drinking and trying to figure it out. For months he tried to figure it out, walking around, muttering stuff like: '. . . my doorman says he didn't see anyone come in. . . . I analyzed the handwriting against Yotti's signature on an old birthday card and it matched. . . .'"

"He never asked Yotti about it?" Jordan asked.

"Of course not," Alan asserted, "that was the premise of the whole prank. Yotti is his friend. He should have simply asked the Yotti about it, but of course he never did. He shunned Yotti even more after that, as you can imagine. And Yotti himself never knew a thing about it. Who would tell him? The joke is riding to this day. We were gonna do one more thing but decided it was too cruel and just plain overdoing it. April first is April Fools. It's also, by coincidence, Warren's birthday. We were gonna leave him a birthday present in Yotti's name—a little heart-shaped locket with a picture of the Yotti inside. We called it the Yocket." Alan now began to redial central booking.

"Too funny," Jordan let out.

"Busy!" Alan exclaimed. "Fuck it. This is ridiculous. This system is just a ploy to keep people from seeing their friends and family."

"So what do we do?" Jordan asked.

"Go to my uncle's house and wait."

After sitting on his aunt and uncle's porch for forty-five minutes, Alan and Jordan watched the white '78 Dodge pull up in front of the house. Alan's aunt and uncle emerged. Uncle Mort suddenly looked older than his forty-eight years, his cheerful, handsome features now bloated and shriveled temporarily out of proportion by the events of the last day and the last year. Alongside him, Alan's Aunt Leah seemed emaciated, her bohemian good looks taxed by the same events.

"Have you seen our jailbird son?" Uncle Mort called out to Alan and Jordan as he and Aunt Leah began to climb the brick stairs to the porch.

"No, they gave us the runaround at the precinct," Jordan responded. Everyone now stood on the porch.

"Well, you'll see that lunatic soon enough," Aunt Leah remarked. "We just paid a lawyer fifteen hundred dollars to get him out. He'll probably make a deal with the Queens D.A. I have no idea where we're going to get the money."

"Hey, I've got it," Alan quipped, ". . . Rick's insurance company."

"Yeah, *that* well has just about run dry," Uncle Mort moaned. "He's on an absolute collision course with oblivion. We've talked to him, let him live here, tried to get him to accept professional counseling, but he won't budge."

"We don't sleep much anymore," Aunt Leah said. "I get sick and all wound up just thinking about it."

"I'm the same way," Alan concurred. "That's why you don't see me over here so often anymore. It's hard for me to confront the whole situation."

"His own brother is the same way," Aunt Leah asserted. "We're sure that's why Randy joined the Krishnas—to escape Rick's mental illness."

"That may be the reason," Jordan mused. "The whole thing confuses me. I mean, they're both intelligent kids. Maybe Randy just needs to do something constructive. He should go to business school."

"Yeah, that's it," Alan quipped. "Why didn't we think of it sooner?"

"He resists any form of help," Uncle Mort said. "That's part of the whole madness. He'll concoct the most elaborate argument for why he's a hundred percent okay."

"uhhh. . . ," Alan began, launching into a near perfect imitation of cousin Rick, gravelly voice and all, "I . . . uhhh, can't go to the substance abuse counselor . . . cuuuuuz . . . I gotta go pick up a nickel bag in Lefrak City."

****

Alan was half asleep in his apartment the following night, Friday, after midnight, when his doorbell rang. Alan stumbled to the door as he groaned and looked out the peep hole. "Ay . . . Alan. . . ." It was cousin Rick. Alan turned on the light and opened the door in one motion.

"I . . . uh . . . gotta use ya' phone," cousin Rick explained with a sense of urgency. Without waiting for a response from Alan, he dashed to the back of the studio apartment and began dialing.

"Hello . . . Candy . . . this is Rick. I couldn't come to yoga today . . . cuz . . . I was in jail." Alan rolled his eyes. Cousin Rick continued: "Yeah . . . they hit me with a billy club . . . three times . . . hey, guess what? I was practicing 'the frog' in my cell! Yeah . . . you have company? Okay, I'll see you at the 'Y.' We have a lot to talk about. Okay, bye."

"Are you out of your fucking mind?" Alan prompted.

"No, I'm the sanest I've ever been. I'm the freest I've ever been. You don't know how good it is to be back out. Even though it was only a day and a half, you don't know what it means to be locked up—in prison—and what it means to be free, until you're in jail."

"So you're all the wiser for it," Alan mused. "Make any good connections on the inside? How'd you get out?"

"My parents took care of it. They started drivin' me crazy the second we got out, tellin' me I have to pay for the lawyer out of my insurance money that I have left over. No way. I'm usin' that money to take Candy on a cruise. I got pissed at them. I just got into my truck and drove off. It wasn't my fault, Alan. All I did was sit in the chiropractor's office so I could get my x-rays. Those fuckin' things are mine. So I just sat in that fuckin' waiting room. And then two cops come in. The big fat white one grabs me by the collar, pushes me across the room, and hits me over the head with a billy club—three times. The last one came when I was already completely down."

"That's terrible," Alan let out. "He had no right. . . ."

"Next thing I knew," cousin Rick continued, "I woke up in a prison cell, on the floor. This Puerto Rican guy in the cell, he's like missing teeth and shit, he starts saying: 'Ooooo, you're pretty, you're the prettiest thin' I seen in here all week.' So you know what I did then? I roared like a lion. I roared . . . so fuckin' loud it scared the shit out of that fuckin' piece o' shit *and* the two cops outside my cell. I went on roarin' for five minutes. They were sayin': 'He's crazy . . . he's crazy.'"

"Sounds like you're ready to move on to bigger prisons," Alan quipped. "You know, you had us all worried out of our minds. Especially your parents."

"Oh, fuck them. They think they know everything—and everything about *me*. But no one's gonna fuckin' analyze *me*."

"How 'bout business school. . . ."

"I'll tell you what I'm gonna do," cousin Rick continued. "When I was on that cell floor, I made three commitments. First, I'm gettin' out of here. Second, I'm gettin' Randy out of the Krishnas, even if I have to blow him out. And third, I'm gonna find that cop that hit me with that billy club and kill him."

"Is that where you're going now?"

"No, not tonight. Tonight I'm celebratin'. I'm a free man."

Chapter Eight

The following Wednesday afternoon at 1:00, Alan pulled up in front of Juan's house in a blue, two-door sedan with a N.Y.C. Department of Sanitation logo on the side. Juan lived in Glendale, Queens, on a middle-to-lower-middle class block of two-story, brick, two-family walk-ups. Alan parked and pulled his bass case out of the back seat. He rang the bell for the lower dwelling and Juan let him in.

"Hey, glad you could make it," Juan blurted out, extending his hand.

"Yeah, I just cruised by my house and picked up my bass. I'm inspecting an old smokestack about two miles from here for possible conversion to a recycling plant. This is my lunch break. Let's rock."

"What's up, man," Gene said in an unexcited tone, extending his hand for the standard "cool shake."

"I learned 'Minds of War' and 'Sanity on the Rag' note for note, and I've got about the first half of 'Roll Call for the Reaper' down. I also learned 'Breakin' the Law,' by Priest and that AC/DC one."

"All right," Gene sighed, "we'll try it. You sure you're not gonna get fired?"

"There's no law saying I can't spend my sixty minutes headbanging instead of slamming fast food down my gullet and getting drunk in yuppie bars like everyone else."

Alan entered Juan's padded, postered bedroom in the back and plugged into the Marshall bass cabinet. Juan's drum kit was massive, with enough symbols, snares, and tom-toms to open up a small specialty store. Alan tuned his bass to Gene's guitar as Gene winced through every one of Alan's adjustments. "Hit the harmonic," Gene lamented. "Sounds good to me," Juan offered. Two minutes later, they launched into Gene's "Minds of War." Juan's double bass drum kit thundered in heavy triplets, with deafening cymbal crashes. Yet all the sounds were somehow controlled and coherent. Gene's guitar playing was efficient, smooth, and angry, going back and forth from rhythm to leads, compensating the best it could for the lack of an extra track as heard on the four-track demo of "Minds of War." Alan's bass playing fleshed out the music reasonably well. Suddenly, Gene frowned and dropped his arms. Juan and Alan stopped playing a moment later.

"That part's in A, not E," Gene complained. "I thought I gave you the tape."

"Hey, sounded pretty good for a first time," Juan noted.

"All right," Alan conceded, "I thought it sounded good when I stayed on the E. But it makes sense. A and E are relative keys."

"I *wrote* it," Gene argued, "I know how it should be played. Just play the A."

"Okay, fine. Take it from the second verse." They resumed playing, with Gene nodding his head in self-congratulation. A minute later, during the lead, Gene stopped again.

"That's not what you're supposed to be playing during the lead," Gene complained. "You have to play thirty-second notes, not sixteenth notes."

"It won't sound clean that way until I have it perfect," Alan countered. "It'll sound muddy. Just let me try it this way for now."

"Are you good enough for this band?" Gene asked rhetorically. "Honestly, I don't know if you're gonna put the time in. You say you're gonna come by once a week. Is that how we're gonna get *signed?*"

"Wait a second," Alan protested diplomatically, "I can rehearse every single night, Monday through Sunday, or weekend *days* if you want. Right now, this is a freebie. I'm squeezing this one in."

"You know I can't do it at night," Gene stated. "That's when I make all my money. Oh, and another thing, that bass is not stageable. You definitely need to get a better bass."

"I *will*, okay? I'll put it on my list. Let me tell you something: I'll eventually be able to go note for note with you, so just relax."

"I don't have time to waste," Gene retorted.

"Okay, okay," Juan interjected, "you're wasting time *now*. Let's try 'You Shook Me All Night Long.'"

"Fine," Gene agreed grudgingly, as he entered with the first string of chords. When the rhythm section came in, the sound was fairly tight, almost doing justice to a distorted live bootleg of the original. A minute into it, Alan became aware of the furious pounding on the window immediately behind Juan. Juan observed Alan's anxiousness and became aware of it himself. Alan's stomach tightened. This was the last thing he needed, he thought. Accruing bad karma in mid-day by disturbing the frail, elderly neighbors. Juan stopped playing and turned around. He drew open the curtains and pushed open the windows. There stood a woman in her early thirties, dressed in biker clothes, with a pretty but weathered face and a bandanna. "Hey," she yelled, "how 'bout some fucking Black Sabbath?!!"

****

Saturday, around noon, Alan and cousin Rick grabbed a few final things from Alan's apartment as they got ready to drive to Rockaway Beach. They would drive around Queens in Rick's pick-up to load in various friends before heading down Woodhaven and Cross-Bay Boulevards toward the shore. As they emerged from the apartment, they crossed paths with Jill's parents, who were on their way in.

"Hi, Mr. and Mrs. Piros," Alan let out.

"Hello, Alan," Jill's mother answered for both herself and her husband. "You are going to the beach?"

"Yup," Alan replied.

"It is nice weather for it," Jill's father noted.

"Maybe your cousin should take a haircut first," Jill's mother remarked. "I think he may be a good looking boy, if he did that and shaved."

"I like it this way," cousin Rick shot back, perturbed. "I have the strength of ten men."

"And the prison record of twenty," Alan quipped, attempting to smooth over the rough exchange.

"You will see," Jill's mother said, half playfully.

"Okay, have a nice day," Alan called out as he and cousin Rick let the service entrance door close behind them.

"What a fuckin' bitch," Rick steamed.

"I know, but control yourself, as a favor to me. (A), she's my landlord, and (B), I might have to be involved with her on a long term basis."

"No fuckin' way," Rick protested, "you don't want to marry her daughter."

"You don't know *what* I want," Alan shot back.

"She's not smart enough for you."

"You know, if you weren't so drugged out, I'd hit you." As they got into cousin Rick's truck, Alan reflected on Jill's parents and her mother in particular. It seemed clear that at least on some level, she didn't like him. There was a good side to that as well as the more obvious negative side. That Jill cared for him this much, even while against the tide, demonstrated a strong allegiance to him—unless of course it was all part of a game.

An hour later, Rick, Alan, Jordan, Zak, Yotti, and Juan emerged from cousin Rick's pick up truck, now parked in the lot near the boardwalk at Rockaway. A few minutes later, as they spread the blankets out on the sand, a thought occurred to Alan: "Did anyone bother to call Warren?"

"I called Warren," Zak explained. "He said he might meet us later. His asshole's flaring up again." Cousin Rick had already opened the cooler and was now pouring a bottle of beer straight down his open throat.

"How much of that insurance money do you still have left, Rick?" Jordan asked.

"Over a thousand," Rick replied, wiping the foam from his scraggly beard with the back of his wrist.

"Where'd the rest of it go?" Juan kidded. "Up in smoke?"

"I made investments you don't even know about," Rick proclaimed.

"Like in cannabis futures?" Jordan remarked.

"If you mean pot, yeah," cousin Rick resounded. "Pot *is* an investment. When I've smoked a few and I'm feelin' good, I think of ideas—brilliant fuckin' ideas no one else could come up with."

"Yeah, too bad you forget them before they even reach your lips," Alan stated.

Within fifteen minutes, Alan had blown up his two-man inflatable boat and pushed off to sea with Tom Ginotti. Since the tide was out, there was a calm plane of water on which to float. A breeze moved the boat slowly south along the beach. From afar, they saw cousin Rick running to tackle Zak, who held the football. "He looks like a madman turned loose," Yotti remarked. "Aren't they supposed to be playing two-hand touch?"

"Yeah," Alan agreed, "but I think he's warming up for something entirely different. That's a sample of what you're gonna see at the Krishna temple any day now."

"He's still talking about getting his brother out?" Yotti asked rhetorically. "I read that they have huge guys guarding the place."

"Oh, he'll get his ass kicked, no doubt," Alan predicted. "It's just a question of how many people he'll injure along the way."

"Well, I hate to change the subject," Yotti began, "but I have to talk to you about something." Oh no. Alan was almost certain the Yotti knew—the Valentine's Day Massacre, the Yocket. And they were together in a tiny boat.

"Yeah. . . ."

"I've been noticing that I've been progressively more depressed over this past year," the Yotti continued.

"Anything I can do?"

"Let me just bounce some thoughts off you," Yotti resumed. "I'm scared of going nowhere in this job and drowning slowly. There was such a clear goal in college and before—a certain number of courses each semester. Now it's open ended . . . every day I feel like I'm looking down a tunnel, looking directly at the end of the line."

"Well put," Alan commended. "I'm going to remember that and try to put that down word for word when we get back to the blanket. I've rarely heard fear of oblivion stated so articulately, and *that's* coming from someone who thinks about it and discusses it a lot. Let me try to break your problem down into its components. First, the smallest component, but still a very real one—money. I know your present salary is small."

"Yeah, that's part of it," Yotti conceded. "It's virtually impossible to save anything on a low level science editor's salary. I basically like my job, though my parents sort of pushed me toward science."

"That's the funny thing about parents," Alan observed. "They'll push you into things like schools, majors, marriages. But can they continue to push that pencil for you every day once you're in a situation you dread? Can they stay on top of your life as it gets more complicated and full of regret? Oh . . . wait a second . . . that's right, you live at home . . . they can."

The Yotti laughed as heartily as he could manage and picked up the train of thought: "You're right. Money is one factor. At the rate I'm going, I'll always be living on a thread. In school, I did well, but I lived from paper to paper, with the notion of 'one screw-up and it's all over.' And it would have been *easy* to screw up and collapse. Now I'm considering—is this all I get for all those years of pushing and averting disaster?"

"Well put again, Yotti," Alan noted, "which leads me directly into the second component of your problem. You feel your struggles of the past were pointless—is this meager experience the reward? And I don't mean money again. I mean the fact that after all this, we have to get up every morning and answer to some angry, mindless supervisor. Personally, I'm at the point where I'll tell him to fuck off if he pulls anything else with me."

"Aren't you afraid of losing your job?"

"Yotti, I think about leaving my *body*. Leaving a job is nothing. And speaking of the 'what was it all for' component, you know how homeless people wind up wearing random clothing, whatever they were given at some forgotten time. . . ."

"Yeah. . . ."

"Well every once in awhile," Alan continued, "I see a vagrant in a Harvard sweatshirt, or a Princeton or Yale one, and I think 'Gee, he must have had a real tough time sophomore year and just kept sliding downhill.' But he's still got that sweatshirt and damn it, that's what makes this country great!" Yotti laughed loudly, over the sound of the gentle waves, and resumed the train of thought:

"Well, what's component number three of my problem? I know what I think it is. In college and before, I was able to study a wide variety of things without having to go to absurd lengths."

"Right," Alan agreed, "you were paid . . . or subsidized to be a Renaissance Man. And now that's shot to hell. You're paid to do one thing and then go home, go to sleep, then come right back in and do it again—day in, day out. Yeah, that's component three all right."

"And I see people ten years down the road in that condition," the Yotti added, "and there doesn't seem to be any alarm going off in their head. No one's telling them or me anything. It's simply not discussed."

"That's another ironic thing about this country," Alan observed. "They tell you to *feed your dreams* . . . but they make hallucinogens illegal. Anyway, Tom, let me tell you my secret, as far as handling component number three is concerned—the death of multifaceted dreams. I keep most of my dreams and aspirations on maintenance—low level maintenance, like the white dot in the middle of an old black and white TV set that lasts about three minutes after you turn it off. I'll do anything to keep that white dot glowing. Even the most minor things, like if the goal is to play organized baseball again someday—I'll keep a little file on where there are semi-pro or adult leagues in the New York City area, or even low level minor league baseball clubs. Keep that white dot burning. It's not easy, but it beats the alternative."

"Your cousin Rick keeps his white dot alive," the Yotti mused, ". . . with a lit joint."

"Very insightful," Alan commended. "I've heard a lot of people talk about him, but no one ever hit the nail on the head like that. Deep down, he knows he's only a shadow of what he used to be, just a couple of years ago. He was a mensch—two jobs, good grades, he was clean cut. He had the looks of a model. He got *me* a job in the summer of '82. No one even remembers *that* Rick anymore, because the images seemingly have no connection. But I think you're right. I think one of the purposes of the pot, damaging though it is, is to let him remember what he once was and envision what he might one day be. Okay, component number four—final component. And this relates to the first thing you complained about—time. You phrased it best . . . 'No more semesters as distractions.' You're now looking down the line at the end. *Now* you know why people pursue advanced degrees. It brings back the distraction and the feeling of not having 'finished' yet."

"It seems the only time a person is truly happy," Yotti observed, "is when he's not aware of time passing or having ever passed."

"Bingo!" Alan exclaimed. "Brilliant. Like the situation we're in this very moment, a perfect example. We're in a little boat, floating along, having a great time. But then we look at the shore and realize we've floated like half a mile away from our group, down the beach, and start recognizing that for every ten feet we float, we have to walk back ten feet, carrying the boat on our backs. That sucks."

"All right," the Yotti sighed, "let's go back." As they neared the shore again, Alan and Tom began to decipher a familiar sound, apparently emanating from the blanket of two young women. The sound became steadily less distorted as they emerged from the water.

"Wait, walk over with me," Alan insisted. "I know exactly which Zeppelin bootleg this is."

"Of course you do," Yotti agreed, "you taped it off of *me.*" The women, like Alan and Tom, were in their early to mid- twenties. Both were seemingly athletic. One had shoulder length auburn hair with mild freckles on an attractive all-American face. The other was short, with straight black hair and a moderately exotic look. Their blanket seemed positioned to maximize simultaneously their distance from all of the surrounding blankets, with none closer than fifty feet. Now, they looked up at Alan and Tom with some trepidation.

"Zeppelin, London, 1969, recorded live in performance for the BBC," Alan stated.

"Oh my God," the one with auburn hair returned, breaking out in a wide smile, "I can't believe anyone knew that."

"Are you from this part of the planet?" the dark haired one asked. "All anyone around here knows is jungle music."

"They don't know that either," the auburn haired one clarified, "they just blast it. We had to move three times today to get away from it."

"I think what you need is a bigger ghetto blaster," Alan suggested.

"That, and a can of mace," the auburn haired one added. "I'm Kim, this is Cheryl." She extended her hand as did her friend. Alan and Tom reciprocated.

"I'm Alan, this is Tom."

"That's probably the best Led Zeppelin bootleg I have," the Yotti asserted. "It was recorded directly from the sound board instead of from a lone microphone in the back with everything booming off of walls. That recording is so clear, you can hear everything individually."

"It took some getting used to, though," Cheryl indicated. "You listen to these songs one way for years, and they're so full. And then you hear this and it's just bass, guitar, drums, vocal—the bare bones."

"But it's a great performance," Alan noted.

"Oh, yeah," Kim agreed, "and you begin to really appreciate it for what it is."

"Exactly," Alan remarked, "and maybe someday you'll feel the same way about the jungle music at Rockaway Beach."

"Never," Cheryl exclaimed.

"Never," Kim echoed. "Where are you guys sitting?"

"About three lifeguard stands that way," Alan replied.

"We might come over later," Kim announced.

"We might need protection," Cheryl quipped.

"Tom'll handle that," Alan returned.

"Fear not," the Yotti proclaimed. As Alan and Tom moved away, they heard one of the two female voices ring out: "Nice chest."

"Now come on," Alan retorted, turning his head for a moment, "Tom can't stand being treated as a sex object."

Several minutes later, as Alan and Tom approached their own blankets, Tom asked the mandatory question: "Do you think they'll really come over?"

"I doubt it," Alan said. "But just in case they're serious, I didn't tell them about my cousin." At the blankets, cousin Rick lay face up and puffed on a joint.

"That's why you had to sit down after only three quarters of touch football!" Jordan barked at Rick. "You're destroying your lungs."

"Ay, who scored on that forty-five yard punt return?" cousin Rick bragged.

"Forget about his lungs, Jordan," Alan advised. "Has anybody read the law lately? Smoking pot is illegal.

Personally, I could care less, but you're gonna get busted out here."

"I don't give a shit," cousin Rick proclaimed. "If they bust me, you can just tell them you don't even know me."

"That *is* what I'll say," Jordan grumbled.

"Can't you just wait till that party we're going to later?" Juan asked.

Alan was half asleep on the blanket an hour later, when he heard Juan's voice express hushed amazement: "Man oh man, they're coming here." Alan looked up and saw Kim and Cheryl, now carrying their beach gear.

"Now don't get too flattered," Kim stated, "we're only here in an attempt to save our lives."

"My cousin here will guard you with what's left of *his* life," Alan asserted.

"There's still time to run, ladies," Juan kidded.

"Ay," cousin Rick let out with a grin, looking up at the women, "my fuckin' fan club."

"How do you know we're not undercover cops?" Cheryl posed.

"Ay, you can get under the covers with me anytime," Rick remarked, coughing up a lung full of smoke.

"Maybe we oughta' go back to the jungle," Cheryl proposed, nudging Kim.

"No, nothing is worse than that," Kim asserted. "We'll stay on one condition. That you give us a hit of that."

"Yeeeooow," cousin Rick let out exuberantly.

"You don't want to get involved with him," Alan warned. "He's wanted in three states."

"Oh yeah?" Kim inquired. "How many states are *you* wanted in?"

"None yet, but damn it, I'm trying."

In the late afternoon, the entire group piled into Rick's pick-up truck. Kim and Cheryl had agreed to come along and go to the party in Manhattan. Rick, Jordan, and Juan rode in the driver's compartment, while everyone else squeezed into the rear camper shell, isolated from the front. Cousin Rick pushed into high gear and hit eighty-five miles an hour on the Crossbay Boulevard.

"Oh God," Cheryl yelped, "does he always drive this fast?"

"Yeah," Zak replied, "except when he's going to Lefrak City on a pot run. Then he floors it."

"Someone please tell me," Kim requested, "what I'm doing in here."

"Clinging to dear life," Alan responded. "Any other questions?"

"Did anyone tell Rick the party's on Astor place?" Yotti asked.

"Yeah," Alan said, "I told him. If he misses it, just bail out at the right time."

"Warren might meet us there," Zak noted. "It's really his friend's party. . . ." Cousin Rick swerved at full speed to pass a vehicle on the right and sent everyone in the back flying to one side and screaming. Kim landed in Alan's lap and remained there a full fifteen seconds after the danger had subsided. Alan left his right hand cradling her head.

"He's not driving me home, I'll tell you that," Kim asserted, still on her back. "Will you drive me home?"

"Sure," Alan answered. "No one should be subjected to this twice in the same lifetime. Fortunately, I've got a little treat for you." He picked up the acoustic guitar that was lying in the back and began to strum an upbeat twelve bar blues. "This is called the 'Cousin Rick Blues'. . . .

Livin' on insurance money, and acting like a slob

Livin' on insurance money, ain't gonna get no job
Ain't never workin' nine to five
I'd rather join the mob.

Use the city sewer, to get from here to there
Lookin' like a vagrant, I never cut my hair
Not into doin' laundry
Just sniff my underwear. . . ."

"Bravo!" Kim shouted, "Bravo! You oughta' do this for a living."

"What do *you* do for a living?" Tom asked.

"We're both dental hygienists," Cheryl replied.

"That's funny," Zak returned, "so are we."

The party was packed. Alan and Kim occupied a corner of their own and watched cousin Rick from across the room, dancing like a wild man with two preppie women in their late teens.

"My friends need him," Alan explained, "so they can feel good about themselves."

"But you love him, don't you?" Kim asked.

"Sure I do," Alan confirmed. "He's my favorite bagman in the whole city. No, seriously, I would take him in if I had to."

"Good," Kim stated, "because I admire compassion. There's not much of it around these days—it's out of style—politically, economically. I don't like the whole time we're living in. I feel like I don't fit in."

"I couldn't agree more," Alan concurred. "I don't even like the lingo and catch-phrases of the era. Like 'quality time.' What's that, the twenty-eight seconds immediately before, during, and after an orgasm?"

"That's funny," Kim exclaimed. "Or a 'power lunch'—that's when you throw up on your date at noon."

"Ho, man, you're amazing," Alan marvelled. "I'm stealing that one and anything else you have."

"Be my guest."

"How 'bout this one?" Alan offered. "'Networking'... that's when you stay home all day and watch "Loveboat" re-runs on ABC."

"'Career move'," Kim returned, ". . . a bowel movement at work."

"Consider it stolen."

"Can I steal you?" Kim replied.

"Let me think it over, while I get us two more beers," Alan suggested. He walked toward the bar area, past dozens of sweaty moving bodies, and reached into a plastic garbage pail filled with ice, water, and bottles of Rolling Rock. When he turned around, Warren was facing him point blank.

"Hi, Reiss."

"Warren," Alan retorted, "you *did* show up. Glad you didn't get *left behind.*"

"Well har-har-hardy-har-har," Warren reeled off, Jackie Gleason style. "Of course I'd show up. It's Ken's party. You remember Ken from the show."

"Oh yeah, he was good."

"Well Reiss, I'll tell you though, I barely made it here on the subway. I'm so doped up on Cleocin 100, the room is spinning. Does Rick have room in his pick-up?"

"Hey, I *know* you're blitzed if you want a ride home with *him,*" Alan quipped. "Yeah, there's room. Between me and Kim."

"That girl you're with?" Warren asked rhetorically. "She's cute, and believe me, she's attracted to you. I was watching her."

"And you weren't even in the truck on the way over," Alan noted.

"Well . . . are you gonna go for her?"

"Warren, Jill is coming home two weeks. Even if it was two months, I'd still have to answer no. I'll admit I'm tempted, but so what? Millions of things tempt me."

"You're sure she hasn't fooled around on you in Greece?"

"Sure?" Alan returned. "Not one hundred percent positive, but probably not. Look, I have to assume the best in other people, especially her. There are only four possibilities. If we're both faithful, that's the ideal outcome—that's what I always set my sights on. If we're both unfaithful, we're both swine rolling around in the same mud. If she's faithful and I'm unfaithful, then I won't be able to look myself in the mirror."

"Just like now," Warren remarked.

"And finally," Alan continued, "if I'm faithful and she's not, I'll be extremely hurt, but I can live with it."

"Okay, Reiss—just as long as you give me this girl's phone number when you're done."

"Her name is Kim," Alan stated flatly. On his way back over to Kim, Alan overheard Jordan, who was in a heated argument with a well dressed man about three inches taller and roughly the same age.

"Don't you tell me about my fucking job!" Jordan shouted.

"First of all, you're in the wrong field," the other one delivered loudly, "and second of all, your firm's second rate."

"You couldn't get my job if you blew all eleven V.P.'s!"

Seconds later, Alan handed Kim a beer. "I thought of another one while I was away," Alan began, ". . . 'the Mommy track' . . . that's the rail system leading into the delivery room."

"Your friend Tom told me you have a girlfriend."

"He *told* you?"

"I was talking to him. It came up."

"Well, it's true," Alan said. ". . . and. . . ."

"And it sucks," Kim asserted, "but this is my life, and welcome to it. Cheers."

"Cheers," Alan returned, clinking his bottle with hers. "Do you have a paper and pen?"

"Sure. I'll give you my number."

"Great. It's also for a list of jokes. I'm trying to get back into. . . ." Alan stopped upon hearing an irregular sound. It was a table hitting the floor. Jordan had punched his adversary several times swiftly and now was all over him. Alan lunged toward the brawl, as Jordan's adversary lay on his back and tried to inch away. The adversary reached for a bottle and struck Jordan on the head. From above, Alan got Jordan in a full nelson and began to pull him aside, though Jordan continued to punch effectively. Juan pushed Jordan's opponent along the tiles toward the wall. Zak held Jordan's legs around the calves.

"I'll fucking kill you now," Jordan screamed, "get off of me."

"Shut up, just shut up!" Alan yelled. Jordan was difficult to hold. Alan looked around. Everyone else had simply watched, except for one other unknown male who was now helping to hold down Jordan's opponent. A bookcase had fallen and destroyed a lamp. There were books, bottles, broken glass, ice cubes, and potato chips all over the floor. Now Zak stood up and put his hand to his left eye. Somewhere along the line, he had taken a hard hit and it was already starting to show. An elegant blonde woman with a beautiful, harsh face—possibly Ken's girlfriend, walked up to the scene and started scolding: "I want you out of my apartment now! This is disgraceful! Who do you think you are? How do you intend to pay for this? You are disgusting animals! I'm calling the police! How were you brought up? I'll give you ten seconds! Who invited you? Do you know what that lamp cost? You are disgusting. . . ."

Alan and Juan took Jordan into the building hallway. Seconds later, the elevator door opened and cousin Rick emerged screaming: "They stole my fucking guitar. I went down to get a joint out of my glove compartment, and some shithead musta' kicked the glass in while I was upstairs. My fucking guitar's gone."

"Is any money missing?" Alan prompted.

"No, it was all at home," Rick replied.

"Well that's good," Juan said.

"I know exactly what to do," Alan asserted. "It may not work, but it's the best shot we have. Let's run three blocks over to St. Marks Street. That's where they sell all the stolen shit. They probably sold the guitar to a street dealer two minutes after the crime. Some junkie probably did it."

"Maybe Rick knows him," Juan kidded.

Seven minutes later, Alan, Juan, and cousin Rick continued to walk up and down St. Marks, looking closely at each blanket spread out on the pavement.

"Ah, I don't see it," cousin Rick complained.

"No," Alan conceded, "but here's a *Life* magazine from 1962 with Marilyn Monroe on the cover."

"What the fuck," Rick sighed, "I saw a nice acoustic guitar for sale at the other end of the block. Not mine, but I liked it. I got a hundred bucks on me. I'll buy it."

"Realistic decision," Alan asserted. "I'm proud of you. You've made not one but two hopeless drug addicts very happy tonight."

"Well, I'm comin' back here tomorrow night, and every night after that," Rick warned, "and if I find that guy, I'm gonna kill him."

"Let's see, Rick: there's him, the chiropractor, the cop that hit you with a billy club, the guy who broke into your locker at the 'Y,' the guards at the Krishna temple. . . ," Alan reeled off. "The list is getting long. How're you gonna find time for all this?"

Back at the party, Jordan had somehow slipped back in and was now calm but still simmering. Alan heard some teasing going on. "Hey, how's the job?" Zak quipped.

"Hey," Yotti chipped in, "I overheard that guy over there say his firm out-earned yours last quarter."

"Hey," Alan offered, "*I* know—your company can challenge his company to a softball game. Settle it like men!"

"I'll sell the beer," Juan added.

"Make that wine coolers," Alan proposed.

At 2:00 A.M., Alan drove his '76 Dodge Aspen through Woodhaven Queens with only Kim, who sat in the front passenger's side. After Rick had dumped everyone off in front of Alan's apartment, Alan had agreed to take Kim and Cheryl home. Alan had dropped Cheryl off first and now pulled up in front of Kim's house.

"Cheryl and I would love to see you do comedy some time," Kim said, "we really would."

"Thanks. I have your number. I'll definitely call you as soon as I have something."

"I'll go even if your girlfriend is there," Kim boasted.

"No problem."

"She better be pretty," Kim teased. She shook Alan's hand and got out. As he watched her turn the key, he felt a merciless wave of sadness lift him off his seat an inch or two and pass through him. Then he recalled one item on a list he had made when Jill left—"become platonic friends with two new women."

Chapter Nine

On Tuesday, August 11, at 5:50 P.M., Alan walked home from the subway expecting the light in Jill's second floor window to be on for the first time in a month. It was. He walked beneath the window, through the service entrance, and into his own apartment. He resolved not to call her on this night. He didn't know why. He considered it childish, not one of his major traits—in fact, outright unusual for him. Still, it had to be done.

Alan was stepping out of the shower when he spotted cousin Rick at his living area window. Rick already had one leg in the window.

"Ay Alan," he began, continuing his climb into the apartment. "I'm goin' to get Randy out. You comin'?"

"Are you going to get violent?" Alan prompted.

"No, no, no, forget about that," cousin Rick assured, "don't worry about that. That's in the past. I was pissed off. After he hears what I'm gonna tell him, he'll come right out with us and probably go pick up a couple girls . . . heh, heh, heh. . . ."

"Sure. What are you gonna tell him?"

"Just wait."

Forty minutes later, at the temple in Brooklyn, Alan and Rick parked, walked toward the entrance, and passed inside without difficulty. They approached the shaven, robed white man sitting at the front desk.

"I need to see Randy Reiss," Rick began.

"Bhakta Randy?" the robed receptionist returned rhetorically.

"Randy Reiss," Rick insisted. "I'm his brother."

"Okay," the receptionist agreed. He began pressing buttons and speaking into the intercom system. Now he looked up: "Bhakta Randy will be with you shortly."

"I can hardly fuckin' wait," cousin Rick stated. "I'm gonna straighten him out."

"By example alone," Alan mused. Randy came floating down the open staircase a minute later, bald and robed. He walked up to his brother and cousin, extended his hand, and spoke:

"Haribol."

"What does *that* mean?" Rick demanded.

"It's invoking the Lord's name," Randy explained. "It's for your benefit."

"Well, I got something for *your* benefit," Rick boasted. "It's some advice from the *Old Testament.*"

"Could you please tell my brother not to patronize me?" Randy requested of Alan.

"Well," Alan replied, "look on the bright side. He's standing on his own two feet and not holding a lit joint."

"'Thou shalt worship no other God before me!'" cousin Rick admonished in a deep, gravelly voice. "That's the first commandment and you're breakin' it. You're prayin' to a plastic statue. I know about what you do. You're goin' straight to hell if you keep that shit up. I'm givin' you one last chance to save yourself."

"Let me explain something," Randy offered calmly. "I haven't violated any commandments. Gazing at that statue is just a way of focusing our meditational energies toward Godhead. I don't go around telling you that you worship a little leather box strapped to your arm."

"That's different. . . ."

"No it's not. I'm not going anywhere with you."

"Oh yeah?" cousin Rick threatened. "I'm tellin' your guru about that girl you fucked, up in Maine."

"Fine," Randy shot back, "that's irrelevant. That's in the past. Do what you want. No one cares."

"I'll tell him everything you did," Rick continued, ". . . from the front, from the back, sitting up . . . you made her suck you. . . ."

"You're a madman," Randy said, now raising his voice.

"And I'll bring her down here," cousin Rick proceeded, "how 'bout that? When you see her, you'll wanna do it all over again!!"

"I don't have to listen to this. . . ."

"Yes you do you fuckin'. . . ." Rick grabbed Randy from behind, around the neck and under the shoulder, and began to pull him toward the door. Quickly, monks came out of the woodwork. One of them—six-foot-four, over two hundred and fifty pounds with a light brown pony tail—took charge. He lifted cousin Rick by the shirt and carried him toward the front door. Rick screamed in protest as his legs dangled: "Get off me motherfucker—I'm warnin' you."

"You're an asshole," Randy shouted as he reassembled himself, "an asshole, and you're coming back as a sewer rat!" The monk bouncer dropped cousin Rick near the door, but Rick got up and charged: "Now you're dead, ya' fuckin' idol worshiper. . . ." Alan watched as the monk bouncer lifted cousin Rick like a sack of potatoes over his shoulder and tossed him out into the street. Through the window, Alan saw cousin Rick run and bounce off the Big Man's chest several times.

"Can I interest you in some literature?" a more delicately built monk inquired of Alan inside.

"Sure," Alan acquiesced, "but I'm on my way out." Alan's gaze was directed toward a table displaying soft and hardcover books with multicolored eastern religious depictions on the front. He spotted various books explaining ancient scriptures and the principles of reincarnation, several of which he already owned.

"How about this one?" Alan inquired, ". . . on vegetarian cooking. I've gotta stop living on pizza and salads."

****

The phone rang in Alan's apartment the following evening.

"Hello," Alan spoke, putting the receiver to his chin.

"Alan, hi . . . it's Jill. What happened yesterday?"

"Oh, it's a long story," Alan responded. "It involves my cousins. That should tell you something."

"Well, I'm coming down."

"Great," Alan said, enthusiastically.

When Alan opened the door four minutes later, Jill threw herself at him mock lustfully and gave him a hard, close-lipped kiss on the lips. Alan looked her up and down once quickly. She was slimmer, tanner, and more fashionably dressed than ever.

"I had such a great time, but it's hard to be back," Jill let out, ". . . but I'm happy to see you. How *are* you?"

"Okay. Not as tanned, rested, and ready as you are," Alan replied. "Saddled with things here and there that I never asked for—like getting my cousin out of jail."

"You're kidding me. . . ."

"Don't worry, he's out—and more confused than ever."

"Well, he's not the only one who's confused," Jill revealed. "It feels strange to be back. I don't know what I'm supposed to be doing."

"Give yourself a break," Alan advised, "you've only been home a little over a day."

"I know, but my mother is on my back already. . . ."

"About what?" Alan asked.

"About everything . . . we'll discuss it some other time. I'd rather tell you all about my trip. Corfu was amazing and I made so many good friends. My friend Sylvia will probably visit over Christmas. I can't wait."

"Good," Alan stated. "Oh, I have one more thing to mention, a bit of potential good news, trivial as it might seem. Looks like my band will be getting this gig out in Long Island."

"Good," Jill said perfunctorily. "I didn't know you had a band." Alan reached over on the couch for the back of Jill's neck and leaned over to kiss her. She acquiesced briefly and pulled her head back.

"I've got a surprise for you," Jill let out. "There's an apartment open on the seventh floor. That's what I came here to tell you. My parents said you could have it if you want it. It's not much more than you're paying now."

"Cool," Alan exclaimed. "I'm definitely interested."

"I have the key," Jill revealed. "We can take a look now if you want."

"Great. I'm excited."

Ten minutes later, as they looked out the seventh story living room window, facing toward the interior of the block, Alan put his hand around Jill's waist. Her body was stiff as a manikin.

"When would I be able to move in?" Alan inquired.

"In a few days," Jill replied. "My father just has to put in some cabinets. I wish I could have this place. My parents . . . they're funny. They could care less if I work. I think it would be fine with them if I took more classes or if I just stayed home. But I really want to work. . . ."

"So do it."

"Then you definitely want the apartment?"

"Hey," Alan quipped, "anything to keep my crazy cousin from climbing in the window." Alan looked around the L-shaped studio and began a mental list: loft near window, couch against back wall, carpet beneath loft providing bedroom feel. . . .

****

Thursday morning at 9:27, in the eleventh floor hallway on his way in, Alan ran into Frank Carillo, the Department of Sanitation Director of Engineering, who normally remained on the eighth floor. Frank was in his early fifties, shiny bald on top, with a distinguished air about him and a bright look in his eyes. "Hello, Alan," he boomed. "How's that bridge in Fresh Kills?"

"Still there," Alan remarked, "but I don't know for how much longer. We took some cores. The deck's going to need replacement."

"The garbage business is hell, isn't it?"

Alan walked down the hallway and caught the usual glare from Dick O'Malley. Alan was now virtually immune to it.

In the latter part of the morning, Alan's concentration was broken by Elena's shrill voice: "Alan, pick up on seven."

"Thanks . . . hello?"

"Reiss? It's Warren. I have great news for you. I have this friend out in California who's an agent—a literary agent. . . ."

"Yeah. . . ."

"I know him from college," Warren continued, "back in Chicago. He was a senior when I was a freshman. Great guy. Well, a couple of months ago, I sent him the first fifty pages of your novel. Remember you lent me a copy?"

"Uh-huh."

"Well, he loved it," Warren revealed, "and he wants to see more. He thinks he can get you a deal."

"All right," Alan let out enthusiastically. "What's our next step? Should I send him the next few chapters?"

"He wants you to call him as soon as possible. Here's the number. Ready? Area code 2-1-3, 7-6-3, 9-0-9-3, and his name is John Wilner."

"Okay," Alan repeated, "2-1-3, 7-6-3, 9-0-9-3."

"Right," Warren confirmed. "Call him as soon as possible. He's coming to New York this weekend. I'm gonna see him. It's a perfect chance for you to meet him."

"Okay, thanks Warren. I have my credit card number. I'll call him now. What is it, 9:30 there? Is he in yet?"

"Probably. Okay, let me know what happens."

"Sure, bye." Alan was dialing within seconds, punching in his calling card number after the beep. The third ring was cut short: "John Wilner. . . ."

"Hi, this is Alan Reiss—Warren's friend."

"Oh, right, I was hoping to hear from you," came John Wilner's deep, soothing Californian voice. "I really like what you're trying to do in your novel. You're definitely pulling it off. Tell you what—I already have a publisher in mind."

"I'm glad to hear that," Alan put forth. "What can I do for you?"

"Well, Alan, I'd like to meet with you. I'm going to be in New York this weekend. Meet me Saturday night, eight-thirtyish, at the Rainbow Room."

"That's right across the street from Rockefeller Center, isn't it?" Alan noted rhetorically.

"That's right. Just ask for John Wilner. I'm looking forward to meeting you."

"Same here," Alan returned. "See you there."

As Alan was winding up the conversation, Salaam, a black engineering technician in his thirties, had stepped up to the desk. He held in his hand a rolled up full-size drawing.

"Hey, Salaam," Alan said as he put down the receiver.

"Alan, man," Salaam began, "Sal's gonna have us workin' on the roadway grade for that haul road today. Two of the vertical curves are being changed."

"Uh-huh," Alan acknowledged.

"Yeah, man," Salaam continued, "I have the proposed changes on this sheet and the current profile and stuff on this drawing."

"So I'll come up with the new points," Alan proposed, "and you check 'em and plot them."

"That's right," Salaam agreed. "I'm gonna make copies of both of these for you down here."

"Okay, thanks a lot." As Salaam stepped over to the Xerox machine, Sal walked in with his usual strained look.

"I need you to replot the points for that roadway," Sal declared.

"I know," Alan replied, "Salaam already went over it with me."

"Don't spend too much time on it."

"I won't spend *any* time on it."

"Just get it done," Sal demanded. "Also, I need your time sheet."

"That makes one of us," Alan quipped.

"I'm not fooling around. I need it as soon as possible."

"They're not even due till the end of tomorrow," Alan complained.

"People have been handing them in late," Sal explained belligerently. "We need them now."

"What if I don't know what I'm gonna be working on tomorrow?" Alan inquired.

"Use the number for the task I just gave you."

"I thought you said not to spend too much time on it," Alan remarked.

"All right, fine," Sal said in a huff. "Hand it in tomorrow." He stormed out the door to the hallway. Near the doorway, Salaam picked his head up from the Xerox machine and stepped up to Alan's desk.

"Man," Salaam let out, "in Nam we woulda' fragged his ass."

"Frag," Alan asked, "what does that mean?"

"Fragged him," Salaam reiterated. "When I was in Viet Nam, and we had a sergeant or leader or somebody actin' like that, hey it's bad enough in an office—in a war, that shit'll getcha' killed! Respect is one thing, but you can't have nobody crawling up ya' ass like that all the time. So when he goes to the latrine, everybody else comes out an' we roll a little grenade in there. Boom, man—problem solved!"

"Holy shit!" Alan marvelled.

"Yeah, man, we woulda' fragged his ass."

****

On Friday evening, Alan and Jill sat at a posh European- style bar off of Varick street in lower Manhattan. Jill poured from the tiny, expensive pitcher of blue marguerites they had just paid for.

"You'd look better with your hair cut differently and combed over to the side and over the top," Jill suggested. "It just kind of hangs there now. You need to do something with it."

"Like one of your cover-guidos from *GQ?*" Alan ribbed.

"Not just *there,*" Jill retorted. "I can show you what I mean from a lot of magazines. Like that guy right over there."

Jill pointed to a *GQ* male in his late twenties with his otherwise straight black hair styled in the way Alan had imagined Jill meant. He felt certain that were Jill here alone or with a female friend, she would have struck up a conversation with Mr. *GQ,* and probably made some sort of date with him.

"And then we've gotta get you some new clothes," Jill proceeded. "You go to work and go out in the same clothes. That *bothers* me."

"It bothers me too," Alan quipped, ". . . deeply."

"It *should* bother you," Jill proclaimed. "Right now, in a way, you're incomplete. I'll show you what to buy."

"Great," Alan asserted. "Then I'll teach you how to read, and we'll be all set."

"Oh, fuck off," Jill said indignantly, "don't give me that shit."

"I really don't want to hear anyone telling me what to do right now," Alan asserted.

"Why not?" Jill demanded. "My mother's always telling *me* what to do."

"What does she tell you to do about *me?*" Alan inquired.

"You . . . nothing," Jill leaked. "What *should* she say?"

"I don't know," Alan returned. "It's not important to *me.*"

"I don't want to get into this now," Jill moaned. She lifted her glass of blue liquid, sipped from it, lowered it, and looked around the room with a glazed expression. "You know, you're different," Jill mused.

"In what way?" Alan asked.

"The other guys I've been with were so much more aggressive," Jill delineated. "Sexually aggressive. If they wanted something, they just *took* it. You don't do that. You're waiting for my reaction. They would never put up with the shit you put up with."

"Is that good or bad?"

"It depends," Jill said carefully.

"For me, it doesn't *depend,*" Alan retorted. "If I have to 'take' anything from another person, I can never genuinely have it anyway."

"And another thing," Jill continued, almost obliviously, "you never talk about your ex-girlfriends."

"That's true," Alan acknowledged. "I've always considered that a cheap way of evoking a reaction."

"Well, I might want to talk about my past relationships," Jill proposed.

"If that's what you want," Alan stated, "I can take it."

"No you *can't,*" Jill said sharply. "There's a guy I met my first year of F.I.T. Do you want to hear what we did between classes?"

"Is there a point to this?" Alan demanded.

"Maybe I've already made my point," Jill speculated.

"Maybe," Alan conceded, "but you made it stupidly and for no reason. Do you think that evoking a reaction equals power? When it's misguided, that power wears off—quickly."

"See, I *knew* you couldn't take it," Jill concluded. Alan felt weak, nauseous, and defenseless against the jealous images in his head. He wished the pain could have been more focused and simple, like that from a knockout punch to the jaw.

****

Saturday night, at 8:23, Alan emerged from the elevator on the floor of the Rainbow Room. He was neatly dressed in a blue sport coat, white shirt, blue and brown silk tie, and grey woolen pants. He walked down the hall, through the open glass doors and faced the dignified looking maitre d'. "Excuse me," Alan began, "I'm looking for a Mr. John Wilner. I'm supposed to meet him here. He should be sitting back there somewhere."

"Yes, I shall look," the maitre d' said with a French accent as he looked down at his guest list. "No, no, he is not here. We don't have anyone like that."

"You're kidding me," Alan returned. "He said he'd be here, and you don't even have a reservation in his name? Could I possibly have a very brief look around?"

"Well, yes . . . all right," the maitre d' acquiesced. Alan recalled that he knew next to nothing about John Wilner's appearance. He gleaned what he could from his memory. He was about three years older than Warren, making him twenty-seven. Over the phone, he had sounded white, genteel, and perhaps even a little portly. As Alan walked around and scanned the crowded, carpet-and-crystal covered room, he saw only one person coming close to that description. There were five people in all sitting at the table. Alan walked toward the table and spoke up as he neared: "John?" A silvery grey-haired man craned his head and looked up.

"No, sorry, looking for somebody else," Alan explained as he walked away. Now he paced in the exterior hallway. As his embarrassment faded, his self-probing thought process took over. He wondered how he had expected such smooth sailing after tinkering with Warren's life twice in the past six months. After twenty minutes, Alan approached the maitre d' again: "Nothing?"

"Nothing."

****

Sunday at midnight, Alan was on his loft and fading fast. The day had been a still and lifeless one. The first few people he had called were unavailable. Jill's mother said her daughter went into the city. Still, Jill's bedroom light was on. There was no answer at Warren's house. Alan tried John Wilner's number in California and got a thirty second opportunity to recount his bafflement to an answering machine. Zak wasn't in. Alan decided not to fight it. He would spend the day with his own uneasy thoughts—face them directly and try to work on a few projects. Strangely, for the first time in many weeks, he wished cousin Rick would come through the window. But somehow it was evident that the phone would not be ringing and no one would be dropping by until his state of mind was very different. He looked around the apartment and considered how he would package various items for the move to the seventh floor.

Now, as Alan continued to drift into sleep, the faint nausea he had felt all day from Jill's recent comments began to be replaced by a dream-like awareness of the same thing: she held her lover's hand in class, and Alan was two rows behind in the same room, nodding in approval. Now her lover got up before the class and said a few words about Jill. She was his seventh girlfriend. His speech was overcome by a high-pitched shriek. Alan lifted his head from the mattress and looked out through the window as he noisily spread several of the metal slats in the blinds with his fingers. He considered whether the dream had continued into his apartment and out onto the walkway as he looked at Ruth, the nineteen-year-old girl from the third floor, and her dark companion. He seemed like her boyfriend of the past few months. Ruth was staggering and moaning as he held her around from the back. Must be the conclusion of an alcohol-soaked date. Alan put his head back down on the mattress and almost as soon, sprang up fully awake, alarmed, and determined. As he whipped open the blinds, from his peripheral vision, he saw the assailant fleeing. Alan jumped out the window, dropping three feet to the concrete walkway, and ran up to Ruth, who was on her back, half-conscious. In a quick glance, he saw the assailant disappear up the hill, around the corner. He looked back down at Ruth. Blood oozed from the back of her head, onto the pavement. "Jill," Alan screamed, "Mr. and Mrs. Piros! Call the police! Call an ambulance! Ruth was attacked!"

Lights went on at the second floor level. Alan jumped back inside and came out with a towel, which he folded and placed beneath Ruth's head. She looked up at him with glazed eyes and spoke: "My head hurts. . . ."

"Just don't move, okay?" Alan advised. "You'll be fine." Jill's mother emerged from the service entrance. "What happened?" she asked.

"A Spanish looking guy," Alan explained, "he attacked her. By the time I got out the window, he was way up the block."

"Well it's a good thing for her you were here," Jill's mother said with a calm air of concern.

"Thanks, but I really wish I'd caught the guy," Alan revealed. Jill and her father, along with several other neighbors, were soon milling about the area. The police and paramedics had come whipping around the corner and now swarmed the area as well. Alan happened to look directly at Jill's face. She stared at him blankly, like a pale ghost, with the truth buried many layers beneath the surface of her eyes. Alan turned away, not as having just looked at the sun, but rather at the moon. The paramedics lifted Ruth on a stretcher and moved her into the back of the ambulance. "One person can come along," one of the paramedics announced. Jill volunteered, as much to get away from Alan, it seemed, as to help Ruth. Alan saw the same apparition inhabiting Jill's body as the ambulance doors closed.

"You're a hero," Mr. Alvarez from the fifth floor proclaimed to Alan.

"Gimme a break," Alan responded.

"No, really," Mr. Alvarez insisted. "Most people would do nothing. Believe me, they don't want to get involved. Her father will be grateful. He's divorced, you know. . . ."

"Excuse me," a sharp looking black officer began, stepping up to Alan, "you saw what happened?"

"Part of it," Alan confirmed. "I'll tell you everything I know."

****

Alan called Jill's number from the office in the morning. He was startled to hear Jill answer.

"Hello. . . ."

"Jill, it's Alan. Is Ruth okay?"

"Yes . . . she's fine," Jill replied uncomfortably, guarding her words just as she had guarded her gaze. "She's awake. This guy grabbed her from behind. She was coming home from work."

"Right, I heard," Alan proceeded. "Listen, I got a call from the police this morning. They caught a bunch of guys roaming around Queens last night. They think they have the one who attacked Ruth. So they want me to come down and identify this guy in a line-up. Can you come with me, just for moral support?"

"I wish I could," Jill said hastily. "We're going somewhere tonight. I can't."

"Okay, no problem. You know, I still feel bad I wasn't more alert and didn't catch the guy. I only really saw him from the back and a little from the side."

"Don't feel bad," Jill advised. "I would have done exactly the same thing. I have to go."

****

"Okay, my name is Saunders. Listen, we've got the guys. We know that." The staunchly built detective with a crew cut addressed seven witnesses in a small room within the 113th Precinct. "We just need you to identify them. We've got three separate line-ups, depending on which crime you witnessed. Your guy is gonna be in there. I want you to look real hard."

"Excuse me," Alan inquired, raising his hand, "should we say anything if we're not a hundred percent sure?"

"No," the detective stated authoritatively, "only if you're sure. Don't make a guess or a wild stab. But don't be afraid either. You can see them, but they can't see you."

Ten minutes later, Alan stared through the small glass hole in the wall and understood that the American justice system had not really decayed entirely. There were five young Hispanic men standing shoulder to shoulder, some looking concerned, others looking bored. There would be no easy way out for Alan. He could narrow it down to only two, taking into account the height and the curly hair.

"No, I'm sorry," Alan said, still looking. "I was told not to guess."

"Are you sure?" a different detective was prompting.

"Yeah. I'm sure that I'm not sure."

"Okay, okay. . . ."

As Alan emerged from the rear of the viewing room, a pretty, bandaged Ruth and her father, Marty Rosenbloom, greeted him.

"Hey, I'm sorry. I couldn't identify him," Alan said. "I had to take this thing seriously."

"That's okay," Ruth's father replied. "Someone else already I.D.'ed him. He'll probably go to jail. Even if it's just a year, that'll teach the bastard."

"I couldn't identify him either," Ruth revealed. "He grabbed me from the back. I never got a good look at him. He started choking me and told me to give him my keys."

"Oh my God," Alan blurted out.

"I got one yell out," Ruth continued. "My father wasn't home. I could have been raped. Thank you so much. I know you have problems of your own. I know you and Jill are breaking up."

"I wanna thank you too," Ruth's father chimed in. "I really do. If everybody was like you, there'd be no crime in this lousy city."

"Yeah," Alan remarked, "no crime . . . but lots of nervous breakdowns."

****

Wednesday, in the early evening, Alan had roughly half his stuff in boxes. Jordan had volunteered to help and was busy breaking down the loft. Jill had been unavailable for three days—shielded in her ethnic family world—but now appeared in the open doorway.

"Hi, Jill," Alan said, almost facetiously.

"I'm sorry I haven't been around," Jill said apologetically. "It's just that . . . I'll try not to be that way anymore."

"Why don't you grab some boxes and start taking them to the seventh floor?" Jordan asked Jill flatly.

"Okay. I'll take this," Jill offered, lifting a box of clothing. Alan handed her an extra key as she wandered out the door.

"No offense," Jordan confided, "but she makes me sick. She's vain, for starters. And she's an airhead."

"First of all, I'm not offended by your opinion," Alan asserted. "Second, she's not an airhead, she's a baby. She's intelligent, but she's not able to galvanize that intelligence into intelligent action. She's sheltered—you know that. She doesn't know how to stand naked in the world."

"Well, I wouldn't trust her as far as I could throw her."

"Let me worry about that, okay?" Alan proposed. "I'll admit she's made me feel terrible lately by being untouchable, unreasonable, and through innuendos. And I'll admit that as a result I've had trouble lately finding the motivation to do things—like packing this box right now!"

"Look, Alan, I know you're worthy of some beautiful woman's love, somewhere, but did you ever think that maybe Jill was attracted to you as 'the boy next door,' and now it'll be different?"

"We'll find out, won't we?" Alan shot back. "She doesn't know what she wants. She just hasn't matured."

"Well, I have something to tell you," Jordan revealed.

"What," Alan quipped, ". . . we're breaking up?"

"No," Jordan continued, "I told Warren about the Valentine's Day prank. That's what that agent thing was all about. That was Warren's way of getting back at you. It was all a prank. That so-called agent was Warren's friend from California, nothing more."

"Why was it any of your business to tell him?" Alan pressed.

"I was pissed at the way you and everybody were teasing me after that fight I had," Jordan explained.

"You *deserved* to be teased," Alan remarked.

"Maybe I did, but I was pissed. So I made Warren into an ally as a reaction. He was fuming, Alan, you wouldn't believe it. But I told him, look, let's just do something back in kind. I feel bad about it now."

"Hey, I don't give a fuck," Alan declared. "It was a good prank. I can appreciate it. You didn't tell Yotti though, right?"

"No, of course not," Jordan confirmed, "that would have been worse for him."

"And you didn't tell Warren about the time Zak and I pretended to see his show."

"Nope, I didn't tell him."

"Good," Alan resounded. "Then I have just one question. Zak was in on the Valentine's Day Massacre. But Warren's not doing anything to him apparently."

"He'll get to Zak."

"*Now* he won't," Alan stated.

A half hour later, Alan was alone with Jill in the seventh floor apartment, with boxes and furniture strewn about.

"I'm sad to see you're moving up here," Jill mused. "Things will be different."

"Yeah. We'll be able to fool around without your parents being next door."

"Mmmm . . . that's good," Jill said without conviction. "How come things never worked out between you and Robin? How did it end?"

"Well," Alan recalled, "the boyfriend-girlfriend thing ended one way, the friendship ended later, much differently. In the boyfriend-girlfriend thing, I told her one day: 'Look, you don't seem to want me around, and I can't stand not being wanted around. It's beneath me.'"

"Hmmm," Jill observed, ". . . you made it easy for her."

"And too bad I did," Alan stated. "That was a stray benefit she got from my attempt to live up to high standards. Today, she's waiting for more unearned benefits to trickle down, from someone else."

"What are you talking about?"

An hour later, Alan stood in his old apartment, which was now half empty and appeared ransacked. Holes were left in the walls where the loft had been nailed in for extra stability. Jill's father had brought two people to look at the apartment: an expansive woman in her late forties with big hair and a refined Queens accent, and her timid post-college daughter—the prospective tenant.

"Sorry everyone," Alan explained. "The place looks trashed, 'cause I'm in the process of moving upstairs."

"Tell me something," the mother asked Alan forcefully, "is there a lot of noise?"

"Yes," Alan replied, "but fortunately most of it's coming from me." Jill's father's face revealed uneasiness.

"Tell me something else," she continued, hushing her voice, walking carefully up to Alan, and now whispering in his ear: "Are there roaches?"

"Some," Alan said softly, "but if you fog once in awhile, it stays pretty good for a few weeks. You just have to be able to tolerate all the dead ones when you first come back."

****

On Saturday afternoon, Alan waited for Juan and cousin Rick to ring his apartment doorbell. He had just buzzed them into the building using the intercom. While he waited, he looked out into the courtyard from his seventh story window, through which came a breeze. Although it was late August and still officially summer, it was really the first day of fall. The daytime temperature had fallen below seventy for the first time in weeks. Something subtle in the air promised a more drastic chill, even though it was a fact that warm weather was on the way back. The associations flew in Alan's mind: winding down the baseball regular season, thinking twice before wearing shorts, insipid back-to-school commercials on television, bracing yourself. . . .

"Okay, okay," Alan yelled, as he heard the bell ring.

"Not bad," Juan said as he entered. "Still a little messy."

"Ay, this is gonna be some fuckin' bachelor pad," cousin Rick observed.

"I can give you guys about two minutes," Alan warned. "I'm getting ready to go into the city with Jill."

"We just came to give you the good news," Juan declared. "We got the gig. At Razor's Edge in Babylon. Three weeks from this Thursday."

"I'm gonna be there pickin' up some a' those groupies," cousin Rick forecasted.

"Great," Alan remarked. "What do we get paid?"

"Oh, the way it works," Juan explained, "is the club gives us blank passes and we fill our band name in and give them out to our friends. Then we get two dollars for every person that comes in."

"Uh-huh," Alan acknowledged. "Just for the ones that have our ticket, huh?"

"Yeah," Juan replied.

"And how much do these people pay?"

"Six bucks apiece," Juan responded.

"I never realized how cheap and sleazy the whole proposition was," Alan remarked, "until this minute. We might as well sell tickets to our friends ourselves and then have them come see us play in our own living room."

"I know," Juan agreed. "It sucks. Just don't let Gene down. He's all worried about how you're going to play that night."

"Let him worry about his own shit," Alan asserted. "By the way, does our band have a name?"

"Yeah," Juan replied, ". . . Iron Curtain."

****

Alan sat in the passenger's seat of Jill's Camaro as Jill cruised down Second Avenue in Manhattan.

"I know exactly what I wanna get," Jill proclaimed. "Brown European sandals at this little store in the Village."

"Uh-huh."

"And then I'm getting a leather handbag. . . ."

"You cheated on me," Alan said forcefully, without warning.

"What?"

"Don't waste your breath denying it," Alan barked. "You had sex with some guy in Greece on or about July 17th."

"What are you talking about?" Jill demanded. "How do you know this?"

"I meditated on it and got the answer—something you could never do. You think my thorough state of mind is limited to making lists, but you're wrong." Jill's face turned from red to normal again as she spoke:

"I didn't want to tell you."

"Always thinking of others," Alan quipped.

"Well, I didn't know if things were going to work out between us. . . ."

"She's the master of self-fulfilling prophesy," Alan proclaimed facetiously. "And *I* thought you were *stupid.* . . ."

"I don't have to take this. . . ."

"Shut up," Alan let out. "You're a shallow, scheming, lying, spoiled brat with nothing to offer the world but a shopping list."

"Oh fuck you," Jill screamed, trying still to concentrate on Second Avenue, "you just can't *take* it. . . ."

"Let me ask you something," Alan returned, "did I make it *easy* for you? Is your convenience requirement satisfied?" As Jill slowed for a red light, Alan whipped open the door of her Camaro and dashed out into the street.

"Don't do that!" Jill shouted angrily. "Come back here!" Alan disappeared into Twenty-Second street.

His subway ride back to Queens was a first taste of hell. Appropriately, it was underground. Tolerance for small annoyances—like waiting on line for a token while the toll booth clerk took his time with the change—was gone. Internal cursing and lamenting abounded inside Alan's head. The subway car was filled with people who did not share his lament. Aging people with maybe five to ten years of physical struggling standing between them and death had it better. They didn't have to wrestle with the image of a self-adoring Greek god sticking it to their girlfriend. People Alan's age had it better, too. They were on dates right now. Or they had perhaps broken up recently too, as a result not of getting burnt to a crisp, but rather of innocuous drifting apart: gravitating toward different music, different movies, different lovers, still friends, smooth transition, no harm done, never missed a beat or went a day without it, better off now, see you at that party. . . . Alan stood there on the moving subway car and gave himself generous credit for not opening fire. Now, an elderly gentleman approached Alan, touched his arm for a moment, and spoke: "Excuse me, does this go to Ely Avenue?"

"Ely Avenue?" Alan replied. "Yes it does, sir. Two more stops."

"Thank you very much."

"That's it," Alan thought, "I've achieved fucking sainthood."

Chapter Ten

As evening approached, Alan stood in the doorway of his apartment and waited for cousin Rick to emerge from the elevator. Now as Rick appeared and proceeded to trudge down the hallway, Alan left the door unlocked and went back inside. "Ay, what's up?" cousin Rick said as he opened the door. Alan had already collapsed on the living room floor, near the stereo.

"I just broke up with Jill, a few hours ago. I told her right to her face that she cheated on me on July 17th and jumped out of her car."

"Holy shit, man," cousin Rick exclaimed, "whad she do?"

"Defended herself and admitted to it at the same time," Alan answered. "It was the hardest thing I ever did, and what's my reward? My reward is that every minute is my enemy now. Each one is agony to get through, and when each minute is conquered or simply borne, the next minute waits."

"You did the right thing," cousin Rick asserted. "She couldn't hold a candle to you."

"Doing the right thing is no consolation now," Alan observed. "Not everything in my life can take the form of doing what's best for the future—I'll go crazy. Besides, I think I loved her, as sick and pathetic as that sounds. And I still want to fuck her."

"Well, at least you're not the only one with problems," cousin Rick revealed. "My parents just kicked me out. They told me they wouldn't support my lifestyle anymore. I have till Wednesday to take my stuff. And they took my truck back and put it up for sale. I fuckin' walked here. So, you're not the only one with problems."

"Yeah," Alan agreed, "but unlike me, you earned yours. Look, you're in luck. I'm applying for sainthood this month and need all the brownie points I can get. You can move in here."

"I can?" cousin Rick said excitedly. "Fuckin' A!"

"I have just one question."

"What's that?" Rick asked.

"You have any pot?"

At 2:00 in the morning, in the dark, Alan and cousin Rick stared at the ceiling from different areas of the apartment as they worked on their fifth joint. Alan knew the first signs of sleep were still hours away. But it didn't matter. The THC was providing a stronger, more thorough mental rinse cycle than sleep alone could have accomplished.

"So now that we're completely stoned," Alan began, "what do we see as the pure truth in this matter? Why did Jill do what she did?"

"Well," cousin Rick responded, "she didn't know how to handle the situation. Her mother wanted to break it up between you two, but Jill didn't wanna . . . be controlled. But she didn't have the strength to go against her mother . . . so she solved it in her own way. She convinced herself she made her own decisions. And in her own stupid way—she did."

"You hit the nail on the head, boy," Alan declared. "Now I know why you smoke so much of this stuff. It lets you see right through to things. That's probably why I stopped smoking it three years ago. You know, I'm already taking in so many things as it is . . . the pot made it all too much."

"Well," cousin Rick mused, "why would you ever wanna be in any state of mind . . . other than seeing the truth?"

"Look at the price *you* pay for it," Alan remarked. "You neglect the material realities of life to such a high degree that someone else has to scoop up the mess. I mean, I'm happy to help you out, but I firmly believe you can attain comparable clarity without the aid of a chemical substance and without sacrificing other abilities. It takes persistence and self-discipline."

"Well," cousin Rick agreed, "you're probably right. But until I feel like makin' that kind of effort . . . I'm gonna stay stoned off my fuckin' ass . . . heh . . . heh . . . heh. . . ." Rick could not control his hysterical laughter.

"Okay, then while you're in this state," Alan proceeded, "functioning as an oracle, let me ask you something else. I'm in incredible pain now. I can see what the near future's going to be like. Little or no escaping the pain. The automatic tasks in life—getting out of bed, brushing your teeth—have already become and will remain almost insurmountable obstacles. And I don't even care about getting through them either. That whole picture is agonizing to even consider, especially for someone like me who takes pride and pleasure in getting things done. The point is, I didn't do anything wrong that I know of, pushed myself to the limit to try to confront head-on an ugly situation that had begun to confront me. But for some bizarre reason, I have to be experiencing the agony while she goes free. Why is that?"

"First of all," cousin Rick pronounced, "you don't know for a fact that she's not in some sort of agony."

"Okay, I'll grant you that. . . ."

"Second of all," cousin Rick continued, "unfortunately . . . we can't always know the big picture. The events . . . of the past few hours could be settin' up something great to happen to you. And another thing, this might be necessary for you . . . to help you develop your character. Who fuckin' cares about Jill? She might be in less pain, but you'll leave her in the fucking dust. You already have. Even though it sucks . . . it's still about *your* progress. . . ."

"Yeah," Alan agreed, "one thing we can certainly say about God—he's very interested in character development."

At five minutes after nine in the morning, Alan crawled to the phone while trying not to jar his state of slumber too drastically. Cousin Rick was still looking at the ceiling, working on another joint.

"Whatcha doin'," cousin Rick asked, "callin' in sick?"

"Yeah," Alan groaned, "like for the next week."

"Aren't you afraid of getting fired or something?" Rick inquired.

"Hey, I once told the Yotti, I think about leaving my body. Leaving a *job* is nothing." Now Alan heard Elena's voice on the other end of the phone and spoke: "Hi, it's Alan Reiss."

"Hello Alan. . . ."

"Hi, listen . . . I won't be in . . . the next two days. I woke up feeling really sick this morning."

"Well, you don't sound so good. . . ."

"I know," Alan agreed. "Hey, why push it? I have some sick time coming to me."

"Nothing serious, I hope," Elena said.

"No, I'll be fine. Thanks."

"Okay," Elena concluded mischievously, "I'll tell Sal."

"You do that." Alan crawled back to his blanket on the floor and passed out.

At 4:00 in the afternoon, Alan and cousin Rick had dragged themselves out of the apartment and down to the field behind Forest Hills High School, where they had arranged to meet the unemployed Zak. Zak hit fungos out to Alan in left field. Cousin Rick took cut-off throws from shortstop. As Alan chased a long fly to his left and let it bounce once before scooping it up, he became disgusted. He was aware that out of perhaps twenty fly balls hit so far, he had failed to make his usual gallant effort on five and let them fall in for base hits. His throws back to the infield were lifeless. Now Alan walked toward the grass near the dugout area and collapsed. He lay on his back.

"Tired already?" Zak called out as he began to walk over.

"I'm not playing like myself," Alan explained. "You can see that—you've been hitting balls to me for a decade and a half. If I'm not playing like myself, I'd rather not even play. Frankly, I'm nauseous. I'm standing on the same field where I gobbled up balls like a vacuum cleaner ten years ago in pony league, and now I'm watching myself boot the same balls while knowing that everything I've accomplished in the interim adds up to zilch. 'Cause I'm merely an adult with a dead-end job and no girlfriend. I have zero motivation. Why push myself? Am I gonna' improve now and work my way into the majors?"

"Don't beat yourself down like that," Zak advised.

"It's the plain truth, kid," Alan reeled off.

"Anyway, were you going to *marry* this girl?" Zak asked, half-rhetorically.

"I don't know," Alan responded. "When it seemed to be a real prospect, it made me very uneasy. Now that it's gone, I'd like to go back in time, to that situation, and try to feel good about it."

"I'll tell you what you should do," cousin Rick suggested. "That girl you met on the beach . . . what's her name. . . ."

"Kim."

"Yeah," cousin Rick continued, "Kim. Call her. Fuck Jill. Just move right ahead, like a fuckin' steamroller."

"Damn good idea," Alan exclaimed. "Must be the pot kicking in."

Back at Alan's apartment, there was one blink on the answering machine, indicating one message. "That would be pretty amazing if it turned out to be Kim," Alan said as he flicked the playback switch and waited for the message: ". . . Alan, this is Cliff. I'm driving up to New York in a couple of days. If I can crash at your pad. . . . please press one . . . now. If you would like Bo Derek to sit on your face... please press two . . . now. . . ."

"You remember my friend Cliff Tate, don't you?" Alan asked cousin Rick. "We did stand-up and improv together in Jersey."

"Yeah, of course," Rick replied. "I saw you guys. He's fuckin' amazing. This is gonna be great. He's comin' up from Florida, right?"

"Yup," Alan confirmed. "This is like another little consolation prize after the big blow. A couple hundred more like that and I'll be fine. I'll call him back, right after I call Kim. It's after 5:30. She might be in." Alan pulled her number from a sheet of paper and dialed. The fourth ring was interrupted.

"Hello. . . ."

"Hello, Kim?"

"Speaking."

"Hi, this is Alan Reiss. We met a few weeks ago. . . ."

"Oh, hi," Kim responded carefully. "It's nice of you to call."

"Would you be interested in going out to dinner tomorrow night?"

"It's so nice of you to ask," Kim returned consolingly, "but I can't. I already have plans."

"Well, maybe some other night. . . ."

"Maybe," Kim continued. "Remember I told you about my ex-boyfriend—Steve?"

"No, not really, but go ahead."

"Well, we got back together," Kim proceeded.

"Think you're gonna break up again soon?"

"I don't think so," Kim answered, "we're engaged. But listen, Cheryl and I would still love to come see you do your comedy."

"You're seeing it now."

"As long as we can bring our boyfriends," Kim added.

"Yeah, sure. Cheryl's seeing someone too?"

"Uh-huh. Steve's brother."

"Does this Steve have any sisters?" Alan asked.

"No. . . ."

"Okay," Alan concluded, "I'll keep you posted."

"Thanks a lot. Bye." Alan put down the receiver.

"Well," cousin Rick asked, "how'd it go?"

"Get out the pot."

****

Alan forced himself into work on Wednesday morning. At 9:15, as he rode the elevator up, Frank Carillo was among the four other people along for the ride.

"How're you doing today?" Frank asked.

"Like the City of New York. Just getting by."

"Well, *damn,* that's not good enough," Frank observed jovially. "We're gonna have to get you on some sort of program."

"Or *off* of one," Alan replied.

Alan juggled some papers at his desk. He wasn't going to hack it today. Elena called out: "Alan, pick up on seven. It's your father."

"Thanks. Hi, Dad?"

"Alan, I got your message. I'm sorry you're going through this."

"Thanks. In all honesty—I'm a mess. I don't have the fight left in me."

"You'll get it back soon enough," Alan's father consoled.

"Soon enough to move my furniture out into the street."

"Well, you must have some fight left in you if you took Rick in," Alan's father observed, "in the midst of all this."

"Hell no. I need the pot."

"Well, I know it hurts, but I firmly believe what happened, happened for the best. . . ."

"Wait, can I call you back?" Alan proposed. "Someone's standing at my desk."

"Sure."

"What do you want?" Alan asked Sal, who looked down and frowned.

"Did you call R.J. Burghoff's office?"

"Not yet today," Alan replied. "I called him six times last week and seven times the week before. He hasn't gotten back to me."

"Well call him again," Sal insisted.

"Sure. I think the fourteenth call is gonna crack this thing wide open."

"They're busy," Sal explained belligerently. "I know. I used to work in a consultant's office. We have to get them to develop a schematic for that roadway."

"*I'll* do it for you in *one day*," Alan proposed.

"How 'bout that traffic diversion plan?" Sal prompted. "Did you finish that?"

"More than half of it."

"You shoulda' had that finished by today," Sal ranted. "But you were out the last two days. How do you expect to get anything done like that?"

"By working from my bed," Alan shot back. "Every couple of hours, I'd lift my head out from under the covers, make a couple of scratch marks on a piece of paper, and go back to sleep."

"You'd never make it in a consultant's office," Sal boasted. "I used to work in a consultant's office."

"Why don't you go back?" Alan remarked.

"No excuses anymore," Sal warned as he turned his back and walked toward the door.

"Oh, one more thing," Alan blurted out, opening his desk drawer and fully exposing his keyboard. "What do you think of this riff?" Alan played four bars of "Smoke on the Water," loud and clear.

"You'd better clean up your act," Sal admonished.

"So I can get that all-important PG-13 rating?"

****

As Alan returned from work in the early evening and walked down the hill alongside the building, her face came into focus. It was Jill, walking up the hill towards him. She was dressed casually and appeared ready to release some well thought out words:

"Hello, Alan. . . ."

"Come off it," Alan shot back dryly, passing her by. He turned around four steps later upon hearing her scream:

"You can't even say hello?!! What's the matter with you?! What's your problem?!!"

"You're the one with the problems," Alan replied calmly, as he turned back around and continued on into the building. As he walked up the stairs, he saw her face in his mind: red, strained, exasperated, furious—for once not calling the shots. In the apartment, cousin Rick had the phone in one hand and a joint in the other as Alan walked in: "That thirty-year-old one was my favorite . . . hey, Juan, I gotta go . . . Alan just walked in . . . yeah, see ya' . . ."

"Guess who I just ran into?" Alan began.

"That bitch?"

"Yup, Jill," Alan confirmed. "She blew up 'cause I wouldn't say hello to her. I just said 'Come off it,' 'cause she's such a phony—even when she's enraged."

"Woooo, man," cousin Rick exclaimed, releasing a huge burst of marijuana smoke, "sounds like she's startin' ta' feel sorry she blew it. Now she's just gonna get madder and madder—unless you do somethin' about it."

"You *know* I'm not," Alan stated. "How could I even touch her or talk to her again as if I respected her? It would disgust me, especially in the long run. I'll admit a small part of me wants to perform some sleazy act on her terms, but so what? At least I feel a little better now. Part of the reason I'm down, in the first place, is from a superficial ego blow. Now I'm back up a bit again from a superficial ego boost. I guess I'll just take it."

"Well, let me ask you something," cousin Rick proceeded. "How long do you plan to live in this building? I mean, Jill's family owns and controls this fuckin' place. They can mess things up for you."

"And I can mess things up for them," Alan retorted. "I'll stay here as long as I feel like it—which may be years."

"All right!" cousin Rick let out, along with more smoke.

"One more thing," Alan related. "I don't want to be a pretentious asshole, but I'd like you to drastically cut down on the pot. I won't be having any more myself—maybe a hit here and there. It could easily become a crutch for me, like it is for you."

"Okay, it's your fuckin' place," Rick said with resignation.

****

Alan and cousin Rick helped Cliff with his bags as they walked into the apartment just after 11:00 that night.

"Nice place you got here," Cliff noted.

"Thanks," Alan acknowledged. "It'll be a little cramped in here. You can have the couch."

"Great," Cliff resounded. "I won't be here all the time anyway. I have gigs at night and a couple of other places to crash at." Cliff appeared as Alan remembered him: a missing link in the Hollywood brat pack, only with tremendous comic ability and without the arrogance.

"Had a long drive," Cliff related, "lots of time to come up with funny stuff. I'm driving through Jersey, along Interstate 295, and I see a sign saying 'New Jersey Works.' Damn, what did it smell like when it was *broken?*"

"Good one," cousin Rick said.

"Ever notice," Cliff continued, in a hybrid voice of Steve Martin and Robin Williams, ". . . ever notice on the highway that you get pulled over by the state troopers for doing sixty, but guys blowing you by at ninety-five are left alone? That's for a good reason. You see, the cops can catch *you*. And there's another reason—they *admire* that guy doing ninety-five. And they admire his car. 'Hey, Joe, check out that '66 Mustang tearin' up the road. Hmmm . . . not bad . . . must be fuel injection.' 'Hell, it's the overhead cam. Hey, wait a second, let's get that faggot doing fifty-eight in a Yugo.'"

"Not bad," Alan said. "I'll make sure you write everything down. By the way, Cliff, you walked into a weird situation. I recently broke up with my girlfriend."

"Robin . . . the psycho?"

"No," Alan explained, "Jill. I haven't kept you up to date. Her father owns this building."

"Sorry to hear that," Cliff stated. "You have a picture of her?"

"Well," Alan remarked, "I bought a picture frame, but the model in the picture that came with it was such a knockout, I left it in."

"Just show me that, then," Cliff quipped. "Hey, look, relationships are tough, but you have to deal with it. My girlfriend bought a special pill for her PMS . . . it knocks me out cold in fifteen minutes."

****

Alan tiptoed around the apartment while getting ready for work in the morning. Cliff and cousin Rick, in different corners of the room, clutched various nearby objects in their sleep and enjoyed their respective cocoons. As Alan closed the apartment door behind him, he felt something strange and then looked. It was a rubber band hanging from the outside doorknob. An attempt at communication from Jill, he thought. Worthless. But not a bad way to start the day.

****

Iron Curtain held a rare Saturday afternoon practice. Cliff had driven Alan and cousin Rick in his jeep over to Juan's house.

"You don't mind these guys sitting in, do you?" Alan asked Gene respectfully.

"As long as they don't waste my time," Gene warned. "I hope *you're* gonna be ready for this gig. If we don't sound good, I might just disband this unit."

"Don't worry, okay?" Alan returned.

"Is my car gonna be safe out there?" Cliff asked Juan.

"Yeah, no problem in the daytime," Juan assured him.

Since Juan's bedroom was too cramped with five people and the drums in it, Cliff and cousin Rick agreed to sit in the living room just outside. Inside, Gene, Juan, and Alan launched into "You Shook Me All Night Long." Alan tried to let his pain and misgivings run out through his fingers, if only to be free for three minutes and forty-seven seconds. When the song was over, Cliff and cousin Rick pushed the door open against Alan's back.

"Sounds real good," Cliff proclaimed. "You guys are just about there."

"Thanks," Gene said.

"Yeah, you oughta blow that place away," cousin Rick chimed in, breathing out pot smoke.

"Let me ask you something out of the blue," Alan said. "There was a rubber band hanging from my outside doorknob a couple of mornings ago. Do you think it was from my ex-girlfriend?"

"She wants to talk," Gene supposed, "but you won't talk anymore...."

"Why should I?" Alan remarked.

"Well," Gene continued, now with a wide boyish grin, "women get angry as hell when you don't talk to them. It's like Jekyll and Hyde. Believe me, I've been through it a dozen times. I *still* go through it."

"So what should I do," Alan ventured sarcastically, "transform myself into the lifeless patsy she thinks she needs?"

"Do whatever you want," Gene shot back.

As Cliff, Alan, and cousin Rick walked from Cliff's parked jeep back to Alan's apartment building later in the afternoon, Alan spotted a piece of paper on the windshield of his own car, parked up the block. Cliff and cousin Rick followed as Alan walked toward it, bass case in hand. The piece of paper was yellow, roughly three inches by three inches, and trapped under one of the wipers. Alan took it out and flipped it over. It was blank on both sides.

"Is this bizarre or what?" Alan asked loudly.

"This girl's bad news," Cliff observed. "Either that or completely illiterate."

"I don't feel sorry for her," cousin Rick said, releasing a burst of smoke. "She's pathetic."

****

When Alan opened the apartment door early Monday evening, cousin Rick was half asleep on the floor mattress. "What's up?" Rick yawned, sticking his head out from under the covers as Alan closed the door behind him.

"Where's Cliff?"

"He's been out all day," cousin Rick responded.

"Well, I'll *tell* you what's up. I smell some kind of weird perfume. I smelled it all the way down the hall, and it's coming from here. You know my sense of smell is superhuman. I can tell when someone three apartments away is lighting up a cigarette."

"Yeah, so. . . ," cousin Rick challenged.

"So I'm gonna take a wild guess. You had a woman up here, and you paid her to have intercourse with you."

"All right... I'll admit it," Rick shot back. "What's the big deal? I still had money left over. It's *my* money, and I already changed the sheets!"

"Yeah, you think it's that simple," Alan pressed. "What if she stabbed you up here? What if she stole something of mine?"

"Get real," cousin Rick shot back.

"I'll get real," Alan said in a raised voice, "...real adamant and kick you out. You probably think that's one strike. Well it's *two* strikes and a half-swing that the home plate umpire is referring to the first base umpire! Where'd you find her—the *Village Voice?*"

"Yeah. You had it lying on the table."

Chapter Eleven

Alan stopped dead in his tracks in front of the building Tuesday morning. Both tires on the left side of his car were slashed. The game plan in his mind changed. Life was going to be different now. He walked somberly over to the scene of the crime for closer inspection: both tires slashed through the side wall, making patching impossible. The sight of the humble '76 Dodge Aspen leaning to its side, crippled, flanked by sleeker, newer, unblemished cars on the street brought sadness to Alan before the anger kicked in.

Five minutes later, Alan swung open his apartment door.

"What happened?" cousin Rick let out, startled.

"My tires were slashed. You get three guesses. . . ."

"Holy shit, she's gone too far," cousin Rick exclaimed. "We should just run her over."

"With my car in its present condition," Alan exclaimed, "I don't think I could catch her. I've got a busy day planned now. I have to call in sick—I'm not gonna get anything done at work in this condition. Then I've gotta call a tow truck and wait downstairs. Damn, if she had nailed one tire instead of two, I could have *driven* it to the gas station.'"

A little after 11:00 A.M., with his car in the shop, Alan walked into the 112th Precinct in Forest Hills. After fifteen minutes of waiting, a semi-official, hefty white woman in her thirties sat him down in the chair alongside her desk.

"What can I do for you?"

"My car tires were slashed," Alan began, "and I know who did it. This crazy girl who lives in my building. Her family owns the building."

"Are there any witnesses?" the woman asked politely.

"Not at the moment," Alan responded. "But she has a motive."

"Ex-girlfriend?" the woman asked.

"Yeah. . . ."

"Well, there's not much we can do without a witness or other concrete evidence," the woman explained. "What I'll do is assign you a case number. If there are any further developments, let me know."

"What am I supposed to do about my car from now on?" Alan asked. "I can't afford to put it into a garage."

"Well," the woman suggested, "try parking it in a different area."

When Alan returned to his apartment at 1:00 P.M., Juan and Cliff were there along with cousin Rick.

"I heard what happened," Cliff offered. "I think she's a sick girl."

"Yeah, well the cops won't do anything unless we catch her red-handed," Alan complained. "What am I gonna' do, stay up all night and stake the car out? I'll probably park it a few blocks away tonight, that's all."

"Well, I'm sure it's her," Juan added. "When I was walking into the building about an hour ago, I heard some girl's voice say 'Ha-ha.' I'm sure it was from around her window on the second floor. When I looked up, I just saw a shadow behind the blinds, running away."

"Yup, that's what she does best," Alan remarked. Alan turned and picked up the phone on the first ring. "Hello. . . ."

"Alan? It's Jordan. You weren't at work, so I called home and your friend Cliff told me what that bitch did. I think we should hold a stakeout on your roof."

"Forget it," Alan replied. "Stay up all night and go into work wasted?"

"Hey, I'll help you," Jordan offered. "We'll do it in shifts."

"Thanks. I'll keep it in mind. Let me go. I'm gonna' try calling the detective who was involved with that rape I broke up. He might be able to help me out."

"Okay," Jordan advised, "keep me posted." Alan redialed without missing a beat. "Hello," a rough male voice said, ". . . hundred thirteenth. . . ."

"Hello," Alan proceeded, "could I please speak with Detective Saunders?"

"I'm sorry, Detective Saunders is on vacation. He won't be back till a week from this coming Monday. Can I take a message?"

"No," Alan said, "I'll call back then. Wait, is there anybody else who worked on the Rosenbloom mugging?"

"Rosenbloom mugging? We get so many cases. . . ."

"It was a few weeks ago," Alan explained, ". . . you caught a bunch of guys. . . ."

"Let me put you in touch with someone who can run it down for you," the voice offered.

"Okay, no," Alan concluded, "it's not worth it. I'll just wait for Detective Saunders to get back."

"Okay." Alan put down the receiver and looked around the room at cousin Rick, Cliff, Juan, and lots of dirty laundry strewn about. "I understand what's happening," Alan announced. She's trying to make *her* disease *our* disease. If she could just get me to do something stupid. Well, it's not going to happen."

****

Cliff's expression was gaunt when Alan opened the apartment door Wednesday after work. "She flattened one of your tires again," Cliff revealed. "The left front one."

"But I parked five blocks away," Alan exclaimed, "near the private homes. How did you even see it?"

"I went out for a jog," Cliff explained. "When I spotted it, I almost got sick to my stomach."

"You sure it was mine?"

"Yeah—it was the one with the flat tire. There was also this note on the front windshield," Cliff revealed, carefully handing Alan a small white sheet of paper. Alan fixed his eyes on the typewriting: "No Place To Hide."

"She's crazier than we thought," Alan observed.

"I've only touched it in the upper left hand corner," Cliff related, "like you're doing now, so that if it's ever analyzed for finger prints. . . ."

"Okay, good," Alan asserted, "I'll put it into an envelope right now. Also, I notice the 'o' is a little high in both the 'No' and the 'To.' That'll come in handy if the police decide to get off their asses when I show this to them. I'll tell you, I'm impressed. I didn't think she could type."

"Let's blow up the building," cousin Rick suggested.

"Do you think talking to her father would help?" Cliff asked.

"No," Alan responded. "I know these Balkan types. They just get offended. Besides, he's probably in on it. And if I confront *her,* it's just giving her the contact she wants, perhaps even encouraging it."

"Can you afford to keep replacing tires?" Cliff asked.

"Of course not," Alan stated. "Right now, my life is on pause. I need that car for the band and a whole bunch of other things. Gentlemen, we're holding a stakeout."

"Fuckin' A!" cousin Rick yelled. "If I catch her, do I get to rape her?"

"Sure," Cliff returned. "On one condition. If it turns out that it's her brother or someone doing it for her, you have to rape *him,* too." Alan now had Jordan on the phone:

"Jordan, we're gonna' go with the stakeout. Tonight. My car comes back to this block. You call Warren and Zak. I'll get the Yotti and everyone else. Bring your camera with the telephoto lens."

****

At five minutes past 10:00 P.M., Jordan looked through the cross hairs of his telephoto lens and brought the '76 Dodge Aspen into focus. Alan looked around the roof. In attendance were just himself, Jordan, cousin Rick, and Zak. Cliff had a gig. Yotti and Warren had difficult workdays ahead but left open the possibility of participating in a future stakeout. Juan promised to drop by later. Still adjusting the lens, Jordan spoke to Alan, who stood next to him along the parapet wall: "Did you think she was this crazy when you first started going out with her?"

"I didn't even know she was this crazy a week ago," Alan replied.

"My question is," Zak asserted, "what do we do if we see her do something? Just take pictures?"

"I'm gettin' my b.b. riffle," cousin Rick declared. "It's in my bedroom at my parents house. I'll shoot her in the tits."

"She's flat," Jordan quipped.

"I don't want to see that gun up here," Alan warned. "How do you think that'll make my case look, you moron? On the other hand, if you want to throw water balloons, you have my full consent."

"So," Zak asked rhetorically, "It'll be me and Jordan from midnight to 3:00 and then you and your cousin from 3:00 till 6:00?"

"Yup," Alan affirmed, "just come downstairs and wake me up at three. Rick'll already be up, watching porn movies on the VCR or something. He doesn't get up until 2:00 in the afternoon anyway."

"If you want," cousin Rick offered, "I can wait inside the car, in the back seat, under a blanket, and then grab her if I hear someone messin' with the car."

"Not a good idea, especially right now," Alan explained. "First of all, I know she's home. I saw her bedroom light on when I went down to the Seven-Eleven. All we need is for her to see someone enter the car. She's already gotta be wondering why the car is back on the block."

"And even if she doesn't see someone entering the car," Zak added, "she might be suspicious when she sees that blanket stretched across the back seat."

"Maybe, maybe not," Rick countered.

"I have the sobering feeling this could go on unfruitfully for days and days," Jordan sighed. "I know I was the one who pushed this idea on you, but now that I think back on stakeouts I've read about—police stakeouts—they usually drag out and get boring. And we're not even getting paid. I mean, I'm looking at the car . . . and nothing, nothing, nothing."

"I watch 'Starsky and Hutch' re-runs too, Jordan," Alan remarked. "Look, if it doesn't yield something in a couple of nights, then forget it."

Jordan was lifting Alan up by the shoulders at three A.M. "Come on," Jordan said, "time for reinforcements. I can't keep listening to old Deep Purple albums on my Walkman." Alan tried to scrape the newly formed crust from his corneas and reorient himself. In a four-minute-old dream, he had just caught Jill towing the car away, with his cousin Rick still sitting in the driver's seat. Now, Alan saw Zak coming down the fire escape and into the open window of Alan's bedroom area.

"Okay, okay," Alan said. "I'm getting up."

"Your cousin's already up there," Jordan informed Alan. "It was boring up there till about half an hour ago. This mafioso looking guy was running down the hill chasing this woman in her twenties. He caught her, hit her, and she started screaming: 'You fucking bastard—I'll rip your heart out!' And he's all of a sudden saying: 'Baby, baby, I'm sorry baby. . . .' It was pathetic."

"Great," Alan said. "All I'm gonna get to see is the sanitation truck arriving at 5:30."

An hour into the new shift, Alan slumped down against the parapet wall. "I'm not gonna make it tonight," he told Rick. "I might just crawl into that car after all."

"Go ahead," cousin Rick consented. "I'll keep watchin' from up here. I'm readin' this *Old Testament* at the same time anyway."

"Is *that* what the blue book lying around the past few days is?" Alan asked rhetorically. "It's good to see you reading something without a centerfold."

"There's a lotta great laws in here," cousin Rick related, "things that tell ya' how to live. Like leavin' the corners of your field unharvested, so the poor people can come and take it."

"That must explain why you leave roaches all over the apartment instead of smoking the whole joint."

"Maybe it does," cousin Rick agreed. "I can't stop reading it. And the strangest thoughts have been popping into my head. I feel like I've been up on this roof before, reading these same commandments."

"I think they call that deja-Jew."

Alan woke up inside his '76 Dodge Aspen at ten after 8:00 in the morning. He had reset his portable alarm clock several times in the last hour, but now there was no more fighting it. He slipped his Nikes on, rolled up his blanket, tasted his own bad breath, and got out of the car. No damage had been done. The light in Jill's bedroom was off, meaning she had probably not gotten up yet. Alan headed upstairs to shower and change for work.

Alan stretched the skin on his face with his hands as he sat at his desk at 9:38. Even if he could work some normal feeling back into the skin, the brain within would still be aching and lethargic. Relief lay as close as the lawn in front of City Hall, downstairs and across the street. Now, Sal Weisel stood up against Alan's desk. "You just get up?" Sal said vindictively.

"Are you kidding?" Alan shot back. "I've been up for ten minutes."

"Do you have the new revisions on the legal grade for that roadway?" Sal pressed. "I asked you for it two days ago. Do you have it?"

"No. It's being worked on."

"When are you gonna be finished?"

"Now," Alan said, lifting his desk from the bottom and turning it over. Sal jumped out of the way and screamed, feeling a toe caught for just a second.

"I should kick the shit out of you right here," Alan said sternly.

"Get away! You're crazy!" Sal let out.

"Don't ever say anything to me again or come near me," Alan warned. "If you do, I'll kill you. On the spot. I promise." Alan walked out the door, catching just a glimpse of Elena's amused face on the way.

****

"What are you gonna do now?" Yotti asked, atop the roof. "You lost your *job?*"

"Oh, please don't get like my grandmother," Alan pleaded sarcastically. "As if one shitty job can't be replaced in two seconds by another shitty job. Everybody from that era is so clingy, like armageddon is always around the corner. Well, I'll tell you something—armageddon is here, and it's been here for awhile." Alan looked around the roof and saw a full house: Jordan, Zak, Juan, Warren, Yotti, Cliff. Cousin Rick had left a half hour earlier to run an errand. Now Warren walked up to Alan. Wearing his Mets cap and a pair of binoculars, Warren looked like a combination of an American tourist and a Cub Scout.

"I always wanted to be part of a stakeout," Warren revealed. "But we're still missing a few things. Like a keg."

"Well, I'm gonna go down to Seven-Eleven in a few minutes and buy a couple of six-packs," Alan assured him. "On one condition—that you promise to throw the bottles off the roof when you're done."

"No problem. You know, I thought about it, Reiss, and the situation you're in right now—it could only happen to you."

"I've got news for you," Alan remarked. "It's happening to you, too, right now."

Just after 11:00 P.M., Alan looked through the glass cooler doors at the Seven-Eleven on Queens Boulevard. With his peripheral vision, he followed a short-haired blonde woman roughly his own age, who was now coming down the same aisle. On his way in, Alan had made brief, explosive eye contact with her. Now she stepped up behind him and spoke: "Get the light beer. It's less filling."

"Tastes great," Alan shot back. He turned around and looked directly into her penetrating green eyes and wide smile. She looked down briefly at the three six-packs Alan was cradling in his arms and looked back up.

"Having a party?" she inquired.

"Actually, a stakeout, on the roof of my building," Alan explained. "Someone's been slashing my tires, and my friends and I want to get it on film. We know who it is."

"Really? Who is it?"

"My landlord," Alan replied. "He wants me out of there so he can re-rent the apartment. It's a long story."

"So I guess you know how to change a tire," the woman mused.

"Are you kidding?" Alan quipped. "I'm the tire changing king of Queens. I have to be."

"Good. My car is sitting on a flat right now, four blocks from here, and I suck at changing them. I mean, I've done it. . . ."

"No problem. I'll fix it right now," Alan declared. "Um. . . ."

"Liz."

"Liz? Alan." They shook hands.

Ten minutes later, Alan had Liz's red '85 Honda wagon up on a jack. He handed Liz the lug nuts one by one as they came off.

"I'm here for six months," Liz explained, "working for IBM in the city. My girlfriend's letting me stay with her."

"Where're you originally from?" Alan asked.

"Bethlehem, Pennsylvania," Liz answered. "I don't know what I'm doing when this internship is up. If they don't offer me a permanent job, I might wind up going back there." Liz looked down to check Alan's progress. "Hey, not bad. That was fast."

"Thanks. Actually, it's my ex-girlfriend slashing my tires. Although, her family does own the building. You probably think I did something terrible to her, but I didn't."

"I believe you," Liz asserted. "There are a lot of crazy people in New York. I can't tell you how many times I've been felt up by some lowlife on the subway. And also,

I went out with this guy for like a week, and he's been harassing me on the phone ever since."

"Really?" Alan asked rhetorically. "Maybe I'll have a little talk with him. And you can do the same with the vulture ruining *my* life."

"Sure," Liz offered. "I'll punch her lights out. She's probably some spoiled, skinny, stuck-up New York bitch anyway."

"She is. You could take her, no problem."

"Actually, I'd like to visit your stakeout for a little while."

When Alan and Liz stepped out onto the roof several minutes later, cousin Rick was clutching his b.b. rifle in one hand and a joint in the other.

"Jordan, did he fire that thing?" Alan pressed.

"No, I wouldn't let him," Jordan assured.

"I ain't gonna fire this thing unless I need to," cousin Rick declared.

"Yeah," Warren quipped, "like if he sees that guy who short-changed him last week on a nickel bag."

"Or his chiropractor," Alan added.

"Ay, who's the pretty girl?" cousin Rick asked, walking up to Alan and Liz.

"Hi, I'm Liz," she said, extending her hand. "Alan told me all about you and your brother in the Krishnas and living in a truck and everything on the way over here."

"Did he tell you I'm gettin' my own pot farm on government land in the Midwest?" cousin Rick asked. Alan drifted over to Jordan, who was keeping watch at the parapet wall. "You know," Jordan said, looking through his camera, "I don't think I've spent one waking minute since Andrea and I broke up not at least marginally pissed off."

"I know it seems like hell," Alan related, "but that's the nature of life. You almost never know when relief is coming. You find yourself in a situation where it's harder and harder to stick to your principles. And when relief finally comes, either you're embarrassed because you wished you had behaved better, or you're proud, because you can identify a particular act of faith you performed while you were waiting. But here's the most frustrating part—as soon as you discover what act passes for faith, it becomes obsolete, and a new, more difficult act is required for the next dry spell."

"This is not the sort of shit you should be telling me while I'm looking off of a roof," Jordan remarked. "Anyway, I know what relief will consist of for me. When I see Jill touching your car—after I get a couple of pictures, I'm gonna nail her with your cousin's b.b. rifle."

"Alan, your cousin Randy's on the phone," Cliff yelled from over near the fire escape. Alan made his way down the fire escape, crawled in through the window, and picked up the receiver.

"I can't believe you're calling at this hour," Alan began. "I thought you guys all went to bed really early."

"I did," Randy affirmed. "I'm already up for the new day. In a couple of minutes, I'm gonna start chanting my rounds. We try to go on four or five hours of sleep. Listen, I heard through my parents that you were holding a stakeout. I have some advice. Why don't you rent a video camera, set it up on the roof, and let it run? That way, you won't have to waste so much time. How can you go to work the next morning?"

"Well, I already lost my job," Alan revealed, "but that's a good idea. I was considering that just this morning."

"Yeah," Randy continued, "what you're doing could take weeks. Sorry about your job."

"Don't be. Any openings at the temple?"

The doorbell rang before Alan got back to the window. When Alan opened the door. Gene walked into the apartment.

"I heard what happened," Gene offered. "I heard you lost your job. Here's a present." He handed Alan a small bag of pot.

"Hmmmm," Alan mused. "Do I know anyone who could use this?"

"One time I had this job," Gene revealed, "at an electronics store. Just in the back, not even in sales. My fucking boss made me cut my hair. And I had it in a ponytail. It wasn't even all over the place. It was neat, and no one gave a shit anyway. But that asshole had to hold my job over my head. I quit a month later. I never threw that pony tail away. I saved it in a bag. When I walked in there, I said: 'Fuck you!' and threw the pony tail in his face. He looked scared, like I was gonna kill him or something, but I just walked out."

Cliff was entertaining several people with a stand-up routine when Alan reappeared on the roof:

". . . sure *playing* golf is fun, but what I really like doing is *watching* golf. I could watch golf all day. Sometimes, I'll tape a whole tournament and watch it back in slow motion. Hey, I even enjoy watching *other* people watch golf. And you know, I don't just watch the ball, like some people. I look for little things . . . like where the infielders set up. What I can't stand, though, is how it always winds up in a brawl. It's getting to the point where I'm afraid to take my sister's kids to a game. . . ."

Alan dropped the bag of pot into cousin Rick's lap and walked away from the immediate area of laughter, towards Liz.

"Your friend Cliff is hysterical," she stated.

"He's a pro," Alan stated. "He has a state license in stand-up."

"You know you're very lucky," Liz continued. "I can't believe how many of your friends came to help you out."

"I *am* lucky," Alan agreed. "But it's a rare moment that I can reflect clear-headedly on that sort of thing. We're always surrounded by complications."

"Reflect on it now."

"Here, I'll show you what I mean." Alan pulled out a list and showed it to Liz. "These are the sort of things cluttering my life. Sometimes I think simply not staying on top of them would allow them all to go away." Liz read from the sheet of paper:

"'Gather receipts for 1040 form, make list of places to gig in Long Island, call Mr. Martin about getting article published, fill out juror questionnaire, call Dartmouth about loan repayments, buy transmission fluid. . . .' Can I hire you?" Liz asked with a short laugh.

At 1:15, Alan returned to the roof after having walked Liz back to her apartment. He noticed a man in his early thirties with a thick beard and a beer belly. Zak began explaining:

"Alan, this is Larry. He lives on the seventh floor, like you. He wandered up here when he couldn't get to sleep. I gave him a beer and told him the whole story."

"You went out with the landlord's daughter?" Larry said in awe. "Holy shit. You must be some kinda' fuckin' stud I don't know about."

"It was nothing really," Alan returned.

"Yeah, right! She's a fuckin' *fox!*"

"You want her number?"

"Alan," cousin Rick yelled in a partially hushed voice, "there's a guy breakin' into a car down there. Not yours. What should I do?" Everyone including Alan rushed to the parapet wall and looked down. A young white man dressed in mostly black clothes was starting to cut a hole in the side window of an '83 Oldsmobile Cutlass.

"Shoot him," Alan said. "But go for his ass." Cousin Rick looked through the sight glass and fired three times. Shot number one hit the side of the Oldsmobile and made a metallic sound. Shot number two bounced off the pavement near the auto thief's feet. Shot number three was a hit, to the back of the head. The thief took off in a frenzy, down the hill.

"Fuckin A!" cousin Rick yelled, for all of Queens to hear. The rest cheered.

Alan woke up in the morning on the floor of his apartment. Jill hadn't gone for the bait. Jordan fretted: "I can't go into work like this. What am I gonna do?"

"Gimme the phone," Alan asserted, "I'll lie to that yuppie scum boss for you." Alan dialed Jordan's general work number. "Hello," Alan began, "this is Jordan Messer's physician, Dr. Reiss. Yes . . . Jordan suffered a severe ulcerative flare-up last night. He's in a great deal of pain. That's right, he won't be coming in till Monday. Okay? Thank you very much, I'll tell him. . . . Your secretary hopes you feel better."

"That sounded like total bullshit."

"Not to her. You had sick days coming, right?" Alan walked over to Yotti, who was half-asleep in the corner and shook his shoulder. "Yotti, wake up. . . ."

"Hmmmm. . . ."

"Yotti, I got an amazing good night kiss last night. Yotti, remember how I told you on the boat that for every ten feet you float in one direction, you have to walk ten feet back, with the boat slung over your shoulder?"

"Mmmm . . . yeah," Yotti groaned.

"Well, I was wrong. Every once in awhile, you get a freebie."

Chapter Twelve

On Sunday evening, Alan walked cousin Rick through the video equipment he had rented and the alarm system he had improvised. The camera stood on a tripod and focused down, over the parapet wall, upon the '76 Dodge Aspen. The camera and VCR were protected from rain by a tarpaulin. A heavy duty extension chord ran from the equipment, across the width of the roof, and down the fire escape into an outlet in Alan's apartment. A five dollar makeshift alarm system was hooked up to the roof door, ringing a bell in Alan's apartment once a circuit was completed by the opening door.

"No more human stakeouts," Alan said to cousin Rick. "We have lives to live. We'll set this up every night until we get something. And if her father or someone comes up on the roof, we'll know immediately. I can't afford to lose that equipment."

"Pretty cool," cousin Rick noted, a copy of the *Old Testament* in his hand. "How're you gonna' review eight hours of tape if you find your tires slashed?"

"Easy," Alan explained. "Just rewind to the four-hour mark and see if the car is damaged yet. Then keep going forward or back in halves till we have the crime narrowed down to a couple of minutes."

"Not bad for a City engineer," cousin Rick beamed. There was one message on the machine when Alan and Rick climbed back downstairs. Alan turned the dial to "playback" and looked in amazement at cousin Rick as the sounds became identifiable. It was Jill, breathing heavily and moaning, as if she were having sex: "Please, please . . . oh, please . . ." In the background was a male voice grunting and yelling: "Katti . . . Katti . . . Katti...." In the distant background, top forty music played. The machine's beep cut off the orgasm.

"Holy shit, she's sick," cousin Rick exclaimed. "Do you think that's real?"

"I don't know," Alan said. "I don't know if she really had sex and taped it, then played it back into the phone; or if she and a male cousin or someone fake it into a tape and play it into a phone. Or if it was fake and live. Or if it was real and live. Wouldn't that be great, if it was real and live: 'Excuse me... would you mind if we phoned my ex-boyfriend during this part?'"

"She's out of bounds," Rick asserted. "What do you think it is ... outa' those possibilities?"

"Well, first of all, that tape is a good item for my police file. I'm taking it out of the machine. Second of all, no matter what it was, it doesn't bother me nearly as much as it's intended to, simply because it's intended to do just that. I think it was faked and taped. It sounds insincere and muffled. What do you think?"

"I think I better get a *real* gun," Rick replied.

****

"How'd your date with Liz go?" cousin Rick asked as Alan walked through the door Monday night. The apartment reeked of pot smoke.

"Great. We had dinner. I told her I was unemployed. She's still crazy about me. She offered to walk past Jill's window with me a few times to piss her off and prompt a sooner conclusion to this mess. She's a cool girl."

"You're gonna marry her," cousin Rick stated.

"Uh-oh. Did you look into your marijuana-smoke-filled crystal ball again?"

"Yeah, sort of. You'll see. I'm sure of it."

"Well, let me bring up something a bit less pleasant," Alan began. "I know you're a bit of a hero for nailing that auto thief, but I don't want to see you resting on your laurels. Maybe you think that somehow earns you the right to hang out here and get stoned a couple of extra weeks, but it doesn't. Why don't you go out and look for a job?"

"Why don't *you?*"

"Oh, that's very funny," Alan shot back, "but I *have* been working for almost two years straight. I'll make sure everything is paid for somehow—will you?"

"I got almost two hundred dollars still left over," cousin Rick agreed.

"Oh, *excuse me,*" Alan exclaimed. "I didn't realize you were independently wealthy. Fuck it—light up another joint."

"I think I will," cousin Rick said defiantly.

"I don't care what you think," Alan declared, "I'm not trying to bust your balls or be your parent. I simply can't stand to see you continue to waste your life."

"You can stand it," cousin Rick returned. "You just want me outa' here so you can start messin' around with Liz."

"That's bullshit," Alan barked. "I could always ask you to leave for a few hours. Anyway, it's a little premature to even joke like that. Lemme see this tape." Alan popped the previous night's video tape into the VCR, which was temporarily hooked back up to the TV set. Alan's '76 Aspen had been found unblemished in the morning. Now Alan watched the TV screen, as a passerby happened to walk in front of the car.

"Not bad," Alan noted, hitting the pause button. "You can make out the car, the person's body shape, and even a little bit of the person's face under the street lighting. It's just a matter of time now. Wanna' help me set up?"

"All right," cousin Rick conceded.

****

Alan and Rick awoke to the startling sound of the alarm Alan had installed. The digital clock read 7:53 A.M. Any reluctance to get up would have to be obliterated instantly.

"Shit, somebody's up there," cousin Rick yelled. "Let's get that equipment."

"At least the thing works," Alan remarked. Rick was first out the window and up the fire escape. Alan was right behind him. As the roof came into view, they saw Jill's father, Mr. Piros, pulling on an extension cord and looking angry enough to start a small revolution in the Balkans. Undaunted, they walked toward him. Mr. Piros managed a few words:

"What are you doing?"

"Videotapin' your daughter," cousin Rick replied.

"I will have you evicted," Jill's father shouted.

"Good luck," Alan said. "Tenants have a lot of political clout in this city. And you're the one harassing *me*."

"You're crazy," Jill's father shouted. "I never do nothing to you. I let you live in a nice apartment..."

"That's bullshit," Alan shot back. "I pay rent. And in exchange, you let your daughter wreak havoc on my life!"

"She never do nothing to your car..."

"My car? My car?!!" Alan repeated. "Did I mention anything about my car? Damn, you must know something I don't, because I never said anything about Jill doing anything to my car!"

"Look," Jill's father began, mock-consolingly, "you find somebody else. Katti no want to see you anymore. She find somebody else. You find somebody else..."

"Hey, I don't *want* your spoiled, JAPy daughter," Alan yelled. "I want her away from my car—got that?"

"Your daughter's a horny little bitch," cousin Rick barked. "Maybe ya' oughta' get to know her."

"I kill you right now," Mr. Piros threatened, lifting his right hand and taking one step forward.

"Go ahead, try it," cousin Rick dared, "you'll go sailin' off this fuckin' roof. Common, get your whole fuckin' family!"

"All right, you'll see," Jill's father warned, backing away and now pointing to the video equipment. "You take this before I throw it... you are in much trouble."

"Hey, I'm shaking," Alan continued. "I know you'd love to re-rent my apartment for another two hundred a month. Well dream on, you fucking moron!"

"You don't touch Katti!" Mr. Piros admonished.

"I won't if you won't," Alan said, spooling up the extension cable around his bent left arm.

****

In the early evening of the same Tuesday, Alan and Liz stepped into the apartment. Alan spotted a note on the table and read it aloud: "'Dear Alan: I'm outa' here for now. There's something I had to do. I'll be calling you. Thanks for helping me out. Love, Rick.'"

"You don't think he's going to hurt himself, do you?" Liz asked, visibly concerned.

"No, no, that's not his style," Alan assured. "I see he's taken most of his clothing. I don't think you need that for the afterlife. He's probably taking up residence with a hooker."

"Well, good, I'm relieved," Liz let out. "He's such a sweet guy. I wouldn't want to see anything happen to him. I got to know him a little during your stakeout. He's a very intelligent man. He's just confused."

"You're right," Alan acknowledged, "but it's even more complicated than that. He's been through at least three distinct phases in his life, and the first two came to fairly abrupt ends. When we were growing up, he was an absolute daredevil. He got in and drove my uncle's car when he was nine. He would balance himself on anything he could find, like a ledge or a rope; he would slide down long banisters. He would go into Chinatown to buy fireworks and get ripped off. He was a small guy physically for most of those years. It wasn't until a couple of years ago that he sprang up. It was as if he was always trying to prove something. Anyway, then when he went off to college down south, he became a southern preppie, like overnight."

"Oh my God, that's hard to imagine," Liz remarked. "I only know him as a bagman-druggie."

"Bizarre, but true," Alan acknowledged. "He threw the New York street kid image out the window almost overnight. He got a crew cut, bought a pick-up truck, dressed in cotton sweaters. Then he hit a breaking point two years ago. He was working two jobs during his senior year, and everything he had earned for six months was wiped out by repairs not covered in the warranty on the truck."

"That's what life is like," Liz commented. "No matter how hard you work, all the money you make goes somewhere—it gets sucked up by something."

"It's true," Alan continued. "On that day, Rick drove me around in his truck. He was really distraught. He told me that at best things were two steps forward, one and nine-tenths of a step back. And that was why he was filled with dread every time he took two steps forward—and why, strangely enough, he relaxed after being set back one and nine-tenths of a step. He said it really didn't matter what he did, as long as he ran his own life. From that day on, he didn't shave or cut his hair. There was nothing I could tell him at the time to console him. I just felt bad for him."

"He gave up, Alan," Liz stated. "That would be all right for some people, but not for him. It's not in his nature."

"Coulda' fooled me, though."

"It's *not* in his nature," Liz continued. "I can tell. He let himself go as if to call attention to himself."

"Well, it worked."

"But if it had *really* worked," Liz resumed, "he wouldn't have smoked all that pot. I used to work in a mental health clinic. They call what he does 'self-medicating.' His pain had to be diffused, because it never actually went away. I feel a lot of pain. I don't even know where I'll be in a few months. But I've always tried to do everything I can about a situation and then let it go. Once I've done that, I can let the situation resolve itself."

"You're right on the money."

"Then why don't you go in and tie up the loose ends at your job?" Liz asked.

"I will, I will, okay?" Alan let out. "You mentioned it four times already. I'll do it when I'm in the mood."

"Even if you clean out your desk, say goodbye, and find out when your last paycheck is coming, I feel like nothing else can move forward for you until you do at least that. I'll go in with you if you want."

"No, you don't have to, Liz. I'll take care of it. Speaking of unpleasant things to take care of, I have to make a phone call." Alan picked up the receiver and dialed the number of Marty Rosenbloom on the third floor.

"Hello, Mr. Rosenbloom, this Alan Reiss. Would it be possible for me to set up some video equipment in your living room for a few days? Mr. Piros's daughter has been vandalizing my car, and I can't use the roof anymore."

"Sure, Alan, come on down."

Downstairs, Alan knelt on the ground and adjusted the tripod near the window.

"Piros is a real bastard," Marty Rosenbloom remarked. "He's been after me for a couple of years. I'm the head of the tenant's committee. He wants me outa' here so bad he can taste it. He turned off the electricity on Mrs. Horowitz on the fifth floor because she had a cat."

"That's sick," Alan boomed. "She's seventy-five years old!"

"You bet it's sick," Marty continued. "She had that cat before he even owned the building. He changed the rules on everybody. But you see *him* with a dog!"

"And that dog has it better than all of us," Alan quipped.

"We sued him and won," Marty revealed. "We settled out of court for five thousand dollars."

"Excellent," Alan declared, adjusting the zoom lens. "Okay everything's set. Do me a favor and hit record around 10:00 tonight. The tape'll run for eight hours. I'll call you at least once a night. I really appreciate this."

"Hey, no problem," Marty said. "I owe you one."

"And I hate to use it up in this manner."

Back upstairs, Liz lay back as Alan kissed her and got used to the scent of her skin. It was different. He wanted never to have to get used to the scent of another woman's skin after this. He wondered if the things that occurred to him followed any set of rules or if the rules were made up later to suit the events.

****

Alan had fought the tenseness in his fingers through most of the one-hour set at the Razor's Edge on Thursday night. He knew his fingers wouldn't relax until he became somewhat indifferent to how his personal performance appeared to others. That would take many stage appearances, and this was only his first. For weeks, he had looked upon this event as "it," but "it" was twenty-eight people standing around at 11:30, yelling and clapping a little between songs. Now, during Black Sabbath's "Paranoid," some relaxation set into Alan's hands. Yet the full fluidity he had attained in practice still wasn't there. The notes were played sequentially with passable timing. Still, Gene seemed elated with the gig.

As Alan stepped down from the stage at the conclusion of the set, there was about fifteen seconds of clapping. Gene reeled off one last lick by himself. Liz walked up to Alan and delivered her assessment: "You guys are good, I really enjoyed it. But the vocals were a little rough. You're gonna' need a lead singer at some point."

"I know," Alan acknowledged.

"Great fucking show, man," Gene said, beaming and extending his hand to Alan. "You and Juan both really showed me something. It sounded great up there."

"Thanks." It occurred to Alan that the whole time, Gene had really been nervous about his own performance and hadn't listened that closely to Alan.

****

Only a single lamp shone in Alan's apartment Sunday night. Alan and Liz lay in bed partially clothed and looked out the window at the other buildings, as the warm air came in.

"When I look outside," Liz observed, "or walk around outside when there's no one around, I consider the stillness, and how these objects out there are exactly the same, day in day out. Everything's calm, and I wonder: 'Where are the problems?'"

"We generate them," Alan stated. "We're damn good at it. I'll be generating some problems of my own tomorrow. I'm going in to clean up my mess."

"Good. I'm glad."

"No problem," Alan asserted. "I always try to be three things: flexible, rational, and moral. The 'flexible' is an important part that most people with the other two never get. That's why I let my cousin open fire on that guy. I'm not into guns, and I'd like to see them banned. But it was called for."

"I only wish I had seen it," Liz said. "It sounded hysterical. So what are you going to do, look for another job?"

"No," Alan replied, "I'm gonna' get into an accident and live off the insurance money like my cousin. Seriously? Find a way to pay the rent and enjoy myself. Everything in this world is based on the concept 'Do your time.' Put in your hours and then die. I won't live with the goal of looking ahead to that wonderful time when I can look back."

"Hey, *I* know," Liz suggested, "I'll move in with you here to really piss Jill off. That'll be fun."

They had let the phone ring four times, and now cousin Rick's voice came over the answering machine: "Ay, Alan, are ya' there?" Alan grabbed the receiver and flicked off the machine.

"Yeah, yeah, where are you?"

"At the Rabbi's house, in Brooklyn," cousin Rick explained. "I'm livin' here. The rent is low, an' all I have to do is study Judaism under Rabbi Linman. He's Hasidic."

"Did he give you the Hasidic garb and everything?" Alan asked.

"Yup," cousin Rick replied, "I'm all neatened up now."

"Hey, and you already have the beard. . . ."

"I really enjoy learnin' this stuff," Rick continued. "I study all day. No more pot—that's for sure."

"Unless it's kosher," Alan quipped. "Well, I'm for anything that helps you out, and this will definitely help you out."

"I wanna help you out, too," cousin Rick added. "I've been readin' some o' these laws, and you know, you're not supposed to have sexual relations with a woman except with the woman on her back and the man on top of her. Anything else, like sittin' up, is a sin."

"You know, I hadn't thought of that," Alan kidded, ". . . sitting up. Thanks for the idea. Now we'll *have* to try it."

"So, I need to pick up the rest of my clothes," Rick indicated. "Can I come by tomorrow night?"

"Yeah, after 8:00. I'm going into work tomorrow to clean out my desk, then I'm gonna hang around the City for awhile."

"Okay, thanks. If you're not there, can I let myself in?"

"No problem. See ya', Rick." Alan put down the phone and looked over at Liz. "He's a Hasidic Jew now. Rick went from being a spaced out, hippie-druggie to being a Hasidic Jew in one week."

"Oh, my God," Liz laughed.

"Do you think somewhere in there, passing through, maybe for thirty seconds, he was normal? You know, just for half a minute he enrolled in college, filled out a credit card application, went out on a date? . . ."

****

Monday afternoon, on his way up to the eleventh floor, Alan stopped off at the eighth floor to give back a reference text he had borrowed and then taken home. He opened the glass door to the main office area of the Department of Sanitation and fixed his eyes straight on the shelf from which he had taken it three months earlier. "Alan, would you step into my office?" It was the voice of Frank Carillo, the Director, coming from behind him. Fine, Alan thought. I'm ready. You want to give me some stupid story about how I let you down and how you're gonna make sure my record of violence will follow me all over the City? Fine. I'll tell you what a joke this office is and how anyone who gives a Sal Weisel responsibility *deserves* to have everything blow up in his face.

"Yeah, okay," Alan responded, walking in behind Carillo, who now motioned with his head to Ben to remain in the room. Ben promptly closed the door behind everyone, as Carillo seated himself. Alan remained standing. Carillo spoke:

"Alan, Sal Weisel is an asshole. You're a bright guy. I've followed you since you started here. You're on top of shit, even when it looks like you're not. We don't wanna lose you, period. And we especially don't wanna lose you because of *that* shmuck."

"But I turned over a desk on him. . . ."

"I don't care what the fuck you did," Carillo exclaimed. "I'm amazed you lasted as long as you did. Ben, tell 'em what you did after three weeks of working with Sal."

"Decked him," Ben said, "right in the face. He was out like a light."

"Ben did Golden Gloves for a year," Carillo noted. "C'mon, turning over a desk is pussy shit. Sal's a real dick."

"Well," Alan inquired, "doesn't he ever learn?"

"No," Carillo barked. "Who the fuck ever learns? Hey, look, you just go back to work, and we'll put that asshole somewhere else. Let him bother someone else. He doesn't care. Just put 'em somewhere else. Hey, I heard some of the things you said to him. You're a funny guy!"

"If you feel this way," Alan asked, "how come you never fired him?"

"Do you know how hard it is to fire someone in civil service?" Carillo shot back. "It'd be easier to kill him. Besides, where else can someone like him work? I'll just shuffle him around."

"Well, what if he brings me up on charges?"

"Forget about it, okay?" Carillo returned. "We got so much stuff on him, we could hang him out to dry."

"I appreciate everything you're saying," Alan propounded, "but I'm still curious why I wasn't warned or anything."

"I don't know," Carillo said. "Ben, why do we do it this way?"

"I don't know, it's like initiation," Ben explained.

"Now you missed a week," Carillo continued. "I can't pay you for that. We'll throw a couple extra sick days in there. Let me ask you something, is something bothering you lately?"

"Yeah," Alan revealed, "this girl I used to go out with. She's slashing my tires. Her father owns my building. There's no getting away from it."

"Whad you do to this girl?" Carillo asked.

"Nothing. Believe me, nothing. She's just crazy. *She* broke up with *me,* really. I just didn't want to get into some pointless discussion ten days later when she suddenly felt like it."

"Oh, they hate that shit," Carillo let out in revelation. "She's not gonna stop until you make love to her."

"In other words, she's not gonna stop," Alan quipped.

"Can't you move? Can't you put your car in a garage?"

"I can't afford either of those options," Alan explained. "There are a few garages in the area, within the buildings, but they're all like a hundred dollars a month."

"I know, I know—we pay you guys shit," Carillo said, looking at his desk and then around the room. "Tell you what. We're gonna' get you a merit increase. Forty bucks a week. It'll take four to six weeks to come through, okay? Now why don't you go upstairs and talk to Sashi?"

"Thanks a lot," Alan said, heading toward the door. "I mean it. I really appreciate it."

"Oh, and one more thing, Alan."

"Yeah?"

"Try to be on time?"

****

It was already fairly dark outside when Alan emerged from the subway in Queens and started walking home. He had gone album and musical equipment shopping in Manhattan and carried two bags in one hand. Liz would most likely be waiting upstairs in his apartment. Not much had sunk in yet. Maybe it would start to when he put the Van Halen album on. He considered the turn of events. Relief had come, and the strange thing was, in spite of all his efforts and planning, he hadn't earned it. By the same token, he hadn't earned the misfortune that preceded it either. But when relief came, the smart ones took it. And the smart ones had done enough while waiting to convince themselves they deserved it.

As he rounded the corner and looked down the hill, a man in a black suit and black hat had Jill pinned against the '76 Dodge Aspen. It was cousin Rick, in full Hasidic regalia. Jill was squirming and yelling: "Let go of me! Let go of me!" Alan ran toward the car.

"Alan, I got her, pullin' off your wipers," cousin Rick shouted. "Not even a minute ago. I was comin' ta' get my stuff and I spotted her. Call the police. Call the police."

"Get the fuck off me, you asshole," Jill screeched. "Let me go, I said."

"Let her go, Rick," Alan said. "We have all we need. I'll call the police from upstairs. If we're lucky, we'll get a restraining order out of it."

"Let her go?" Rick repeated with an air of disappointment. "She'll deny everything."

"A witness is a witness," Alan related, "especially when he's dressed like you. Let her go." Cousin Rick released his grip reluctantly. Jill darted off and shook like a leaf as she fumbled for her keys at the front entrance. "I'll kill you," she grumbled as she disappeared.

"Rick, let's surprise Liz," Alan suggested. "Before we go all the way upstairs, come to the third floor with me."

"Okay."

Ten minutes later, Alan and Rick opened the door to the apartment. Cousin Rick was carrying the VCR, with the tape inside. Liz was near the desk, reading a computer textbook.

"Hi," Liz exclaimed. "Rick—you look so different. I can't believe this. I don't know if I would have recognized you on the street."

"It's the new me," Rick said.

"Liz," Alan revealed in a hurry, "I didn't lose my job. I owe you one. And Rick just caught the bitchwoman in the act."

"Oh my God!" Liz let out in near rapture.

"And guess what?" Alan continued. "Marty Rosenbloom put the tape on a little early tonight because he didn't know if he'd be home at 10:00. We're gonna check the tape right now. . . ."

Once Alan had everything hooked up and rewound, he joined Liz and cousin Rick on the couch. He still held the remote control in his hand. "Here it is," Alan indicated. On the screen, beneath a street light, Jill walked into view and looked around nervously. Once secure, she went right for a wiper and started twisting it off. Another ten seconds of mangling went by until cousin Rick appeared in the picture. In full black, at a full clip, he flew into Jill and brought her down.

"Damn, Rick—*nice tackle,*" Alan marvelled.

"Thanks," Rick acknowledged. Liz exploded with laughter. Now, on the screen, cousin Rick stood Jill up and put her against the car.

"You should be showin' up any second," Rick noted.

"Yup, there I am," Alan confirmed, "albums and all."

"You guys should bootleg this tape," Liz urged. "You'd make a million."

"Let's look at that one again, Frank Gifford," Alan said, rewinding and then replaying in slow motion: "Okay, here's Rick Reiss, the young middle linebacker from the Lubavitchers putting the hit on the runner. Reiss is second year out of Yeshiva. Notice how he gets down and puts that front shoulder right into the knees. . . . Gee Frank, that musta' hurt. . . ."

"Fuckin' A!" cousin Rick yelled, "Let's see that again."

"We're moving outa' here," Alan said, walking over to the file cabinet and pulling open a drawer. "Nothing left to prove. We'll move like a mile away and leave no forwarding address."

"I'll miss this apartment," Liz said.

"We'll get a better one in one day," Alan retorted. "And one more thing. No more focusing on things left undone. I wanna enjoy my life for awhile." Alan held a sheaf of papers and stood near the window. "This is virtually every list I've compiled for the last two years." He tore the sheaf lengthwise, then widthwise, and tossed it out the seventh story window.

"Well," Liz offered, a little choked up, "I know that must have been very hard for you."

"Not at all," Alan replied. "I have a Xeroxed copy of everything over at Zak's house."